THE
ROSE
REAPER

OTHER TITLES BY JENNIFER HUNTER

THE RYAN STRICKLAND SERIES

The Lost Victim

THE
ROSE
REAPER

A THRILLER

JENNIFER HUNTER

 THOMAS & MERCER

Text copyright © 2024 by Jennifer Hunter
All rights reserved.

Published by Thomas & Mercer, Seattle

www.apub.com

Amazon, the Amazon logo, and Thomas & Mercer are trademarks of Amazon.com, Inc., or its affiliates.

ISBN-13: 9781662509353 (paperback)
ISBN-13: 9781662509346 (digital)

Cover design by Damon Freeman
Cover image: © lenetstan, © Den Edryshov / Shutterstock; © Karina Vegas / ArcAngel

Printed in the United States of America

For you, the reader.
Thank you for continuing this series with me.
Enjoy the dark and twisted ride.

Prologue

Finished with her again, her attacker slid down her body, his sweaty chest and face dragging over her stomach, her crossed and bound ankles dragging over his back and shoulders, until he was free and stood at the end of the plastic-covered bed and stared down at her. The frenzy in him had dissipated to a calm that unsettled her. She knew the end was near and welcomed the relief it would bring, even as she fought to compartmentalize what was happening to her. He'd violated her body, hurt it in the worst way, but she tried to keep her wits about her. She desperately wanted to find a way out of this impossible situation.

It hurt to breathe.

He liked to punch her in the side when she struggled, so she'd stopped doing that to save her strength.

For what, she didn't know. It seemed there was no way out of this living hell except for death, which she'd wished for but then took back as she rallied to live to see a better day. One where this monster was behind bars for life. Or dead.

He walked over to one of the two chairs at the table in the single-room shack. The room was clean, but worn. Time had dulled the wood walls and floor. The two small windows on either side of the door barely let in any light in the day. At night, they reflected back the horrible scene of a crime she believed would end in her death very soon.

She wasn't getting out of here alive.

What would her life look like now after all this anyway?

The tears started again, though they were useless. He didn't care if she cried. He didn't care if she screamed. She was nothing to him. Just an object to be used to fulfill whatever fantasy played in his head, whatever disturbing need ate away at him that would make him do this.

He opened the only door to the cabin and stood out on the rickety porch smoking a cigarette, nude, like he didn't have a care in the world.

We're somewhere secluded.

He's not afraid of getting caught.

No one knows I'm here.

She held back the hysteria, choking it down, trying her best to find a clear thought that might lead to a plan of escape.

Since he was far enough away not to hear her if she made a soft noise and he had his back to her, she pushed with her feet to alleviate the tension on her wrists and arms. She shifted to ease the pain aching in her whole body and noticed something above her. The knot that held her to the old metal bedframe had come loose. Not all the way, but enough that if she worked at it, she just might free herself.

Then what?

How would she get past him? She couldn't fight him. He was too strong. She didn't have the stamina or speed to outrun him.

But if she didn't try, she'd regret it later whether she lived or died. Because she didn't want to go down without a fight. Or at least an attempt at one.

So she watched him through the open door as he blew smoke into the night and looked up at the stars, humming that strange tune. And when he tensed, then came back into the cabin to pull on his jeans and shoes, grab the knife he'd left on the table beside the bed, and rushed out again, leaving the door open, she wondered, *Is this a test? Some other kind of torment?*

Did he expect her to try to escape just so he could chase and kill her?

If she stayed put, would he reward her by not killing her?

2

It would probably just be more of the same until he tired of her and killed her anyway.

With her thoughts occupying her chaotic mind, it took her a second to realize she'd freed her hands from the metal headboard, though they remained tied at the wrists. She sat up and worked at the knot on her right ankle, then the left, her heart jackhammering, making it hard to breathe or hear past the beat pounding in her ears.

The plastic beneath her crinkled as she moved. She didn't dare take the time to try to find something to wear. He'd shredded her clothes, taking them off her with that knife. She had a few nicks still bleeding on her arms, torso, and legs. They were nothing compared to the raw skin around her ankles and wrists. She found her shoes tucked under the bed, pulled them on, and tiptoed to the open door, her heavy breathing giving her away if he was close enough to hear it. She couldn't help it. Fear and adrenaline wanted to halt her in her tracks and make her run at the same time. She thought the best way to go was to make a mad dash for it, because stealth seemed impossible.

And if this was her one and only chance to get away, then she was going to run until her lungs exploded if that's what it took.

With that thought in mind, she bolted out the door and hooked a left just off the porch, knowing he'd gone the other way and hoping he hadn't circled around the back of the shack to capture her as she ran right for him.

"I knew I'd find you here." A strange voice came out of the darkness from close by.

Stunned, she stopped in her tracks.

Who is that?

A savior?

Another monster like him?

She tried to see through the darkness, to gauge where they were and if she had a chance of still getting away.

"You shouldn't be out here. This is none of your concern." Was that *him*? He'd never spoken to her.

"I know why you're doing this, but you don't have to. You can stop."

Who is that?

"I need this!"

She didn't wait around to hear more. He wouldn't stop. He couldn't. And she wasn't sticking around to find out what happened next. So she ran like her life depended on it, because if he caught her now, it was over.

She didn't know where she was or what direction to go, but it didn't really matter, so long as he didn't find her. She ran and ran and ran, stumbling over tree roots, the brush whipping at her body, her legs aching along with her lungs. Every noise terrified her more. She imagined him chasing her down, though she couldn't really distinguish between the sounds she made and the noises around her muffled under the sound of her heavy breathing and her heartbeat pounding in her ears. The terror inside her fueled her mad dash.

She came to a steep incline and dug her feet in, dirt and gravel getting into her shoes, under her nails, but she kept going, grabbing on to tree limbs, the tall grass, anything to give her a handhold so she didn't slip back down the slope. And then she came over the rise and found herself standing behind a guardrail on the curve of a road, headlights headed her way.

She didn't think, she just ran out into the road, waving her hands, feeling like her attacker was right behind her, ready to pounce and drag her back to that shack and the death that awaited her there.

The car drew closer and skidded to a stop, the headlights glaringly bright. She covered her face with her arms and backed away, even though she desperately wanted help.

"Hey, are you okay?" a man's voice rang out.

"Stop," a woman said. "We can help."

Kate dropped one arm and used her other hand to shield her eyes from the blinding light. "He's coming. Please. Get me out of here." The rushing sound in her ears began to fade along with what little energy she had left.

"Mile-marker twelve on the big curve. She's naked and bleeding. Send an ambulance." The man's desperate voice made her still. He really did want to help.

The woman moved forward, her body blocking one headlight, making her appear more like a dark figure walking out of the light.

Kate tried to rein in the need to run away again. Her whole body vibrated.

"It's okay. I won't hurt you," the woman said, inching closer, taking her time, hands up like she meant no harm.

Kate wanted to trust that this would end well, but it was so hard to make her mind believe that when everything inside her told her to escape, just keep going. Far away wasn't far enough.

The woman stood in front of her. Dark hair, brown skin, warm, kind eyes. "I am not going to hurt you." She held open a black cardigan. "Let me help you put this on. You're trembling."

Kate managed to turn to the side as the woman stepped closer. She draped the cardigan over Kate's shoulders. Kate realized her wrists were still bound.

"Let me take that off." The woman worked quickly and gently to undo the intricate knot and unwind the rope from Kate's wrists. She tucked the rope in her back pocket.

Kate tried to put one hand in the sleeve, but it seemed her arms didn't work properly anymore and she missed.

The woman took Kate's fingertips and gently put her hand into the sleeve and pulled the material up her arm. "There now. One done. Let's do the other together, too." She repeated the action with Kate's other arm and settled the material on her shoulders. "All done."

Kate immediately gripped both sides of the open sweater and folded her arms, closing the material tightly around her middle.

"Come. Let's have you lean against the car just to steady you until the police and ambulance get here." The woman held her hand out toward the front of the car. "I promise, no one will touch you. We'll just watch over you until help arrives." The woman took a step toward the car.

Kate followed, letting her go first, while she kept her eye on the man still standing behind the door of the driver's side. In the back of her mind, she understood he was trying to give her space, to not be threatening. But it didn't stop the overwhelming feeling that she needed to flee. This wasn't safe. No place was safe with *him* still out there.

"My name is Vivian. That's my husband, Jamal. What's your name?"

She kept scanning the side of the road, the forested area beyond. "K-Kate."

Sirens grew louder in the distance, coming toward them. But it was the truck pulling in behind them that set off a new round of alertness and dread.

Jamal called out, "Go around," and waved his arm.

Something deep inside Kate screamed at her to run. She began backing away from the car, the headlights pinning her in their beams, spotlighting her futile escape, because she knew he'd found her.

Suddenly, the suspicious truck revved, then sped forward around Jamal's car and cut in between her and them. The monster opened the truck door and stepped out wearing just jeans, his work boots, and a look that said it all.

You're dead.

He didn't have to say it. It rang in her head.

He prowled toward her, a predator about to pounce on his prey.

Jamal stepped around his vehicle and into the headlights, calling out, "Hey, stop. You're scaring her."

The sirens grew louder.

She kept backing up, heading in their direction.

"Kate. Come here," the monster called.

She could only make out his dark shape, but it was enough to scare her senseless. She shook her head and kept a death grip on the sweater around her, knowing the thin barrier was no match for his blade and what he wanted to do to her.

"Kate," he warned again.

And then it was like the world turned to chaos as not one but several cars halted behind her and several more suddenly appeared behind Jamal's car, their emergency lights swirling and lighting up this lonely patch of road.

Voices rose over each other.

"Police. Stop right there."

"FBI. Stop right there. Put your hands up."

FBI? Why would 911 send the FBI?

Kate pulled her thoughts off that sidetrack and back to the drama at hand. She did not stop. She kept backing up toward the officers, keeping her eyes on him.

He put one hand at his back.

"Sir. Put your hands up." The voice came from a loudspeaker.

"Kate. You're almost to me, keep coming," someone called to her.

How do they know my name?

"Kate," *he* called.

Suddenly a man with FBI on his back appeared in front of her with a shield, blocking her from the monster, who growled in frustration.

"She's mine."

The raw declaration unsettled her even more and made her whole body tremble.

The man in front of her backed up a step. She did the same. And then again he retreated up a step, and so did she.

And *he* prowled forward, coming for her despite the odds, the hunger in him too voracious for him to ignore.

He glared at those behind her, then suddenly stopped.

So did she, transfixed by the look in his eyes.

The FBI man bumped into her.

She held her ground, protected by his crouched body and the shield, but witness to everything *he* did.

7

He put one hand at his back again.

The officers behind her shuffled and moved about. She imagined them going on guard against whatever he had behind him.

Was it the knife? A gun?

"Put your hands up and get on your knees." The order came over the loudspeaker.

Kate studied *him*, knowing he wouldn't comply, waiting for the inevitable outcome when he didn't.

"Hands up. On your knees," they repeated.

It happened so fast and in slow motion all at the same time. He rushed her, pulling his hand from behind him. All the sound went out of everything, then exploded with gunshots. Dots of blood expanded to streams of it running down his chest and abdomen. He finally did fall to his knees, then crumple to his side, his arms flung out beside him. Nothing in his hands.

It shook her to her core, seeing the life drain out of him.

He stared blankly at the pavement spreading out before him, at the officers and cars blocking the road.

She dropped her head back and stared up at the night sky, exhaling for the first time in she didn't know how long, knowing the monster got what was coming, but also better than he deserved.

After that, it was a whirlwind of activity, her mind filled with disjointed images of being placed in the ambulance, the paramedic gently assessing her, an FBI agent asking her questions she couldn't seem to find words to answer, then nothing.

She couldn't remember the last few hours.

She awoke in a quiet room in the hospital, the lights kept low, the nurse a constant presence. Time had no meaning as it passed.

All she saw in her mind was the face of the monster who took and hurt her. It was *him* constantly calling her name.

And then someone new walked in the door. His voice, the way he said her name, brought her out of her nightmare. "Kate, I'm Ryan Strickland. I'm here to help you."

The Rose Reaper's Journal Entry

Roses are red,

Violets are blue.

If you see me . . .

It's too late for you.

It's a stupid rhyme. I don't know when it came to me. It's been echoing inside me, and now I can't get it out of my head. I hear it when I watch them. I want them to know I'm there. I want them to feel me. Because I am watching. And waiting. And hunting for that perfect someone to be my first.

I can't hold back anymore.

I can't watch them walk away.

I can't appease this ache, this want, this gnawing desire just thinking about what I want to do to them.

I want to feel her anticipating me, afraid of me, under me, bleeding for me. Dying for me. Tonight.

Chapter One

He hummed the tune as he worked. He couldn't get it out of his head. Not since the first time he'd read the rhyme and an awakening came over him. All those twisted thoughts in his mind, the urges he held on lockdown, the need clawing at him . . . he wasn't losing his mind. He wasn't deranged or psychotic.

He was born this way.

And now that he knew that, he was finally free.

The world was filled with possibilities now that he had a road map to his future.

He'd been in the dark, but now he lived in the light.

He had a plan and it started tonight.

With her.

She was perfect. A rose he picked among all the weeds.

Not the one he ultimately wanted. He'd get to her later. When the time was right. When he'd completed the work of the one who showed him the way.

Then he'd be greater than the past.

He'd carry on the legacy.

Starting with this one.

The anticipation built as he tied the final knot around her ankle.

His heart raced. Sweat beaded on his forehead.

This was it.

He put his hand on her bare leg and stared up into her terrified gaze as she whimpered behind the gag, tears rolling down her cheeks. She shook her head, hoping he'd stop. Wishing he'd let her go.

"You're mine now. One of seven that I owe him. Then I can continue in the way I want. And you'll be the one who started it all."

Just the thought of what he was going to do made him hard and desperately want.

She lay on the bed with her wrists bound together and tethered to the top of the headboard. The gag kept her pleas and mewling muffled. He'd crossed her legs and tied rope around each ankle, giving her just enough play that he could slip in between her legs and her ankles would cross at his waist or the backs of his thighs, keeping him right where he wanted to be and her unable to escape.

His balls ached with the release he desperately needed.

But first, he wanted to enjoy every second of this. Savor it.

Because there was only one first.

He planned to make it count.

She was at his mercy, and would soon find out he had none.

The second he put his knee on the plastic-covered bed, she squirmed and tried to get away. But there was nowhere for her to go, and the perfect spot for him was in the cradle of her creamy thighs.

He gripped her under her knees and shoved her legs up as far as he could before the bindings on her ankles prevented him from going any farther. She screamed. Or tried to anyway. Already her voice was hoarse. The seemingly endless tears drying up as her eyes went wide.

She sensed his intent. Feared it. Wanted to make it stop before it even happened.

But no. One look at her with her cunt bare to him, her breasts bouncing as she struggled, the look of fear in her eyes, all of it only made him want her more.

So he took it, not caring that the bindings tore her ankles to shreds. The scent of blood in the air only drove him on and made him buck harder and faster even though he wanted this to last.

He couldn't get enough of her screams, the plea and terror in her eyes.

It didn't live up to the flat words in the journal. It surpassed it.

The power that surged through his body, the thrill of it, excited him until the pleasure swamped him.

His breath came in gasps, then slowed to pants as the buzz waned. He shoved her legs out of his way and fell on his back beside her.

He thought it funny she tried to curl and turn away, locking her legs to her chest and using her feet to block him from the cunt he'd used so well and wanted again.

Because he didn't like this feeling of it being over way too soon.

It didn't have to be. She was his until he was done with her. Then, and only then, would he complete the final act.

Settling in for the night, he pressed up on his hands and stared down at his rose, now a little wilted, but still so sweet and tempting.

The smell of sex and blood filled the room. Her whimpers music to his ears.

And when he reached for her again, she still had some fight left in her and kicked at him.

He rolled her over, smacked her on the ass, pulled her hips up and her onto her knees. That nice round rump, her sex glistening . . . begging for him. He licked his lips and stared at her naked body, wanting all over again.

✿

Hours later, he came one last time, his wilted rose staring up at him, nothing but desolation and surrender in her eyes.

She never saw it coming, but he watched as dawning understanding came with the pinch of pain as he slid the dagger under her ribs and right into her heart. A clean, simple kill. A mercy his predecessor gave those who served him. One he'd give his seven tributes and no more. And for a split second he saw the thank-you and peace come into her eyes that he'd finally set her free.

As her last breath left her, he kissed her forehead.

"Thank you for making this so memorable."

He'd like to leave her just like that. He could come back to this magical place and see her there.

But the plan was clear. And if he stuck to it, he'd get to that seventh victim.

The one who got away.

Then he'd be free to expand his horizons.

But this one would live in his mind and dreams forever.

He'd made her immortal.

He planned to do the same thing for himself.

He pulled out his phone and took a picture of his rose lying naked, her eyes open and staring back at him, lifeless and empty.

She'd given him the greatest night of his life.

He'd sent her to a better place.

And he couldn't wait to do it again.

First, he needed to clean up and start looking for the next rose to pluck from the weeds.

He gathered his supplies, came back, gave her one last longing-filled gaze, and wished he'd gone one more round with her. It wouldn't have been enough. But there were more to come. He sprayed her with bleach and wiped her down with a small towel, making sure every inch of her was clean. He didn't want to leave any trace of himself on her.

He stood back and stared at the empty shell of her, remembering the time they'd spent together, savoring this one last look.

He needed to go, do it now, before sunup.

He pulled the plastic up from the bottom of the bed and covered her feet. He did the same at her head. Then he pulled both sides over and tied the whole thing closed with nylon rope around her neck and ankles.

He picked up the bindings and towel and tossed them into the woodstove. They immediately caught fire. In seconds they were nothing but ash.

He dressed, then looked around the cabin, searching for anything he'd missed. Not that he needed to worry about anyone finding this place. It had remained hidden all these years, until he'd gone looking for answers and found himself.

He dragged his plastic-wrapped dead rose down the bed, lifted her shoulders, pulled her up and over his shoulder, then stood with her and turned for the door. He missed the cabin already, but headed out to finish his task.

The walk took longer than expected with the deadweight.

But once he arrived at the spot he'd scouted, he stood on the stone overhang and stared down at the black water rushing by, the surface nothing more than swirls and ripples in the dark night, serene compared to the swift undercurrent of the river.

He shifted his heavy burden down his body until her feet hit the edge of the rock and he held her in a hug, her face plain to see through the thin plastic. He brushed his hand over her head. "Thank you for unleashing me."

He pushed her off the rock, her body making a splash before the river quickly sucked her under and away. She'd probably end up miles downriver, the plastic stripped from her nude body by rocks and debris. Any evidence of him on her that he'd missed washed away.

He didn't want to think about her bloated and rotted body being found later.

He wanted to remember her the way she was when he took her. His beautiful rose.

With his task done, he turned back to the cabin. The walk soothed him and gave him time to remember this very special night.

He pushed up the tailgate on his truck, closed the camper shell's back window, then climbed behind the wheel and headed home, no one the wiser that the new and improved Rose Reaper had taken another life.

But first, he had to make one pit stop.

A very special someone needed to know about his rebirth.

She'd see him coming, but that wouldn't stop him from taking what he wanted and finishing what the Rose Reaper started.

Chapter Two

The next day . . .

Kate Doyle walked out her front door and stared down the path that led to the cute little garden gate at the sidewalk. She stared at the single red rose lying on the pavement and fell back in time to three years ago, when the Rose Reaper abducted her from her driveway, leaving a single red rose behind.

His signature.

Well, one of them.

He held her in a cabin for two days, until she escaped.

And he died.

He died.

So who would leave this rose on her path? Who would taunt her like this?

It had taken weeks for her body to heal. It took months before she could think clearly about anything other than what had happened to her. It took a year and a half before she was able to go back to work and begin to rebuild her life.

Why would someone want to tear her world apart again?

She felt the panic rising and ran back inside, closing and locking the door. She went for the phone and called the police.

"Nine one one, what is your emergency?"

"Someone left a rose in my front yard."

"What is the emergency?" the dispatcher asked again.

"The rose. Someone left a rose." Her voice went shrill with hysteria.

"Are you hurt, ma'am?"

"No."

"Are you feeling disoriented or confused?"

"No. Don't you see? He left a rose!" The panic set in even as she tried to hold herself together.

"I'm sorry, ma'am, but that is not an emergency. If you'd like to call the nonemergency number to file a littering complaint, I can give you the number."

Kate hung up. They didn't believe her. They didn't understand.

She held on to her purse, walked out the door, picked up the rose, and ran to her car. She climbed in, started it, and backed out of her driveway, looking everywhere, hoping to see someone, anyone, she could make pay for doing this to her.

The drive to the police station took only a few minutes. She parked and rushed inside, coming to a halt at the front desk. "I need to see Lieutenant—"

"Kate, is that you?"

She turned and found Lieutenant Griffin behind her. She rushed to him and held his forearm in a tight grip. "I need your help."

"Sure. Come with me back to my office. I'll get us a cup of coffee. We'll talk."

She frantically shook her head. "You don't understand. There's no time. You need to stop him."

The lieutenant cocked his head, briefly glanced at the officer at the desk behind her, then back to her. "Stop who?"

She pulled the rose from her purse and held it up, a stark reminder of her past. *"Him."*

The lieutenant waved his hand out toward his office. "Come with me."

She followed him and fell into the visitor's seat in front of his desk.

He took the time to pour her coffee with two creams at the credenza behind his desk, just the way she liked it. He held it out to her, forcing her to unclench her fist and set the rose on the desk.

She held the cup in both her shaking hands as he took his seat and stared at her.

"Tell me about the rose." The gentle tone didn't soothe her.

"I found it in the yard, on the path from the front door to the gate at the sidewalk. It was just lying there." The familiar tremor of dread rocketed through her again.

"Were you or one of your neighbors doing any gardening lately? Maybe it got left behind when you or a neighbor cleaned up."

She shook her head. "Why don't you believe me?"

"I believe you. But he's dead. So has there been anyone new in your life, or on your street?"

She went still. "I met someone," she admitted. The first someone who'd had kind eyes and a warm smile and gave her the space and time to ease into the relationship.

"What's he like?"

"Nice. Normal. A contractor." He fixed and built things. She liked that idea because she'd been working on fixing herself and building a new life.

"How long have you been seeing him?"

"A couple of weeks." At first, they met for coffee. The first time, she bolted after fifteen minutes. He'd called her later to make sure she got home okay and to ask if she'd like to meet him again. She thought the gesture kind. He didn't think she was a freak for scampering away like a scared rabbit. Instead, he'd said it seemed like she'd had a rough past. He said he didn't mind taking things slow because he really wanted to get to know the woman with the beautiful, sad eyes.

"Did he leave you the flower?"

It never occurred to her that he'd do something like that.

She'd agreed to a dinner date just two days ago and even took the step of letting him pick her up at her house. At the time, she'd thought it a big move forward in her very guarded life.

Now, it could be the stupidest mistake she'd ever made if he turned out to be the one taunting her.

Or romancing her?

Had she completely misjudged this whole situation?

She pulled out her cell phone and called him, hoping he wasn't busy on a jobsite and unable to take her call.

"Good morning, Kate. It's good to hear from you."

She never called him. She always waited for him to call her. "Hi. Um . . . Did you come by my house last night or this morning?"

"No. Why? Did you want me to?" He sounded genuinely perplexed.

"No. It's just . . . something happened."

"Are you okay?" Pure concern filled his urgent words.

"Yes. Maybe. I don't know."

"Sweetheart, tell me what's happened. How can I help?"

She bit her lip, wondering how she could suspect, even for a second, this wonderful man. "Did you leave a red rose by my gate?" *Please say yes.*

"No. Though I suppose if someone else is doing that, I need to step up my game."

"No, you don't," she assured him. She appreciated his patience more than anything.

"I thought all women loved receiving flowers."

"This is different. I can't explain right now." She hadn't told him about her past.

"Let's talk about it over dinner tonight."

It wasn't him. It couldn't be him. "Um. Okay."

"I can't wait. Are you sure you're all right?" The worry in his voice touched her.

"I will be. Thank you for picking up."

"Always and anytime. I mean that, Kate. You can count on me."

She really wanted to believe him.

"I'll pick you up at six thirty."

That sounded nice. Normal. Something to look forward to, if only her past weren't threatening to send her into a tailspin. "See you then."

"Call me back if you need me before then."

She hesitated. "Don't you have a lot of work to do?"

"I'm always available anytime for you, Kate. I mean it."

Tears gathered in her eyes. "Thank you."

"Thank me later with one of your elusive smiles."

She found one now, even though he couldn't see it. "Bye, Reed."

"See you soon, sweetheart." He'd called her that twice. He'd never done that before.

She liked it.

The lieutenant eyed her. "So not the boyfriend."

He wasn't quite her boyfriend. Yet. But she hoped.

She shook her head, trying to stay present and in the moment instead of letting her thoughts spin out. Despite wanting to hold on to the little bit of happy Reed made her feel on that call, she refocused on the possible nightmare unfolding. "I haven't noticed anyone on the street. It's quiet. Just the neighbors, nothing out of the ordinary."

"Any strange mail or calls?"

"No."

"Anyone approach you when you're out running errands?"

"No." She couldn't explain it, but she knew this was tied to *him*.

"If there was no message or someone trying to get your attention, then isn't the logical answer that someone dropped that by accident?"

She snatched up the rose and shook it. "This is the message."

"I know to *you* it feels that way, but without any other information to confirm someone is either messing with you or threatening you, there's nothing I can investigate."

Her heart sank as the dread took hold inside her.

"But what I will do is increase patrols on your street to help you feel safe."

She appreciated it and gave him a nod. "Thank you."

"Now, tell me, how have you been these last few years? Getting on okay, I hope." When she'd moved to town, she'd taken her therapist's advice and introduced herself to the lieutenant. It gave her peace of mind to have someone in law enforcement who knew her story and could help if she suffered a flashback in public. Or if someone came looking for a story or to get close to the Rose Reaper's only surviving victim.

Apparently, even evil had fans.

"Yes. Things are different now. I have my work, my house, my life back."

"A new guy." The lieutenant grinned, looking happy for her.

Yes. Reed was the first man since her ordeal who she actually liked and wanted to get closer to.

She wanted a life. One filled with love and happiness and someday a family. But for her, with her past, it wasn't easy to trust others.

The lieutenant leaned forward on his arms on the desk. "And this spooked you. I get it. I don't blame you one bit for being cautious. And I will be, too, by sending those patrol cars your way and making sure you're safe."

That was the thing—she'd just gotten to the point over the last six months where she had slowly let her guard down.

Now, she felt like someone had opened a door to the past.

One she'd like to slam shut again.

The Rose Reaper's Journal Entry

The first one was a rush. Everything heightened.

I still remember the look in her eyes when I slid the knife into her beating heart. I felt it thud to a stop.

I watched her in the stillness and silence knowing I'd been the one to end it.

And for a moment the need turned to pure relief. I felt the high of it.

And then it was gone.

I need it back.

The roses are calling to me.

I want to make them hurt, make them bleed.

I want to hear their last gasp.

I want to be the last thing they see as the light dies in their eyes.

And then I want to do it all over again.

Chapter Three

Eleven weeks and five days later . . .

He stood in line, a predator among prey, needing his caffeine fix as much as the others packed into the busy coffee shop. No one knew what lurked among them. The pretty rose in front of him had no idea how perfect she looked among all the weeds.

He hadn't come here for her.

He'd followed someone else.

But now that he'd seen her, he wanted her.

He slipped out his phone and used the sleeves of his hoodie pulled down over his hands to clean the screen. His perfect rose finished placing her order and turned to the side to walk to the other end of the counter to pick it up when she *accidentally* bumped his hands. The second she touched him, a bolt of electricity shot through him, confirming she was his, and knocking the phone right to the floor exactly as he planned.

"Oh, I'm so sorry." Her sweet voice filled his ears like a soft lullaby, soothing him. Oh yes, she'd moan and sigh and whimper so prettily for him.

"No worries." He turned to the person behind him. "Mind grabbing that for me? I've got a bad back. Bending over suuucks," he exaggerated.

The helpful fellow customer snatched up his phone and dropped it in his sleeve-covered palm.

"Thanks." He stepped up to order his coffee. "I'll take a tall Americano." He turned to the person who'd helped him. "Yours is on me."

"Oh, you don't have to do that."

"Happy to. You saved my poor back."

"Thanks. I'll have a grande dark roast."

He handed the barista a twenty. "Keep the change." He went and stood behind his rose, waiting. She left a minute before him, but he quickly caught up to her in the parking lot, noting her car, and getting behind the wheel of his own to follow her.

What a productive morning.

He'd accomplished what he'd set out to do, and now he could spend the day watching his rose and finding the perfect way to pluck her from the weeds so he could really get to know her.

And end her.

Chapter Four

Five days later . . .

He stared down at his coffee-shop rose tied to the plastic-covered bed and grinned. She was perfect. He'd seen others who compared to the Rose Reaper's second victim. He'd nearly taken one of them, but he'd held out to find just the right rose among the weeds.

The one who called to him.

He did not want just anyone. She needed to be as close to perfect as possible, so he could walk in his predecessor's shoes and complete what he'd started. His gift to *him*. Though he didn't plan to stretch this out over years. No. He had his own plans for what came after the seven.

The need inside him hadn't waned but grown to gnawing proportions over the last few days. He'd watched and waited and picked just the right moment to pluck her from her life.

He'd studied her routine. Up at 6:00 a.m. Out the door by 6:30 for a run. Back to the house by 7:15. Shower, change, pour a cup of coffee to go, in the car by 8:20, and off to work at some office. He'd leave her there for the day, then meet up with her as she arrived home again at just before 6:00 p.m.

She didn't seem to be dating anyone. Lived alone. No pets.

She made enough to either rent or buy the house she was living in.

More than likely, she'd be missed at work before a neighbor noticed anything off.

She never sensed him peeking through her windows, watching her live out her life inside the house, watching TV, making a meal, sorting through mail, all the mundane things people did.

He liked to watch her sleep. She seemed so peaceful.

His dreams were filled with dark desires. Ones he wanted to play out with her.

The craving had overcome him as he grabbed her just outside her front door. No one saw a thing, thanks to the private courtyard that blocked the view to the street and neighbors beyond. It had been a risk, carrying her out to his truck, but at that time in the morning, most everyone was asleep or getting ready for their day, not staring out their own front windows.

And the danger thrilled him.

Once he had her in his truck, he enjoyed the drive to the cabin, thinking about all the things he wanted to do with her. How he'd have her at his mercy.

And there she lay, gagged, whimpering, tears trailing down the sides of her face and into her short dark hair. Wrists bound, arms stretched up to the metal headboard, ankles crossed and tied to the sides of the bottom of the bedframe. Naked. Exposed. Trembling with fear.

For him, it was anticipation.

Yes, he liked her like this.

And oh the things he planned to do to her. Today. Tomorrow. Until he tired of her.

Until she bled for him.

Until she died for him.

He hummed the tune stuck in his head over and over again, stroking his hard cock.

Her eyes widened at the sight of him. She could see how much he wanted her.

Oh, how he wanted to do all the dark and dirty things in his head. The rush built to a fever pitch and he reached for her.

She screamed.

Music to his ears.

He pushed her legs up, slipped between her soft thighs even as she tried to fight and buck him off, but it didn't work with her ankles locked at his lower back, his hips cradled by those lush thighs. He took her and everything he wanted to the sounds of her pleas and gasps and moans and whimpers and the inevitable silence of surrender.

And he wasn't done yet.

Chapter Five

Six days later . . .

"*The body of a young woman was found on the shore of the river this morning by two fishermen. The victim is believed to be Kelly Russell. Kelly was reported missing after she failed to show up at work two days in a row without calling in sick or answering calls from her supervisor or friends. Family members became concerned when they found Kelly's car still parked at her home, no indication that she'd packed for an impromptu vacation, and all signs appeared that she'd simply vanished.*

"*The coroner reports that the body was found nude with multiple abrasions, most seeming to have come from rocks and debris in the river, though she did comment there were ligature marks on the victim's wrists and ankles, along with what appears to be a single stab wound to the chest.*

"*The coroner and police department will be making a statement later today and we will carry it live at three p.m., as well as keep you updated with any breaking news in the case.*

"*And now, the weather. Tom, tell us this heat wave we've all been feeling the last two days will end soon.*"

Kate tuned out the rest of the news broadcast and stared down at the article about another missing person.

Denise Simmons went missing thirteen weeks ago. Her body was found in the same river, though in a completely different area. In fact, the two bodies had been found nearly twenty miles apart.

"He could have dumped them anywhere." She stared at the map where she'd marked the two spots the bodies had been found with red *X*s. Most likely, he'd dumped them upriver and let the current take them. The water would wash away evidence, contaminate anything that was left, and because the bodies were found in different police jurisdictions, no one would realize they were connected until a pattern emerged.

But she saw it.

Because six days ago she'd found not one, but two roses on the path outside her house.

For the last three months, she'd held fast to the lieutenant's notion that the first rose was innocuous. Someone dropped it by accident. Someone thought it kind to leave it for her. Maybe a gardener from a nearby house was cleaning up and dropped it.

Every day when she left her house, she looked for a new one. Each day that passed without a rose reinforced the idea that it had nothing to do with the Rose Reaper.

She told herself over and over again, day after day, it didn't mean anything. But it did to her.

And whoever left it and the two she'd received nearly a week ago knew she understood exactly what it meant.

The Rose Reaper was back and wanted her to know he was killing again.

But that seemed impossible. She'd seen him die right before her eyes. She still remembered the gruesome scene, the way he'd looked right at her, the way his eyes went vacant, and the wave of utter relief that came over her that he was gone and couldn't hurt her or anyone else ever again.

But someone was out there hunting and killing.

They were close enough to leave those roses for her.

Of course, she'd called and told the lieutenant about the two roses last week. He chalked it up to a prank. Someone in the neighborhood had discovered her past and was messing with her.

Or perhaps someone from work was taunting her for some perceived slight.

She couldn't remember upsetting anyone, but perhaps she'd misspoken or inadvertently said something that hurt their feelings without knowing it.

It could be anything that set this in motion.

But now, with another body discovered along the river, she believed this was just the beginning.

Why let her know about the two victims? Why give her a chance to alert authorities that the women were connected, even if they had seemingly nothing in common?

Why pull her into this deadly game?

Because she'd gotten away. She'd survived.

And maybe whoever was doing this wanted her to know they knew where she lived, and they were coming to finish what the Rose Reaper started.

She trembled and wrapped her arms around her middle. She needed to dress and go to work, but all she could do was stare at those two red Xs on the map and wonder how many more she would mark before the murderer was caught.

Who would mark her spot?

She snatched her cell phone off the table and hit the speed dial for her therapist. This early in the morning, her office was closed. So she left a message. "Rebecca, I told you the roses meant something. They've found another body. Why is this happening again?" She hung up, feeling like nothing she said or did would convince others that she was right. There was a serial killer out there hunting.

And he was showing off for her.

Why leave her the roses and not leave them where he'd captured his prey, like the Rose Reaper used to do?

Were they some kind of twisted gift for her?

Or were they a countdown for when he'd come for her?

Chapter Six

Ten weeks and five days later . . .

Kate found three red roses by her gate.

She contacted the lieutenant. "He's kidnapped another woman. Watch the river. You'll find her soon."

"Kate. Let me send an officer to the house."

"Why? This is victim number three. I'm number seven." She hung up on him, hoping he started looking for another missing woman. Praying he got to her in time. But she could be from anywhere. The first two victims lived in different towns. That's how the Rose Reaper got away with it for so long. He didn't hunt in one area. He spread it out. He made sure no one saw him coming until it was too late.

It was too late for whoever he'd taken this time.

✻

Thirteen days later . . .

"This is the third body found in the river in the last six and a half months, though authorities have not confirmed a link between them."

Kate turned off the news report. She already knew what had happened to Tina Parker. She didn't survive or escape. She'd ended up in the river like the others. Kate didn't need to hear the details. She'd lived that hell and knew the coroner's report would include everything about the contusions and abrasions from the rapes, the ligature marks around the wrists and ankles, the stab wound to the heart, but not the damage done to the psyche and soul. All that you couldn't adequately describe on a form in sentences or paragraphs.

That was the kind of thing that rippled through your life, touching every aspect of it, unless you were dead. She had to live with it. She had to work around the triggers and anxiety and trust issues that crept up unannounced and unwelcomed in her life. Everything could be going fine one day, or even one minute, and then the next, she was right back in the pain and trauma, fighting to gain control or simply get through it until she could cope again.

She'd been doing so well.

And then she'd gotten that first rose.

It began the slow erosion of her new life.

But she was fighting to stay in the present. She worked with her therapist on techniques to stay in the here and now and find joy in the simple things.

Today it was hard to find reason to this tragedy.

A family lost a beloved daughter.

Others lost a dear friend.

Tina Parker's patients lost a dedicated nursing professional, who showed up for them when they needed her.

The world lost another precious soul.

And Kate wept for all of them, most especially for Denise, Kelly, and now Tina.

Three lives cut short.

And *he* was getting away with it.

Kate walked out her front door an hour later, determined to get to work, do her job, and live her life like a normal person. Her instinct was to check the walkway for another bunch of roses, but instead her eyes were glued to the man sitting on her porch with his back to her.

Reed turned and smiled up at her. "Good morning, sweetheart." He held up a coffee to-go cup. "Your favorite caramel macchiato."

"Thank you." She took the coffee, stepped down one step, then sat next to him, since he didn't seem inclined to stand with her. "How long have you been waiting out here?"

"Ten minutes. I knocked, but you were probably getting ready and didn't hear me."

"Why didn't you ring the bell?"

He turned his head and held her gaze. "I didn't want to spook you. Not today."

She sighed. "You heard." After the second victim was found, she'd confessed to him about the roses and what they meant to her. He was the first person in her new life she'd told about her past.

Reed eyed her. "They found another body."

"She's number three."

He stared out toward the quiet street. "I don't know what to do to make this better for you."

She dropped her purse next to her, put her coffee in the other hand, then slipped the one closest to him through his arm and leaned her head on his shoulder.

He went still, as if surprised she'd reached for him, then simply leaned his head to hers.

"You showed up. You're here." It meant so much to her. She slid her fingers down his arm and right into his hand, linking her fingers with his. "Thank you for coming."

He kissed her on the head. "Always and anytime for you, Kate." He meant that.

She knew that now.

He let her set the pace. For him, it had to feel painfully slow. But he never complained. He never pushed. This was as close as she'd been to him and for the longest time without her backing away, putting distance between them so she felt comfortable. In this moment, it felt good. It felt right to lean on him, to want to feel his strength and infinite patience.

He kissed her on the head again. He did so often. Sometimes on the forehead at the end of a date. Every time, he had to sense her hesitation for something more, but he never said anything about it. But there was always a pause before he pulled away completely, like he was giving her a chance to take things another step further into intimacy. Something that wasn't easy for her now, no matter how much she wanted to feel normal and close to him.

But today she found the courage to express her need to show him how much she appreciated him being here for her this morning. When her world felt like it was falling back into the darkest time in her life, he was an anchor holding her in the present, in this moment of peace she always found with him.

She turned and met his steady, warm gaze. "Reed."

"Yeah."

"Kiss me."

He leaned in and touched his lips to hers in a soft caress, taking his time, letting her feel his lips on hers as their breath mingled.

"More," she requested, searching his eyes for something she didn't want to see, but finding nothing but joy and desire reflected back at her.

He kissed her again, this time pressing his lips to hers with just the barest hint of his tongue tasting her.

She liked it. A lot. And wanted more. So she took over the kiss, leaning into him, sliding her tongue tentatively against his lips. He opened to her, and she slid her tongue along his and the kiss became something shared equally. It went on and on, until they both ended it with a press of their foreheads together. She opened her eyes and found him staring at her in awe.

He sighed with contentment. "I've wanted to do that for a long time."

"I'm sorry I made you wait."

"It was worth it."

"Good." She grinned, then confessed, "Because I hope we get to do that again soon."

He smiled. It lit up her heart.

She sat back, but kept his hand in hers and leaned against him. "I should get to work."

"Me too."

She laid her head against his shoulder. "Can I have just a couple more minutes?"

He pressed his cheek to her hair. "I'm happy right here with you."

She believed him. And in turn that made her realize that even with a killer hiding in the shadows she could still find the light and joy in life.

She'd fought to get free of one monster.

She wouldn't let another one steal her new life and the happiness she'd finally found.

Not this time.

I know what you are. I see you coming.

I'll find a way to stop you.

Chapter Seven

Ryan Strickland stepped off the elevator, spotted Agent Chapman across the office, and headed toward him.

Agent Chapman hadn't changed much in the last three and a half years. His dark hair had a few grays. The lines around his eyes were more pronounced. He'd added a couple of pounds around the waist. But the easygoing smile remained, telling Ryan the tough and emotional job Chapman did day in and day out hadn't dimmed his ability to be happy.

Victim number three, Tina Parker, had been found early this morning, prompting Agent Chapman to pull Ryan in to consult on the developing case.

Ryan wasn't an FBI agent but a psychologist. He had a PsyD degree, his specialties in forensic and child and adolescent psychology. Basically, he knew how to talk to people and get them to open up about their trauma, then better understand their symptoms and how to manage them with time. Because trauma never went away.

In this case, he'd use his forensic psychology knowledge to help Agent Chapman interview potential people of interest and determine if their behavior and age made them likely to commit this crime.

He used to be in private practice while completing his training, but because of his sister's kidnapping and murder, he'd always wanted to work with law enforcement. He'd worked hard to earn a spot as an FBI consultant.

"Thank you for coming on such short notice." Agent Chapman shook Ryan's hand.

"I was in the neighborhood." So to speak. His job coaxing reluctant witnesses and traumatized victims to talk and help investigators required a lot of travel. It had been a short flight from New York to Maine. Ryan had been helping on another case there when Agent Chapman requested his assistance with two potential suspects.

Agent Chapman led him into a conference room. "Like I told you on the phone—"

"You have a copycat serial killer." Ryan remembered vividly helping Kate unlock the nightmare of what happened to her.

Now they had three victims spread out over the last six and a half months.

The Rose Reaper, on the other hand, had raped and killed six victims over a span of about eight years, dumping their bodies in the river. He had long cooling-off periods, nine to fifteen months, between kills. Kate, the Rose Reaper's seventh victim, had been taken after one of those long dormant periods and was the only known survivor, due to her daring escape.

This killer . . . he couldn't seem to wait. He'd already taken his third victim in less time than had elapsed between the Rose Reaper's first and second victims.

Ryan understood why Agent Chapman wanted as much help as he could get to take this guy down quickly. He stared at the three pictures and files spread out on the conference table. "You're right. The new victims look eerily similar to the Rose Reaper's first three victims."

"The case was a sensation, especially after Kate's escape and the Reaper's death. Easy enough for someone to look up the information online and see pictures of the past victims, then hunt for new ones." Agent Chapman pulled the third file closer. "Tina Parker went missing from her home two weeks ago without a trace."

"And Kate Doyle received three roses." Traumatizing the poor woman who'd survived one killer only to be taunted by another.

"Yes. Kate notified law enforcement each time she received the roses. After the first body was found, we immediately started looking for victims two and three after the roses were left for Kate. Not easy to do when, like the Rose Reaper, this guy takes his victims from different towns and counties along the river." Agent Chapman's frustration drew lines on his forehead. It couldn't be easy to find a missing person when they were looking at over a hundred miles of river. "Just like the Rose Reaper, he holds them a few days, kills them, then dumps them in the water upriver from where they are eventually found."

"Is everything else about the killings the same?"

Agent Chapman's grim expression said yes. "The major elements are present, but there are subtle differences. What I hope you can help me determine is which one of my two persons of interest has the capacity to carry out these crimes." The agent already knew everyone had the capacity to commit atrocities given the right circumstances, provocation, and desire.

What he wanted to know was which of the two men he had called in for questioning should be his focus, because time was running out for whoever was being hunted as the next victim.

"Let's go meet the first candidate." Ryan followed the agent to a room with a door and no windows. The only things in the room: a table, four chairs, a video camera in the corner by the door, and Todd Lane.

According to the report Agent Chapman had sent Ryan to study on the plane, Todd had been arrested multiple times for assault, battery, domestic abuse, and attempted murder, though not all the charges stuck. He got off on a technicality for the attempted murder and was still suspected of the killing of one of his girlfriends, though there wasn't enough evidence he committed the crime to bring charges.

Todd Lane was a predator who liked to taunt and hurt his prey. The women in his life didn't stick around because of his kind caring. He beat them into submission.

At least one of those women who'd had the misfortune of ending up in Todd's brutal hands had been found beaten, strangled, and dumped in the river. Even if the cops couldn't prove it, it didn't mean he hadn't done it.

But did that make him their copycat?

Agent Chapman took the seat next to Ryan and dove right in, placing the photos of the three victims in front of Todd.

Todd stared directly at the agent, contempt on his face, without looking at the photos. "Why am I here?"

"Do you know these women?"

"No." Todd didn't even look at the pictures spread before him.

Agent Chapman didn't back down. "Do you know them?"

"No."

"Have you ever seen or met them?"

Todd pointed to Tina's picture on the table without actually looking at it. "Saw this one on the news this morning. They pulled her out of the river." The slightest lift appeared at the corner of Todd's mouth. Not enough to make it an actual grin, but enough that Ryan saw the unconscious action before Todd caught himself.

Could be he put Tina in the river. Or maybe he was thinking of the other woman law enforcement suspected him of killing. Either way, that slight grin said a lot about Todd.

Agent Chapman pulled out a piece of paper and read through the notes written on it. "Thank you for providing my colleague with the information regarding your whereabouts when these women went missing."

"As you can see, I wasn't anywhere near where they lived."

Ryan caught the same thing the agent did.

"How do you know where they lived?"

Todd glared. "I'm not an idiot. Your guy asks me for my whereabouts on three dates, if I've worked in three different towns, then you pull out photos of three women, one of them dead."

"All of them dead," Agent Chapman corrected. "But I think you know that."

Todd's gaze narrowed. "I don't know anything about any of them."

"You travel to a lot of different towns along the river."

"It's my job. I go where my boss sends me." Todd worked for a heating and air-conditioning company for both commercial and residential. He could have met the victims on the job or while working in their locations. According to the notes Agent Chapman had sent Ryan, Todd's boss used him for commercial jobs exclusively. Ryan guessed because of Todd's history of abusing women. His boss didn't want to risk Todd doing something in a customer's home. More witnesses at a commercial building, less possibility of Todd cornering a lone person and putting the business at risk of being sued.

Todd being in the same town on the same day as one of the victims' abduction wasn't enough to hold him.

"What do you know about the Rose Reaper?" Agent Chapman tossed out the question like he was asking the time.

Todd went still. "He got away with murder. Until that last one." The barest hint of admiration in Todd's eyes before he banked it. "Are you charging me with something?"

"We're just talking." Agent Chapman kept his tone conversational.

"Yeah, well, I'm not talking about dead girls and serial killers anymore. You know where I was on the days you asked. I didn't do whatever you think I did. I'm outta here." Todd stood and moved toward the door, stopping at Agent Chapman's next words.

"You'll need to get a ride. Your company vehicle is being searched."

Red rage colored Todd's face. "You can't do that."

"The owner of the company gave his permission."

Todd stormed out, though it was not as effective given the agent escorting him to the elevator and out of the building.

"Your thoughts?" Agent Chapman sat back and held Ryan's gaze.

"He's been interviewed by cops enough to know the routine and his rights. The women don't mean anything to him. He has no sympathy. More than likely, he thinks they got what they deserved. Not only does he know about the Rose Reaper, he admires him for getting away with the crimes. He also thinks he's better than the Rose Reaper because the Reaper got caught."

"Todd's been caught many times."

"But not for the murder he's suspected of committing. He loves that he got that one over on law enforcement."

"Which could mean he's taken things to a whole new level and is copying the Rose Reaper and thumbing his nose at law enforcement again by getting away with these murders."

Possibly. "Right now, you don't have enough to hold him, let alone charge him. But there's something there. When he said the Rose Reaper got away with the crimes 'until that last one,' that hinted to Kate specifically."

Agent Chapman frowned. "Maybe he wants to punish her for taking the Rose Reaper down."

"Taunting her is a good way to start." Ryan thought about what else they knew about Todd. "He's in his late twenties. That's usually when serial killers start killing. He shows no empathy for the victims. In all the cases where he was charged, his response was always along the lines of *they had it coming, they provoked me, it wasn't my fault.* His crimes have escalated over time. And if he did kill that woman and dump her in the river, it's not a far stretch to think he's decided he likes the kill and is now pursuing that thrill."

"I'll keep digging on him, see if I can tie him to any one of the victims in some specific way." Agent Chapman stood. "Contestant number two is next door."

Ryan followed the agent to the next room where Ed Silva sat drumming his fingers on the table.

"Did you know there are a hundred and twelve tiles on the ceiling?" Ed glanced up, then back at them.

The room was exactly the same as the one they'd just been in. Agent Chapman took a seat across from Ed. Ryan took the seat beside him and across from the empty chair on the other side.

Ed assessed both of them with a cool look. "Why am I here? If you're trying to torture me by keeping me in this tiny room, it's working." His fingers continued to drum on the table.

"We just have a few questions for you."

"The other guy already asked where I've been and what I was doing on the dates those women went missing."

Ryan didn't think the agent who'd asked the initial questions would have stated why those dates were important.

Apparently, Agent Chapman thought the same. "How do you know those dates were when the women went missing?"

"I'm into those true crime podcasts and stuff. You can learn a lot about your local community by monitoring the crime that happens where you live."

"And what have you learned about these murders?" Agent Chapman's genuine interest made Ed still and focus on him.

"Someone is hunting."

"Like you?" Agent Chapman kept his voice quiet and inquisitive.

Ed grinned. "Nah. I ain't got caught doing nothing in a long time."

According to his record, Ed hadn't been caught peeping in women's windows in the last three and a half months. Before that, he'd been charged numerous times for trespassing, peeping, masturbating in public, and theft when he took something of his victims, usually an item of clothing from an unlocked car. In the beginning, the charges were either dropped or pled down to nothing but a small fine. Recently, he'd been given a light sentence of three days in jail for using a camera to take pictures up a woman's skirt. The last charge had been for groping a woman in the public bathroom at a local park two towns over from where he lived.

Ed, so far, hadn't been violent. But maybe something had changed they didn't know about and he'd escalated from watching and groping to raping and killing.

Agent Chapman must have had the same thought as him. "Last time, you got up close and personal. You couldn't control yourself with her. You had to touch her."

Ed rubbed his thumb and middle finger together, his eyes glazing over with the memory of touching his victim.

Ryan kneed the leg of the table, making it squeak as it scuffed the floor, bringing Ed out of his revelry and back to reality.

Ed shifted uncomfortably in his seat. "So I got a little handsy. She wanted it."

"That's why she pressed charges?" Agent Chapman raised a brow.

"Women. They tease and taunt." Ed drummed his fingers on the desk again.

Agent Chapman laid out the three files, the women's pictures turned toward Ed. "Maybe you got tired of the teasing and you took what you wanted this time."

Eyes wide, Ed shook his head. "Nope. Not me." Those fingers drummed faster on the table. Ed couldn't take his eyes off the women.

"They're pretty, huh?" Agent Chapman stared at Ed. "They look a lot like the women you like to follow around and watch."

Ed shrugged a shoulder, then quick as lightning touched victim number one's photo. His fingertip touched Denise's mouth before he went back to drumming his fingers on the table. "She's pretty." He leaned in, staring. Intent. Captivated.

"Did you take her and touch her and kill her?"

Ed's gaze shot to Agent Chapman's, narrowing to a glare. "You can't pin that on me."

Agent Chapman tipped his head to the side. "According to your response to the questions you were asked earlier, you were working two blocks from the victim's house the day she was kidnapped."

Fingers drumming on the table, Ed shook his head. "Uh-uh. Not me. You want to ask me anything more, I want a lawyer." His fingers stilled. "Now."

Agent Chapman held his gaze for a long moment, waiting to see if Ed filled the silence. For someone who'd practically been in constant motion since they walked in, it seemed odd and eerie to see him so still, his stare focused on the agent. A predator waiting.

Agent Chapman smiled at Ed. "We're just talking."

"Not anymore. You ain't got no proof. You're fishing. And I ain't stupid enough to bite at that bait." Ed looked at the pictures on the table. "Besides, they're not my type."

Denise certainly was based on Ed's past victim's descriptions and his reaction to her today. But the other two were not his usual type. One blonde, the other with light brown hair. Both pretty, but more petite and slender than Denise.

"I've been working on me," Ed announced. "I've got an online therapist who's been helping me curb my urges. So you see, I didn't do this. I'm better now."

If Ed was telling the truth about seeing a therapist to help him with his deviant behavior, Ryan suspected Ed believed he'd tamed his urges. But the reality was Ed would have to fight those desires while he learned to recognize his triggers and stop himself from acting impulsively. It would take time and a lot of hard work to overcome his predilection before he could learn to interact with women in appropriate ways and not see them as objects.

Ed put both hands flat on the table. "Am I free to go?"

Agent Chapman nodded, knowing they didn't have enough to hold him either.

Ed walked out, escorted by another agent to the elevator and out of the building.

Ryan stood and turned to Agent Chapman. "I wish I could say he absolutely isn't your killer. Too young."

Ed was only twenty-three. Not out of the realm of possibility, but not seasoned enough either.

Ryan put his impressions into an assessment. "His crimes are purposeful in the way he stalks his victims and watches them, but there's an impulsive component to his groping, which was done in public. Much higher chance of being caught. If he'd gone into his victims' homes and assaulted them, then I could see him escalating to kidnapping them. I just don't see him escalating from peeping and groping to rape and murder so quickly."

"He wasn't my first choice over Todd, but there's something about him that makes me think I'm not seeing all he's capable of."

"Probably because you sense in him all the things he'd like to do to the women he targets. Without help, he will escalate and try to fulfill those fantasies in his head."

"Maybe he already has. Maybe all he needed was a road map and used the Rose Reaper's MO to finally fulfill his needs."

"It's possible." Ryan had to agree for such a leap to take place in Ed's behavior, copying someone else would be a path more easily followed than simply giving in to his impulses as it seemed he'd been doing for the last many years. "But if you want me to say it's Ed or Todd right now, I can't. They both have a keen interest in the Rose Reaper. Natural since they've lived in the area all their lives and the Rose Reaper was a huge case. They couldn't have avoided the media and talk about the case at the height of its sensationalism. I'm guessing the case has been talked about and dissected on a lot of podcasts that originate in this region. So the fact they know about the Rose Reaper doesn't mean they're such fans that now they want to emulate him and use his notoriety to gain some for themselves. Todd has a much higher regard for himself than Ed. He seems particularly arrogant about getting away with murder. Maybe he thinks he can keep getting away with it."

Ryan thought more about their younger suspect. "Ed, on the other hand, if he is seeking help for his problem and he's earnest about it, wants to change. Has he changed? Time will tell."

Agent Chapman stood. "I'll keep an eye on both of them, though right now, Todd is my number one suspect."

Ryan stuffed his hands in his pockets and nodded. "He's the logical choice, but I think you knew that before you brought me here."

Agent Chapman shrugged. "The Rose Reaper case consumed my life like no other case. I used to lie awake at night thinking I'd never get the son of a bitch. Then Kate escaped and all of a sudden it was over with six women dead and a survivor who saved herself. Now it's happening again. I want this guy before he takes the next victim. I'll do whatever is necessary, use whatever resources we have, to stop this guy. Maybe having you here was overkill for such mundane interviews, but if you saw or heard something I missed and it holds the key to an arrest, then . . ." The agent shrugged again.

"The most telling thing to me was that Todd hinted at Kate. Ed knows the case. He's probably listened to and read everything about the case, but he didn't mention her. But he was drawn to Denise. He had to touch her picture like a compulsion. Just like he did the woman at the park, who by the way looked a lot like Denise."

Agent Chapman's eyes went wide. "You're right. They did look similar."

"Whoever is doing this is obsessed with Kate knowing they're killing women. I'm guessing Todd has boasted to someone, in some way, that he got away with killing that woman. Maybe the way to get him for these murders, if he committed them, is to find out who he told about the one we know he committed and see if he's talked about the new ones, too."

"Have you ever thought about being an agent?" Agent Chapman asked.

Ryan shook his head. "I prefer helping the victims." He held out his hand and shook the agent's. "Call me if you need me."

"Have a safe flight back to New York."

"I hope you catch this guy soon." Before another victim was taken and killed.

The Rose Reaper's Journal Entry

The more I take, the more I want. I can't help myself. Nothing else matters now. They are all I think about.

I feel like I should regret it, but I don't. I need this so badly to stay sane, to find the calm that soothes me. They are the only cure for the nightmares that haunt me. Where I was weak in my youth, I am strong now. Grown. In control.

I AM NOT A SERVANT TO HER DARKNESS ANYMORE!!!

I take what I want. I show them, they can't hurt me.

Their pain is my pleasure.

And though I see that was what fed her, I can't help feeding it in me.

In more ways than one, she made me.

Finding my path, my roses, is the only thing that saved me.

Chapter Eight

Eight weeks and four days later . . .

"Police are searching for a missing woman after a neighbor heard a scream in the early-morning hours yesterday. Later that afternoon, a friend discovered a cell phone smashed on the victim's back patio where authorities believe she was kidnapped from. Cathy Evans, twenty-eight, is five-foot-six with dark brown shoulder-length hair and brown eyes." Kate stared at the picture of the victim that popped up on the screen next to the broadcaster's head. *"She worked at a nearby restaurant as a chef. Friends and family are asking anyone who might have seen her in the last two days to contact authorities with any information."*

Kate left her untouched coffee on the table and walked to the front door, clenching her trembling right hand. She looked out the window and spotted the four roses immediately.

Hands settled on her shoulders and she jumped and spun around with a gasp, raising her hands to ward off an attack that wasn't coming.

Reed released her and held up his hands in surrender. "It's just me."

She tried to catch her breath, but hyperventilated instead.

Reed reached for her again. This time, she didn't shy away or startle, but went into his arms and held on to him for dear life. "What's wrong?" He held her tighter as she trembled.

"Look out front." She knew the second he saw the roses by the way his body stiffened.

"Fuck. Again."

"He's just getting started." *Two more to go before he comes for me.*

This wasn't the first time Reed had spent the night. But it was new and getting better every time he stayed.

Intimacy wasn't easy, but luckily for her, Reed's patience never waned. And last night had been so easy and wonderful. She hadn't thought at all about the past. She'd stayed in the moment. She'd found pleasure and joy in his arms.

And as the echoes of the past faded as her ability to trust Reed increased, the killer out there kept re-ringing the bell, calling up all her old nightmares.

Reed cupped her face and made her look up at him. "I'm sorry, sweetheart. I hate this for you. What can I do? Let me call the lieutenant for you. I'll check the video camera. We should have a picture of him this time."

Reed had been a huge help in making her feel safe at home. He upgraded all the locks on her doors and windows. Installed a new security system. He even set up cameras at the front and back of the house. He refused to let her pay for any of it, and said that it was for his own peace of mind.

How did she get so lucky?

She didn't know. But it was getting harder and harder to be here without him.

The phone rang. She ran into the kitchen where she'd left it on the charger. She read the caller ID and answered but didn't get a word out.

Lieutenant Griffin jumped right in. "Did you receive four roses this morning?"

"They're on the walkway. I haven't gone out to get them yet. I saw the news about Cathy Evans."

"It has to be her. Four women. Four different towns along the river, though the crimes are subtly different from the Rose Reaper."

She wanted to ask, *How so?* but figured he wouldn't give her any details the press didn't already report.

The lieutenant's sigh rang with frustration and exhaustion. "Do you think that because the abduction was reported so early compared to the other victims he's already killed her?"

Kate shook her head, though the lieutenant couldn't see her. "No." Not yet, anyway. "Not if he really does know what the Rose Reaper did to his victims. He seems to enjoy re-creating it."

"How would he know that kind of detail?"

"Maybe someone got a copy of the police or FBI file. Maybe he knew Freddy Poole," she guessed.

"But waited three years to copy him?"

"I don't know." She wished she had all the answers and this was over already.

"And you haven't told anyone in detail about your experience with the Rose Reaper?" It didn't sound like an accusation, more a quest for a thread he could pull that would lead him to the killer.

"I told the FBI psychologist, Ryan Strickland, who came to see me in the hospital. He was the first person I spoke to after I escaped. I was the only one left to tell him what that monster did to his victims. I've also told my therapist, Rebecca. Other than those two people and anyone in law enforcement who listened to the recording of my conversation with Ryan, I've only told one other person who is not bound by confidentiality."

"Reed," the lieutenant guessed.

"He needed to know why I am the way I am now." She couldn't hide it from him, so she found the courage to share the worst thing that had ever happened to her.

"I know this has shaken you to the core. I wish I could do more."

"I wish I could tell you who is doing this. I wish I could save Cathy Evans."

The lieutenant didn't say anything for a moment. "They never located the cabin where he held you." The statement sounded more like him speaking his thoughts out loud.

"No. At the time, and even now, I can't remember very much about that night, other than the fact that I ran, ended up on the road, and watched the Rose Reaper take the easy way out and die."

"You don't think he got what he deserved?"

"I spent two days at his mercy. Thirty years in prison wouldn't have been enough to make up for what he did to me. The three seconds it took for him to make a move and the officers to shoot him dead was better than he deserved and far less than I wanted. I'm still living with what he did. He should be, too, in a tiny cell, alone, with no one coming to help him and nothing but his unfulfilled desire eating away at him. Because for him, that would be torture. Someone like him doesn't have control or remorse. Their need to hurt others rules them. You take that away and they're left with a need that can't be filled or tamed. Whoever is doing this has to do it. And I hope when he's caught, he's put in a cage and never let out. And still, that won't be enough for me or the families of the victims. This killer has taken four lives. He won't stop until someone stops him."

"Agent Chapman officially took the case after Tina's body was found. He's dogged in his pursuit to find this guy."

It didn't surprise her that the agent in charge of the Rose Reaper case was assigned to this one, too. "Because number three made this monster a serial killer."

"Yes." The lieutenant paused. "I can't imagine the nightmares this brings up for you. How are you doing?"

She stared down at her shaking hand. "It's getting harder to focus and concentrate on anything else. I've worked hard to leave the past locked away where it belongs. I thought I finally had my life back. But *he* won't let me move on."

Reed walked into the kitchen with her tablet in his hand. He held it up to her.

She studied the man standing at her gate. She couldn't make out anything other than the completely black outfit. Jeans, hoodie, gloves, even a ski mask or something obscuring what little she could see of his face through the hood's opening. He stared at the front door like he knew the camera was there. Slowly, he brought the roses to his face, as if he smelled them. Or kissed them. Then he laid them on the path.

But the truly chilling part came when he stood and pointed right at the camera, as if he knew she'd be watching.

Reed set the tablet on the counter and pulled her into his arms. She didn't mean to stiffen at his touch. He didn't seem to take it personally, but lightened his hold, letting her decide if she wanted to step away or not. When she leaned into him, he hugged her close. "I'm so sorry, sweetheart. I wish we had something that identified him conclusively."

"What did he say?" Lieutenant Griffin asked. "Does he have a photo?"

Kate gathered herself. "No. Not exactly. Reed installed a camera out front and in the backyard. We have a video, but there's really nothing there. The man is completely covered from head to foot."

"Send it to me. Maybe we can identify something, anything that will clue us in to who he is." The lieutenant's very optimistic outlook spoke of hope where Kate had none. Not right now. Not with another woman missing and about to be dead.

"Reed is emailing it to you now. I have to go. I'm going to be late for work."

"Kate . . ." The lieutenant probably wanted to give her assurances, but apparently couldn't seem to come up with anything she'd believe at this point. "I wish I could do more."

"I just want to know why."

"You know already. He can't help himself."

"Yeah, well, he can leave me out of it." She hung up, immediately feeling guilty for taking out her frustration on the man who was only trying to do his job.

Reed leaned back against the counter. "Stay home today."

"Why? He knows where I live. He comes at will without any real expectation of being caught. Even if he is, what would they charge him with? Littering?" She thought of that first call to 911. The operator thought she was nuts. Or at least out of her mind for reporting a litterbug.

But this was so much more.

And the carefully constructed walls she kept repairing to hold back the nightmares and memories and all-out terror that wanted to take her under were beginning to crumble faster than she could shore them up with her resolve and optimism that she'd survive this because she'd survived last time.

What did he want from her?

She feared she knew the answer and it would come true.

Chapter Nine

Five weeks and one day later . . .

Kate stepped out onto her porch with the same sense of dread she'd had every day for months coiling her stomach. She spotted the roses immediately and stood frozen in the morbid reality of what something so pretty and innocuous meant to her.

Another woman was taken yesterday.

Whoever it was had endured a night in hell, her world shattered, her body hurt and violated, her future stolen.

Cathy Evans had been found in the river nine days after her abduction. They'd find this victim in the days or weeks to come.

Kate knew it in her bones and all the way to her soul.

The ache in her chest grew. The dread intensified. The sadness threatened to swamp her.

The now-familiar tremble in her right hand quaked.

All the progress she'd made in learning to live a carefree life disappeared beneath the nightmares, anxiety, hyperawareness, and constant vigilance.

Even breathing became harder and harder.

She scanned the quiet street where she lived but saw nothing and no one that looked out of the ordinary.

How could the world look so peaceful when the darkness had invaded her mind again and all she did was look for monsters?

The door opened behind her and she jumped.

"Kate, honey, I thought you were leaving for work?" Reed. Her eye of the storm. He'd been so patient and kind and loving.

He was everything she thought she'd never have after what happened to her.

Over the past few weeks, it seemed they spent more time together than apart, but he never made it feel like he was here protecting her.

But that's what he did. Without being asked. Without her having to say that's what she needed. He understood all the turmoil inside her without her having to say a word.

And when the pressure got to be too much and she railed at whoever was doing this to her and all those women, he added his voice to her concerns and recriminations. He supported her need to try to hold on to the life she'd built while it felt like this monster was tearing it down one victim, one death at a time.

He didn't mind the added police patrols on the street, or that for his own peace of mind he had to text her several times a day just to be sure she was okay and alleviate his own building anxiety. He didn't even mind that she'd come up with a secret code to use with him in case she was under duress and couldn't tell him she was in trouble.

Because trouble was coming.

Reed wanted to take her away.

She couldn't ask him to leave his life here.

She didn't want to leave hers.

She just wanted this to be over.

And they were getting close.

She stepped aside and revealed the five red roses on the path, along with something new. A note written on a large piece of paper and propped against the gate. Black marker warned her of what was coming.

You and Me

Soon

Reed gasped and reached for her, taking her arm and pulling her toward him. "Come inside. Now. We'll call the police."

She walked inside, her mind reeling.

Reed slammed the door like that would keep the danger at bay. Like she'd be safe.

She wasn't. That was the message.

He was coming.

"I'll of course notify the lieutenant, but I don't see what good it will do. They have no leads. *He* comes here at will. He's not afraid of being caught."

Reed had already grabbed the tablet and pulled up the video feed from last night. "Maybe this time . . ."

She shook her head even though he was scanning the video.

She felt like she was losing her mind.

Her therapist, Rebecca, talked about using her coping strategies. But how did you cope with a killer taunting you?

He wanted her to know he was coming for her.

He wanted her to know he'd killed five women.

He wanted her to know she wasn't getting away this time.

Her heart pounded and her chest went tight. The panic attacks came more regularly. She tried to hide them by locking herself in the restroom at work and around Reed, though sometimes, like now, her obvious distress overwhelmed her.

Reed set the tablet on the table and rushed to her. "Take a slow, deep breath."

"I need my phone."

"You need to breathe." He helped her to the sofa and sat beside her, holding her hand.

Such a comfort, even though she felt ridiculous and out of control. His steady presence grounded her.

"There you go, sweetheart. Better. A few more. We'll get through this."

"How do you put up with me?"

"I love you," he said plainly.

She lost her breath again. He'd never said that to her. He showed it in the way he cared for her. She loved all the little things he did to make her happy and brighten her day. The texts he sent to check on her were always disguised as something else.

Do you think Skittles really come from rainbows?

I saw a bunny on the jobsite today. She had your eyes.

Why is lunch meat round and bread is square or rectangular?

Are donuts breakfast or dessert?

You like tea. I'm installing an instant hot-water dispenser for you tonight.

Random stuff, but also a way for him to check in with her, because he knew she'd answer. He didn't want her to feel like he was being overprotective. She didn't want to be asked ten times a day if she was all right. She wasn't. He knew that. But so long as she answered those texts, he knew nothing terrible happened to her.

She knew she could count on him to be there for her.

But right now, she was spiraling.

She needed more.

So she pulled her phone from her purse and called the one person who would understand because he'd been there when she escaped. He'd helped her find her way out of hell and crippling terror.

"Who are you calling?"

"A lifeline."

Chapter Ten

Ryan Strickland scratched his stubbly jaw and poured his first cup of coffee. He leaned back against the new countertop and surveyed the unfinished work in his living room. His best friend, Ash, was doing a great job fixing up his place.

It needed it.

Though the new wood on the ceiling in the living room caught his eye, he couldn't help focusing on the date he had with Molly last night. She'd asked for fun, not complicated. He hoped he gave her that and more. She loved music, so he took her to the fair where they stuffed themselves on surprisingly decent fair food, rode the rides—the picture in his head of her riding the merry-go-round, a huge smile on her face, would stay with him forever—and ended the night in the amphitheater listening to three local rock bands.

They were good.

Time out with Molly—amazing.

It had been a long time since he dated.

And after he spent the last couple of weeks helping take down the Copeland County Killer, finding the remains of not only his missing sister but those of the other thirty-three victims, and laying his sister to rest, he needed some fun, not complicated in his life.

He couldn't wait to see Molly again.

But with him back to work so soon and her late-night work hours, finding the time might be difficult.

His phone rang. He grabbed it off the breakfast bar and checked the caller ID, wondering who would call this early in the morning, hoping it wasn't anything dire.

He didn't recognize the number, but answered anyway. "Hello."

"Ryan, thank God," the woman said in a rush, panic and desperation in her voice. "He's dead, but he's back. At least someone wants me to believe that. He came to my house. He won't stop. He's coming for me. There are five now."

Ryan's heart sped up as his mind tried to decipher what this woman was trying to tell him. "Hold on. Slow down. Who is this?"

"It's Kate. Kate Doyle. The Rose Reaper, he's back. He left me roses."

Ryan went perfectly still. "Kate, Freddy Poole was shot and killed by the police. You were there. You saw it."

"I know. You're right. *He's* dead. But someone is killing again. Someone who knows how he did it. Someone who's been leaving me roses."

"Agent Chapman contacted me about the case a couple of months ago and told me what's been happening." He didn't mention the two potential suspects Agent Chapman interviewed.

He forgot about his coffee and headed for his office, where he unlocked his file cabinet and pulled out the Rose Reaper case file. He flipped it open. Freddy Poole stared back at him from his driver's license photo.

There were many more photos in the file of his seven victims.

"Today, I found five roses. And a note. *You and me. Soon.* I . . . I can't do this again, Ryan. Make it stop. You have to make him stop." The panic in her voice made his heart beat faster as he got caught up in her emotional state.

He tried to remain impartial and detached so he could help. "Kate, I need you to take a deep breath. It is going to be okay. We'll figure this out."

"Someone is killing women and making sure I know about it."

"I understand." And it meant trouble.

Someone had fixated on Kate. Another murderer who also admired the Rose Reaper. Or at least wanted to use his notoriety to build his own.

"Do you get it? Because it's obvious to me that he's working his way to victim number seven. Me, Ryan. He's coming for me."

And if he was already at number five, they didn't have much time to stop him before he came for Kate. "What are the police doing about it?"

"All that they can and nothing that leads to an arrest." Frustration and fear made Kate's voice snap with urgency. "They have regular patrols in the neighborhood. We have a camera at the front and back of the house and still *he* comes."

Ryan took that to mean the guy disguised his appearance enough that they couldn't ID him.

"He's at number five and escalating the time between murders. He only waited five weeks this time. It won't be long now. I don't know what to do. I want to run. But will anyplace be far enough, or safe enough, from *him*? I'm scared that no matter what I do, he'll find me. And I'm angry. Why is this happening to me again? Why can't I just live the life I've rebuilt? Why is he tearing it all down?" Her voice cracked on a sob.

Ryan understood everything she was feeling. "Let me contact Agent Chapman."

"He won't tell me anything."

"He can't divulge information about an ongoing case, but maybe I can find out something to ease your mind. Give me just a little bit of time to get caught up on what's been happening, then I'll call you back. Until then, do you have someone who can stay with you?"

"Yes. Reed is here."

"Who is Reed?" The name didn't sound familiar. He didn't think Kate had any family with that name.

"He's my boyfriend."

That surprised him.

Kate had been a wreck after she escaped. She was afraid to trust herself and everyone else. Ryan had set her up with a psychologist who specialized in trauma. Apparently, she'd healed enough in the last three-plus years to find a partner. "Congratulations. I'm so happy to hear that you're doing well and that rebuilding your life included letting others in."

Ryan hoped Reed was a good guy, one who would stick by Kate.

"I'm trying. But this . . . I feel like I'm spiraling. The past . . . it's coming back to me so clearly. It's like it just happened."

When Ryan first met Kate almost four years ago after her escape, he'd gotten enough information out of her to ID the killer and the general area where she'd been held. The police searched for days, but never found the cabin in the woods where all the women had been held, raped, and murdered.

At first, Kate hadn't been able to speak. It took days to get her to open up even a little bit, until finally she was able to recall bits and pieces of what happened. Enough details to give them the big picture and match the evidence, but not the complete story.

Not much was known about why Freddy Poole did what he did.

What made him a monster?

Who was killing now and taunting Kate?

What kind of person not only kills but re-traumatizes a victim over and over again?

Someone who needed to be stopped.

And if Kate was right, they were running out of time before he got to her.

"Once I talk to Agent Chapman, I'll have a better handle on the situation. I know you don't want to hide from this, but it may be time to put you in protective custody."

She answered with her soft crying.

"I'm sorry, Kate. You endured a terrible experience and came out the other side. I know you're worried and scared and wondering if this will ever end again. It will. And I'm going to make sure you're safe. Keep your phone with you. I'll be in touch."

"Thank you, Ryan. I just . . . I need to know if they have something, anything on whoever is doing this, and when they'll stop him."

It wasn't lost on Ryan that she understood all too well that someone like this wouldn't stop unless stopped.

"We'll talk soon." And if he could convince his boss, he'd be there to see her in person.

He hung up with Kate and made the call.

His boss, Special Agent in Charge Emily Booker, answered on the second ring. "Ryan. It's early. Is everything all right?"

"Yes. I'm good."

"I'm happy to hear that. How is your family?"

He appreciated that his well-being mattered enough for her to ask before they dove into talk about work. "We're all getting better a little each day."

"That's good news."

They laid his sister to rest several days ago. It was a long time coming. And he and his family were finally able to let the past go.

He was ready to help a new victim.

Or in this case, a past victim.

"Kate Doyle just reached out to me."

"The victim who survived Freddy Poole, the Rose Reaper."

He appreciated that his boss took an active interest in all the cases her agents were assigned. "Yes. She's scared because a copycat killer is reaching out to her. She's understandably upset."

"Agent Chapman has the case in hand." Of course his boss knew that. "He's been focused on the women, trying to find links between them. He hasn't ruled out the two men you interviewed with him. Just like with the Rose Reaper, he's got nothing so far."

"Kate says things are coming back to her like this just happened."

"If you want to jump into the case, maybe see if there's something more Kate knows that can help, that can be arranged."

He sighed out his relief. "Yes. She trusts me. If someone is trying to connect with her and killing women, and possibly making her a target, I want to be there to help her through this."

"If you feel that strongly about it, okay. I'll assign you to what, at this point, is a fact-finding mission. I'm sure Agent Chapman will see the value in having a second pair of eyes and ears on the case."

"Thank you."

"It's our job. I'll get the ball rolling."

"I appreciate it."

"Keep in touch. But also take care of yourself, Ryan." With that, his boss hung up on him.

He didn't want to get sucked back into thoughts and feelings about the Copeland County Killer case. He wanted to focus on Kate and a killer who needed to be stopped before it was too late.

He wanted to focus on what he needed right now: a plane ticket to Maine, a rental car, and his go-bag, which he'd already repacked, even though he'd been planning on being home for another week.

Not anymore.

Chapter Eleven

Ryan wanted to go straight to Kate, but decided it best to check in with Agent Chapman. Ryan wasn't here to step on any toes. Agent Chapman had welcomed his help with Kate nearly four years ago and again with the two suspect interviews. He hoped the agent did so now, too.

He found Agent Chapman in a conference room at the FBI field office, waiting for him.

"Ryan, good to see you again. Sorry it's under these circumstances."

He shook the agent's outstretched hand and glanced at the five sets of case files laid out on the table and displayed on the five boards behind the agent.

Five women's faces stared back at him.

"You ready to do this?" the agent asked.

Ryan turned his attention to him. "Start at the beginning."

Agent Chapman went to the first victim. "Denise Simmons. Single. Taken, we believe, from her house. It's unclear how he got in, or if he took her from outside. Just like the Rose Reaper's first victim, she was bound by her wrists and ankles, raped, then stabbed through the heart, a clean kill."

"Any hesitation in the stabbing? Any signs he hit her?"

"No. None. We're not sure if he knocked them out with a drug or simply grabbed them and took them."

Ryan suspected he used something.

They never found anything in the Rose Reaper's victims' systems, but things like benzodiazepines were rarely detected in the blood because they were quickly metabolized. That's why so many date-rape victims woke up confused and foggy about what happened, sure they'd been drugged, even though a blood test showed nothing in their system.

"Any evidence left behind during the rape?" Maybe they had DNA, but not a person in the system or of interest to match it to.

"Either the river washed it all away, or he used a condom."

"Same as the original killer." Ryan's frustration grew. "So the abduction, rape, and kill all feel like the Rose Reaper. What else is the same?"

"They're kept for several days without food or water, single penetrating wound to the heart with a sharp, thin blade, then dumped in the river." Those details had been released to the press, so it seemed obvious and easy to copy those details.

"The Rose Reaper kept Kate in a cabin in the woods. He wasn't afraid of anyone hearing her screams or coming upon them."

Agent Chapman stared at a map of the river where the bodies were dumped and found along the more than one hundred miles. "We have no clue where our new guy is taking them or how. Every home he's taken the women from has no video cameras. Not even the neighbors have cameras."

"So he's stalking his victims long enough to scope out the neighborhood and his victims' homes."

Agent Chapman nodded. "Yet not a single person in the neighborhoods saw a suspicious or even just unfamiliar person on the street or out for a walk. No strange cars. Nothing."

"He's got to be going in the dead of night."

"No reports of dogs barking at night either," the agent added.

Ryan looked at all the women's faces again. "How is he finding them?"

"They have nothing in common. None of them even visit the same coffee place. They live in different towns."

"All along the river, like before, right?"

Agent Chapman pointed at the map. "Green *X*s show where they lived. Blue where they worked. Red where they were found."

Ryan couldn't see a discernible pattern.

Agent Chapman continued. "It's smart. More than one woman goes missing in a single town, that raises a red flag to the police. But you take one from a small town upriver on one shore, then another three months later downriver fifty miles on the opposite shore, no one thinks they're connected."

"Unless you leave a rose for the last victim of the man you're emulating."

"Exactly." Agent Chapman stared at the boards, where five women stared back at him. "Why let the authorities know these victims are connected when you could get away with it for months, even years before the connection is made?"

"Because he wants Kate's attention. He wants recognition for what he's doing. And taunting her gives him a thrill," Ryan said matter-of-factly.

"It's a huge risk. So why do it?"

Ryan shrugged. "Because she's the one who got away. She's the one he needs to finish."

"Like some fucked-up gift to the Rose Reaper?"

Ryan hated to think it, but it was the only thing that really fit. Copycats wanted the notoriety of the original killer. They used their playbook but improved upon it so they wouldn't get caught.

"What about the two persons of interest we interviewed?"

"Todd Lane, the heating and air guy, is still number one on my list."

Ryan shrugged one shoulder. "No one would look twice at a work truck parked on a street too long."

"Exactly. I had the vehicle searched when we questioned him. It came back clean. Nothing to indicate any of the victims had been inside. No receipts that matched up to any of the victims either. While

I can put him in close proximity to the last two victims' homes on jobs he's done, I can't tie him specifically to them."

"And the other guy?"

"Ed Silva," the agent supplied. "Still clean. No new arrests or reports of him trespassing or peeping into windows. Which only makes me wonder more if he's our guy and getting his fix by taking and killing these women, though he hasn't missed any work."

"Maybe therapy is working for him." Ryan hoped so. For Ed's sake, and his potential victims.

Agent Chapman shrugged.

With no evidence on the victim to point them to a suspect, they were left with two men who could have done it, but no proof one of them did do it. "So we know what the killer copied. What's different? Besides him leaving the roses for Kate and not where he took the women from."

Agent Chapman leaned forward, studying the five photos. "That's just it, everything else is nearly identical except the mark he leaves on them."

The Rose Reaper drew on his victims. A rose. Right on their chest above their left breast. It was done in green and red permanent ink. And even though the bodies were left in the river, the mark was usually discernible. A rose with the stem and two leaves on the right side of it.

Kate had it on her chest when he met her in the hospital. He'd asked the nurse to find some rubbing alcohol and clean it off.

But that information had never been released to the public. The news reports focused on the roses left at the scene of the abduction. Some newbie reporter thought it ingenious to be the first to give the killer his own moniker after the seemingly random cases were connected.

"Does he leave a mark?"

"He brands them." Agent Chapman pulled out a photo of Denise Simmons, the first victim.

Ryan took it and couldn't believe his eyes. "It's the exact same drawing the original killer put on his victims." He studied it. "How could the copycat know that?"

"That's what I'd like to know. The two leaves on the right isn't common. Usually, you'll see a rose with leaves on both sides of the stem, or just on one. Even if there are two, this is very specific as far as one leaf being larger than the other. The distance between the leaves is also identical. Then look at the petals. All of them are identical to the original rose drawings the Reaper did on his victims. He drew it the same every damn time. It's too many matches to be coincidental. Either the new killer knew the Reaper and saw him drawing this, or someone who has access to the Rose Reaper file is our copycat."

"It's been over three years since the Rose Reaper took Kate. The cases go back further than that. Most copycat killings happen within the first two years. Yet this guy started long after the Rose Reaper died."

"Something set him off and onto this path. When we catch him, we'll ask him."

Ryan felt like they were missing something. "What about Freddy Poole's friends, known associates, and family?"

Agent Chapman opened another file. "The Reaper had been fired from his job more than a year before he started killing. He got in a fight with a customer, busted the guy's lip and cracked one of his ribs. He had several priors for minor assaults. He got five months for the latest one and got out in"—the agent whistled—"two months due to overcrowding. No known associates. No close friends. He didn't even have a permanent address at the time of his arrest. The dude was a loner."

"More than likely he was living in the remote cabin."

"Yeah. How was it hidden so well that no one in law enforcement out looking for it found it?"

"Kate couldn't remember how long or how far she ran. She said she dodged trees and brush and felt like she zigzagged around obstacles until she came to the hill that led up to the road. She didn't even know the road was there until she stumbled onto it and a car stopped for her."

Agent Chapman frowned. "I bet she was quite the sight, standing there naked and bleeding."

"After two days with no food or water, I'm surprised she made it at all."

"If she hadn't gotten out then, she probably would have been killed soon. Based on how long the bodies were estimated to have been in the river and the dates they were abducted, the Reaper didn't keep them more than three days."

"What about our new guy?"

"Hard to tell because of decomp, bloating from them being in the river, and damage to the bodies due to debris in the water, but the coroners all agree they're held long enough to digest all the contents in their stomachs. Best estimates come in anywhere from a day to four days. Victim number one was probably dumped after less than a day."

"He got excited. He didn't have the patience to keep her. He wanted the kill."

Agent Chapman rubbed the back of his neck. "With victim two, Kelly, he kept her probably about four days."

"He couldn't get back that same level of excitement as he had with the first."

Agent Chapman cringed. "The others it seems to be around two to three days."

"He's getting used to having them and what feels right. The first two days, they're still able to fight and scream and do whatever it is he wants them to do. By day three, their energy is waning. Some of them might even be drowsy and sick and emotionally drained to the point they just shut down. It's no fun to play with something that doesn't play with you." Ryan's stomach turned at the thought of what the women endured.

"That's some fucked-up shit."

No doubt.

Agent Chapman shrugged. "So why not feed them? He could keep them longer."

"They serve a purpose. They are objects. He doesn't care about them. They fill his needs. And when he's done, he tosses them out. He does it in a way almost guaranteed to ensure he's not caught. He wants to keep doing it. He *needs* to keep doing it."

"But our new guy seems to want to get caught. Why else leave the roses and note for Kate?"

"When we catch him, we can ask him." Ryan mimicked the agent's earlier sentiment.

Agent Chapman glanced from the case files to the boards again. "At this point, we don't have a single person of interest or lead to follow."

What he didn't say was that they were waiting for another body to wash up. Or for this guy to make a mistake. Which at this point seemed unlikely. Unless he got cocky. There was always something that led to their downfall.

Ryan hoped it happened soon. He didn't want another woman to lose her life. He didn't want Kate to have to endure any more reminders of her past.

Like getting another bouquet of death roses.

Chapter Twelve

Ryan pulled up in front of Kate's house and parked just outside the garden gate. He sat for a moment and took in the quiet street with the modest homes. The yards were all kept tidy. The houses in good repair. At nearly six in the evening, the street was anything but bustling, with a teenage boy several houses down playing basketball in the driveway, someone pulling into another driveway at the end of the street, and a mom taking groceries from her car and into the house as a toddler tried to "help" by holding on to one of the bags. Really, she was making it harder on the mom by making her tug the toddler along without dropping the other bags. But Mom remained patient and the two disappeared into the house.

But the people who lived here didn't hold his attention. He was looking for someone who didn't belong. Someone who somehow watched Kate's house without being seen.

So he did what most people don't and looked up and out around the neighborhood, noting the tallest trees, the highest roof peaks. Anywhere that the killer could roost and see Kate's place.

He found a couple of potential places to check out.

"Are we going in?" Agent Chapman asked.

He turned to the agent with the notion that they could be being watched right now and not wanting to give anything away. "I'm going to point out a few places of interest around us, but I don't want you to make it obvious you're looking at what I describe."

"Okay." Agent Chapman's hesitancy showed on his face and in his voice.

"At my nine o'clock, so to your left out the window, there's a huge towering tree between the two homes on that side of the street. A perfect place to climb up, be obscured by the branches and foliage, but also to watch Kate's house."

Dawning understanding lit the agent's eyes.

"Down the street four houses on your left is a house up for sale. From the second-story windows, you'd be able to see Kate's house."

"We'll have to see if the owners are still occupying the house or if it's vacant." Agent Chapman took out a notebook and started writing everything down.

Ryan appreciated that the agent wasn't dismissing him. "Behind Kate's home are two other large mature trees. Their foliage is less concealing, but a camera up there pointed at her place would do the trick."

Agent Chapman put pen to paper again and shook his head. "You really do think like them."

"You'd be amazed at some of the things I've learned on the job."

"I don't doubt it with the cases you've helped close."

Ryan continued. "I also think you should check the houses that surround Kate's for cameras that the owners didn't put up themselves. It needs to be discreet. We don't want to tip our guy off that we're onto him if he's using some kind of surveillance to watch her."

"With the latest threat, we need to talk to her about protective custody."

Ryan nodded. "I hope she takes it."

"But you're skeptical she will."

"Kate's a fighter. She's angry this is happening again as much as she is scared. She just started getting her life back on track. She doesn't want someone to take her freedom from her again. She's angry someone has made her scared to exist again."

"From what I've learned about her these last many months, she likes her job, doesn't go out a lot, but she's got a boyfriend now who seems to be supportive. I imagine after what she's been through, trusting people isn't easy. A close relationship even harder to create."

Ryan nodded. "She's also had to learn to trust herself again when everything inside her tells her there's danger, even if it's not really there. Trauma like she's suffered rewires you to always feel that fight-or-flight response, to be constantly vigilant. It takes time and a lot of mental work to rewire that again."

"And now she's in danger once more. This guy wants her to know he's coming for her. The Rose Reaper took random women. This guy is doing the same thing, but also pulling Kate into it, too."

"He's letting her know she's not going to get away this time. He knows where she is and he's watching."

Agent Chapman frowned. "So if we try to move her, he might see that."

"If we move her, we'll need to be discreet and make sure no one can follow."

"Do you think he'll come after her with law enforcement watching?" Agent Chapman sounded skeptical.

"I'm not sure yet if he's willing to do anything and everything to get to her. I find it very odd that he's shown his hand this way. Why tell us the endgame? He could have hidden these murders for a long time if not for leaving the roses for Kate because they're in multiple counties and jurisdictions."

"Criminals are stupid." Agent Chapman backed up that statement with a *duh* look.

In some cases, maybe. But for the most part, criminals were human. Sometimes impulsive, other times savvy. It was usually the little things that tripped them up. Adrenaline making them act too quickly and clouding their judgment. An overlooked detail. Poor planning. And even when everything goes right, the unexpected happens.

And with technology today, the smallest bit of evidence could convict you.

The killer knew that. The river was a great way to mask and eliminate evidence.

What Ryan wouldn't give to get a lead on where he took the victims after he abducted them. It had to be secluded enough that no one saw or heard anything.

Just like the Rose Reaper.

Agent Chapman knocked on Kate's door. "Do you think he's watching right now?"

"If I were you, I'd assume he is."

"Do you think Kate knows he's probably watching her?"

"She knows. And the fact it hasn't driven her away from here or from living her life shows how strong she is. I hope she holds on to that strength until we get this guy."

Chapter Thirteen

Ryan smiled the second Kate opened the door to put her at ease. "Hello, Kate."

She sighed and stared at him, her gaze earnest and hopeful. "Ryan. Thank you for coming. Please, come in." She stood back and let them pass into the living room.

Ryan met the inquisitive stranger's stare. "You must be Reed." Ryan shook the guy's hand, not surprised at all that he was here with Kate.

"She's been anxious all day for you to get here." Reed put his arm around Kate's shoulders, holding her close, even though she stood with her hands locked in front of her.

Ryan took the lead. "Kate, you remember Agent Chapman."

She scrunched her lips. "I'm sorry I've been—"

"Perfectly within your right to be upset, insistent that we do something, and impatient for it to happen. Believe me, I feel your frustration. I wish I could assuage it, but as we've spoken about, this guy is as good as the Rose Reaper at keeping his secrets."

"Except he keeps telling me what he's done."

Ryan understood how much that scared her. "Just as much as he wants the notoriety of the Rose Reaper, he wants your attention as well. It's a thrill for him to brag to you, Kate. It's even more pleasing to know you fear him. You think about him. You're waiting for him."

Kate rubbed her hands over her face, then let them drop back to her sides. "I hate this. I don't know what to do."

"Let's sit." Reed led Kate to the sofa and sat beside her.

Ryan took the seat on the other side of Kate and Agent Chapman took the chair off to the side next to Reed.

Kate turned to Ryan. "He's killed five women. One more and I'm next."

"We don't know that for sure," Agent Chapman said.

Kate turned to him. "Why else would he leave me the roses and the note? *You and me. Soon.* He's coming for me. And though I've been lucky so far, it won't be long before the media is after me, too. They've already picked up the story that the stabbing murders are connected. It's only a matter of time before they make the connection to the Rose Reaper and me. I wouldn't be surprised if someone in any one of the police departments investigating the cases or from the FBI leaks that the killer is leaving me roses." Kate looked terrified of that happening.

Agent Chapman leaned forward. "Only you, Reed, Ryan, Lieutenant Griffin, and I know about the roses. Another officer overheard it at the lieutenant's station, but he's assured me he'll keep it quiet."

Ryan steered the conversation in a new direction. "Kate, tell me how you're holding up."

"I'm . . . scared. Really scared. I can't even walk out my front door without bracing myself. On the one hand, I'm so happy when there's nothing there, but on the other, I know in the back of my mind that he's out there hunting for another woman. I constantly ask myself, *Is it today? Will it be tomorrow? How long can he go before he kills someone else? How long until he decides I'm his next target? After number six? How long after her? Will it be before? Will it stop with me? Or will he keep killing until finally someone stops him? How will that happen when he's so careful?* He's getting away with it." She held Ryan's gaze.

He reached over and put his hand atop hers on the cushion. "There are a lot of people working on this case. Most especially Agent Chapman. And I'm here to help you in any way I can."

"I want to help, too, but I feel so helpless. I don't know who's doing this. I wish I did. I wish I could point to him and say, *That's him! Put him away forever.*" Kate pressed both hands to the sides of her face. "I escaped the cabin. I watched him die. I feel like he's still with me."

"His memory is with you, Kate. You don't forget something like that. You learn to live with it, then you learn to put it away."

"I had put it away. I was living a normal life again. I wasn't looking over my shoulder, or second-guessing the meaning of everything someone said. I wasn't locked up in my house, trying to hide from my feelings and thoughts and the world anymore. I worked so hard for every little inch of my life I took back. *He* ruined all of it."

"That's not true," Reed interjected. "You've been going to work. We go out to eat. You run errands. I know you're always cautious and aware of your surroundings, but you do it. It impresses me every day that you're able to walk out the door knowing that maniac is out there."

Kate threw up her hands and let them drop. "That's only because I know he's not coming for me yet. Let him watch. Let him leave me those flowers. It doesn't matter, until he gets to me. It's just a matter of time. The last victim came only five weeks after the one before. He's escalating. It won't be long."

The ominous words held a certainty and understanding Kate couldn't ignore but had accepted.

Ryan didn't know how to reassure her, except to say, "The police and FBI will do everything in their power to make sure that doesn't happen."

"He literally walks up to my house and leaves roses. What makes you think he won't drop that half dozen roses on the walkway in the morning and continue right up to my door, bust it open, and take me?"

Agent Chapman leaned in. "Because as of ten minutes ago there are FBI agents watching your house. You won't see them, but they're there."

"What?" Reed asked.

Agent Chapman explained, "Kate is right. We haven't been concerned until now that the killer would take her before he finished with his sixth victim. He has a plan. This is his game. And he's been playing it this way from the beginning. We have no reason to believe he'll change it now."

"But if he knows the FBI is watching . . ." Reed stared at the agent with an expectant gaze that he fill in the blank.

"He's known from the beginning that law enforcement would get involved and protect Kate. He's probably counting on it and has planned for it."

Reed raised a brow. "How could he possibly take her if she's got protection?"

Agent Chapman nodded. "That's the question I've been racking my brain over for months. His endgame with Kate is taking her as the seventh victim and finishing what the Rose Reaper started. But how is he going to get her when he's made himself known to her and law enforcement? He has a plan. We just need to figure out what it is."

Ryan took over. "That's what I want to talk to you about, Kate."

"What could I possibly know about that?"

Ryan shrugged. "I don't know. When we originally talked about your kidnapping and time with the Rose Reaper, you weren't in the best frame of mind. You were traumatized and still trying to process. Your description of what happened came out in random thoughts, out of order, and with little detail. You gave me enough to piece together to understand the Rose Reaper's methodology."

"But you think I know more."

"You knew it then and now, you just weren't able to articulate it all at the time."

Kate pinched her bottom lip between her thumb and forefinger. "Even in therapy with Rebecca I've never gone through it step by step in every detail. I talk about my fear, the pain, the flashes of memories that haunt me. She teaches me how to cope, how to look at something, feel it, process it, then set it aside when I understand why it comes up and what triggers me. Sometimes, it can be something as little as a smell. Reed coming in smelling like fresh-cut wood. Suddenly I'm back in the cabin staring at the pinewood walls."

Reed swore under his breath. "Kate. I'm sorry. Why didn't you ever say anything?"

She hooked her arm through his and slid her hand into his palm. "It's not your fault. You don't mean to do it."

"Triggers are like that." Ryan tried to help ease Reed. "Most days, when Kate smells wood on you, maybe it's pleasant and reminds her that you work with your hands. She wonders what you built that day. But another day, it takes her back there."

"Burned coffee makes me want to gag. He'd make it in the morning and then he'd come at me . . ." Kate went quiet for a long moment.

They all let her have the time and space she needed to either finish that sentence or let it go.

She mustered her courage with a deep inhale. "By the afternoon, the burned-coffee smell would fill the room. I'd try to focus on that and not . . . the other."

"I didn't know that," Ryan said softly. "Which means there's a lot of other things you could probably tell me. Maybe even something that helps us figure this out."

Kate met his gaze. "Okay. If you think it will help. Ask away."

Ryan gave her a reassuring smile. "Not tonight. I just wanted to come by and check on you."

"You thought your presence here would bring me back to the night we met."

"It has, hasn't it?" He could see it in her eyes.

"Yes. But with the memories of that night come the feelings I had when you walked in the door and sat next to my bed. One look at your kind eyes and I felt a little bit of calm come into the room with you. Everyone else seemed so urgent and excited for answers. You talked about how pretty the night sky was outside and the landscape on your drive to see me. It felt like you'd keep talking about pretty things until I was ready to talk."

"I would have, because I could see you didn't want the silence. You needed a soft voice to drown out everything else."

"I needed one person to see that I was trying to piece back together the shambles of my mind."

"And you did. And then we talked. We'll talk again. And we'll go slow. You'll decide when you've had enough and need a break. At any time, you can say you don't want to talk about it at all anymore."

Anger and frustration flashed in her eyes. "We don't have time for that."

Ryan gentled his voice. "There is always time for you to take care of yourself. I'm here to help, Kate, not force you to do anything you don't want to do."

She deflated, her body relaxing into Reed's again. "I'll try anything if it means stopping this monster."

"Is there a good time for us to meet tomorrow?" Ryan asked.

"I don't want to waste your time. I know you came here for me and probably have other cases and people who need you, so let's meet first thing in the morning. Say, nine?"

"Perfect. I'll bring the chocolate croissants."

Kate found a smile. "You remember."

"Your mother used to make them in her shop. You liked them best fresh out of the oven."

Nostalgia filled her soft gaze. "I still do."

Ryan stood. Everyone else followed suit.

Kate walked him and the agent to the door, Reed right at her side.

Ryan met Kate's worried gaze. "You have my number. If you change your mind about talking to me, I won't take offense or be upset. I know what I'm asking isn't easy for you."

"I want to do this. I want this to end with Anne Murphy."

It didn't surprise him that Kate knew the last victim's, and probably all the other victims', names.

Ryan gave her a smile goodbye and walked down the steps to the path and gate. He turned back and waved at her, then went to the car as she closed the door behind him.

Agent Chapman glanced at him over the hood of the car. "So what did you learn in there?"

Ryan grinned. "She's still as tough and determined as I remember. She's not afraid to say something about Reed in front of him, even though she knew that comment about him smelling like wood triggering her would upset him. He's patient. He let her talk. He didn't try to keep her from agreeing to talk to us. He wants this solved and her out of danger, and if that means her talking to me about her past and bringing that all up, he's okay with it. She knows she can count on him. She reached for his hand when she needed comfort. He offered it without hesitation. They're good together."

"And?" the agent prompted, sensing Ryan held something back.

"I want to know more about how and when he came into her life."

"I've checked him out." Not an ounce of remorse filled the agent's voice about that intrusion into Reed's life. "He's squeaky clean. No tickets or arrests. No domestic disturbance calls. Nothing to show he's abusive or a hothead. He pays his bills and his taxes. He works hard, has a good reputation among his coworkers and friends. He owns his own place and drives a newish truck."

"And after all that, you're still a little suspicious about him," Ryan pointed out.

"He's perfect for her."

Ryan understood exactly what the agent didn't say.

Kate deserved someone like Reed. Kind. Caring. Patient. Hardworking. Protective but not overbearing. An upstanding citizen. A good friend. A catch for any woman.

A stand-up guy.

But maybe a little too perfect.

Chapter Fourteen

Agent Chapman dropped Ryan off at his hotel. Ryan couldn't stop thinking about Kate and the Rose Reaper case. He wanted to believe that Reed was exactly what he seemed to be: the perfect guy for Kate.

She deserved that, and more, after what she'd been through with the Rose Reaper and now this copycat killer.

He wanted to dive deeper into the case and possible suspects, but right now, after everything he went through on the Copeland County Killer case and burying his sister, he needed to shut down for a while.

He flipped the duvet and top sheet back on the king-size bed in his hotel room, sat on the clean sheet, and looked over the menu before picking up the phone on the nightstand and tapping 7 for room service.

"Good evening, Mr. Strickland, what can I get you tonight?"

Ryan ordered the chicken dinner with fingerling potatoes and broccoli. To unwind, he added a beer. Nothing wrong with ending his day with a cold one and a call to Molly. He hoped she picked up, but understood she might be working and unable to talk.

"Any dessert for you tonight? We have a really good fresh strawberry shortcake, as well as a double chocolate cake that's to die for."

"I'll take the strawberry one." Why not? Tomorrow was bound to be another long day. Asking Kate to open up about the past wasn't going to be easy for her, or him. Listening to the evil things people do sometimes made it feel like there was no good left in the world.

He was going to try to remain impartial. He always tried. But it was hard when you opened up people's wounds and trauma and their emotions infected yours. It always happened, because he was human and most people empathized with others in some way.

He did so easily because he'd seen firsthand the kinds of things monsters could do to their victims and what they left behind in their wake.

He hung up with room service and grabbed his cell, hoping to reach Molly.

"Hello, stranger." Her soft, sweet voice rolled through him.

"It's quiet there. You must not be at work." They met at the bar Molly worked at near his condo. Cocktail Corner. He loved the local place. He used to go in all the time with his buddies. They'd play Ping-Pong and pool and hang out. He never noticed the cute bartender until he went in after a particularly bad couple of days. She'd inadvertently helped him on the Copeland County Killer case when they got to talking about the news reports playing on the TV in the bar.

But they'd also shared a moment when she offered her condolences for the loss of his sister. They'd toasted to the Copeland County Killer's angels.

Somehow, that simple gesture had made him feel better when everything else in his life felt dark, his grief overwhelming.

"I'm off tonight. Want to do something? Please say yes. I've been in my apartment all day being an adult. I've cleaned the whole place, including the refrigerator. You don't want to know what I found in there. I couldn't even identify some of the stuff. I paid bills, went grocery shopping for real food, and was just about to reward myself with a movie and pizza. You're welcome to join me, or we could go out."

He grinned so hard his cheeks hurt. All that sounded so normal and uncomplicated. "I wish I could be with you right now."

"So come over." She paused, then quickly said, "Maybe it's too soon for that. We hardly know each other. I'd say you could be a serial killer or something, but I know you work for the FBI, so that's probably not true. Maybe. I mean, that would be the perfect cover. Who would suspect you?"

He chuckled. "I'm not a serial killer."

"Of course you'd say that." Humor, not suspicion, infused her voice.

"But I am working a case in Maine."

"Oh. So you're not here."

He hated hearing her disappointment. "Sorry. No."

"Don't apologize. You're working. You're helping people. That's your job. So what is it?"

"Serial killer," he confirmed.

"You're joking."

"I'm not. It's actually an old case. And a new one."

"What does that mean?" She paused again. "You probably can't say."

He couldn't tell her everything, but he could give her some details so she didn't feel like he was holding out on her. "I worked a case over three years ago. One victim survived. I helped her open up to tell us what happened so that the FBI could understand the killer's methods and be sure they'd linked all the victims to him. That woman has been receiving messages. Each time she does, a new victim is found. She's concerned, and so is law enforcement, that the new killer is targeting her."

"Sounds like the evil bastard is taunting her."

"Exactly. She's scared. She called me."

"Because you helped her before." Molly's understanding touched him. "She's hoping you can help her again."

"She's starting to recall more details. Maybe something she remembers now that she didn't back then will help law enforcement figure out who and why someone is copying the killer."

"She trusts you more than the cops."

"Yes. I think she felt like they weren't doing enough."

"If the guy is still leaving her messages and killing people, they aren't. He's still out there." Molly let him hear her frustration and sympathy for Kate, a stranger.

"They're as frustrated as the victim and I are. But I'm hoping we can protect her until we put this guy behind bars."

"In the ground would be better." She had a point, though he tried really hard not to think like that and keep focused on getting justice for the victims and their loved ones. "Are you done for the night?"

"Yeah. I'm in my hotel room waiting for room service."

"If you're not doing anything, and I'm here doing nothing, and you want to, we could find something to watch on TV together."

He liked that idea. "Okay. What's on?" A knock sounded on his door. "You find something for us to watch. I need to answer the door and grab my food."

"Okay."

He set his cell on the nightstand, went to the door, and let the young woman in with the tray. "Just set it on the coffee table."

She set it down, pulled the lid off the plate to show him the meal to be sure it was correct, then handed him the folder with the receipt to sign. While she used a bottle opener on his beer, he charged everything to the room, added a tip, signed, and handed it back to her.

"Thank you, Mr. Strickland. Have a good night."

He walked her to the door, put the Do Not Disturb sign on the outside handle, closed and locked the door, then retrieved his phone. "What's on tonight?"

"Do you have HBO?"

"Let me check." He sat on the sofa, pointed the remote at the TV, put his phone on speaker, set it on the table, and took a swig of his beer. He sighed out his joy at the first cold, crisp taste of it.

"What was that?"

"Me drinking a beer."

"I've got a glass of wine. Pizza's in the oven."

"I wish I was there with you."

"I'm betting you have something better to eat than a frozen pizza."

"Is there anything better than a pizza?"

She giggled. "No. Still. It'd be nice to be there with you, too."

He looked around the hotel room and at the empty bed. "Yeah. I'd like that."

He found HBO, clicked the channel, and laughed. "*Happy Gilmore.*"

"Something funny and light and uncomplicated."

"I love it." He especially liked it that she thought about what he was doing here and found a way to lighten his mood and be with him, even if she wasn't with him. He took another swig of his beer, set the lid over his plate aside, and dug into his food. He loved the dinner and a movie date, even more because Molly didn't make a big deal about him being out of town.

She didn't even ask how long he'd be gone.

She accepted his job and that he was where he needed to be right now.

What a relief.

What a gift.

"Look at those gorgeous hydrangeas in his grandmother's yard."

He caught a glimpse of the big clusters of flowers right before Happy Gilmore used that hockey-style swing to shoot a golf ball into a window way down the street. "How long do you think he practiced that unconventional golf swing?"

"I don't know. But he got paid a hell of a lot to do it."

And that's how his night went. He and Molly having dinner, talking about the movie, laughing together, and just hanging out until it ended.

"You know, Ryan, as dates go, this one isn't even close to the top ten worst I've had."

"Is it in the top ten good ones?" He didn't think so. He could do a hell of a lot better than this.

"No. But that's only because I'm going to say good night in a minute and I don't get to kiss you. And I've been thinking about kissing you for a long time now." The shy confession made him hard and desperate for her touch.

"So you're just going to send me off to bed alone thinking about that."

"Sweet dreams." She hung up on him.

He laughed and it felt good.

Most of his cases took everything out of him.

Tonight, she'd made him forget for a little while why he was here and made him want to be there with her. She gave him something to think about other than the case. And oh how he liked thinking about Molly.

Chapter Fifteen

Ryan arrived on time to Kate's house. He stood outside her home on the very path where the killer kept leaving her roses and listened to the quiet morning, searching along the street and neighbors' homes for anything suspicious.

He'd check in with Agent Chapman after his visit with Kate to determine if they'd found anything in their discreet search around Kate's home. He hoped they did without exposing their quest to the killer. With no leads or evidence pointing them in any one direction, their only hope of finding the killer was to discover something he left behind, something he was using to keep tabs on Kate.

Ryan had no doubt that whoever was doing this was drawn to Kate. She was his link to the Rose Reaper. She represented the end of his killing spree. He may even want revenge on her for what she'd done to the Rose Reaper, leading him to his death, though he was the one who chose that way out. But a twisted mind could easily place blame on her.

Which made Ryan think that the Rose Reaper had gone after her that night because he'd had a clawing need to finish what he'd started with her. He couldn't walk away or run. He needed to kill her to fulfill that need. Maybe he'd been looking for a way out all along.

Ryan didn't know if the new killer felt that way, too.

But it was interesting on an academic level that this killer stuck so closely to the Rose Reaper's MO.

How did he know so much about the other killer?

Ryan walked up the path. He didn't need to knock today.

Kate opened the door with a smile, though he sensed her anxiety. "Good morning, Ryan."

"Morning." He held up the small pink box of pastries. "As promised."

Her smile remained. "I'm not sure even chocolate croissants will make this any easier."

"They can't hurt."

"Except my waistline."

He stepped into the entry. "Everyone should treat themselves once in a while."

"Especially when you don't know how much time you have left." Kate closed the door and stared at him. "Sorry. That was morbid."

"You're worried about the threat against you. Reality isn't always easy to face. You've been living with this for months now. The strain must be tremendous."

She held her hand out toward the kitchen. "I thought we'd sit in there and pretend we're catching up on old times."

"I wish those old times were happy memories."

"You and me both. But this is important. I know it needs to be done." Her resolve impressed him.

They sat at the breakfast table by the windows. Kate had already left a thermal pot of coffee and two mugs. She poured for both of them. "Milk or sugar?"

"Black is fine." Ryan looked around the cozy kitchen. "You've got a beautiful home."

"I fell in love with it the second I saw it. It was just right for me. Not too big, not too small. I wanted to feel right here, like this was my second act. I thought here I could rediscover myself and start over."

"And you did. You worked on your mental health. You overcame the debilitating trauma and learned to live with it." Because trauma didn't disappear. You didn't forget it. It was always there. Anything could trigger it again. But you could learn to cope and do what you needed to do to understand what those triggers were telling you.

Were the perceived threats real or echoes from the past?

Right now, the threat was very real.

"Will Reed be joining us?"

Kate shook her head and sipped her coffee. "He's at work. I wanted to do this alone with you. I didn't want to upset him with all the details."

It surprised Ryan that Reed wasn't here, but he left it alone.

Ryan wanted to start with something easy and led Kate back into the past slowly. "How did you and Reed meet?"

She turned thoughtful. "The law firm I work for is building a new office. It's nearly complete now. Reed is the general contractor on the project. I'm the liaison between him and the partners."

"I imagine, at first, that wasn't a comfortable position for you to be in sometimes."

"It wasn't. I didn't expect them to ask me to do it. But I run the offices so well, I know what people need and how the spaces are used, it made sense that I'd help with designing the new floor plan and layout. The partners were concerned about their offices and how big they were and making sure we had enough space for the growing staff, but they don't know where the copy machines need to be and how many are needed, or what a pain it is for the administrative assistants to be away from their desks to get coffee for clients when the kitchen is all the way across the building."

"You see the big picture of the office and the details."

"I try to make the office run efficiently for the employees so their jobs are easier."

"So you interacted with Reed more than the partners."

"Yes. Though most of the meetings were a group of us and them."

"And he liked you."

She tried to hide a smile. "I suppose so. He kept asking me out. I'd politely decline. He'd ask again."

"Did you feel like he was being pushy?"

"Never. It always seemed genuine. He didn't crowd me or make me feel uncomfortable. In fact, he kept things professional when others were around and friendly when we were alone. He'd ask personal questions. Simple things. What did I like to do in the evening and on the weekend? Had I seen the latest blockbuster movie? Did I know of a good Italian place nearby? And did I want to go with him to dinner?"

Ryan grinned. "He wanted to get to know you and make you feel comfortable with him."

"He sensed my hesitation around new people."

"And then you said yes to a date."

Kate blushed and looked away for a moment. "It didn't go well. I ran out of the coffee shop without finishing my drink."

"Why?"

It took Kate a few seconds to answer. "Because it felt so good to be there with him. It felt . . . normal."

"And you weren't sure how to handle that." Ryan understood how foreign that would have felt to her after what she'd been through.

"It took a long time working in an office surrounded by so many people to feel normal. Even being around my old friends didn't feel normal. I felt like they were always looking at me with pity and concern. Most of those relationships ended because I couldn't take them treating me so differently. Like I was fragile. Even if I was. But Reed . . . he treated me normal. He thought I was just shy and reserved. But he liked me anyway. It didn't deter him. He wanted to be with me. I didn't know what to do with that." She pulled a pastry from the box, set it on his plate, then got one for herself.

"So you took a chance on him." Ryan took a bite, letting Kate settle into the casual conversation.

"He sensed something in my reticence, though he never asked. He just kept coming back. He'd say things like, *just a few minutes with you makes my day.*" A grin tugged at her lips.

Ryan thought that sweet and exactly what someone with Kate's past would need in a partner. "Are you happy with him?"

"Yes." She didn't hesitate at all. She took a bite of the croissant and hummed her pleasure at the sweet and buttery treat. "Once I told him about the roses and what they meant to me, he understood why I act the way I do sometimes. He checks in on me more often. He lets me lead in the relationship. I feel like I'm in control." She leaned in. "There's this thing he always says to me. *Always and anytime for you, Kate.* He means that. When I call, he picks up. When I ask him to stay or go home, he does it. When I just want to be quiet, he's quiet with me. When I feel like going out, he's ready to go. When the past overwhelms me, he holds me or gives me the space I need. He doesn't push for answers or details. He's just there for me." Distress creased lines in her forehead.

She raked her fingers through her hair. "And now that I've said all that, I feel like maybe I'm not holding up my end of the relationship. It kind of makes me feel like I'm this needy person asking him all the time to be what I need him to be."

Ryan finished another bite. "Do you ask him about his day?"

"Of course." Kate picked at her food.

"Does he ever say he wants to do something and you do it with him?"

She eyed him. "Well, yes. Most of the time."

"When he's had a hard day or is wrestling with a dilemma, do you listen and try to help?"

"Yes. Of course. I love that we talk so much and share our days together."

"Does he ever express any feelings or comments that you're not listening or giving him what he wants and needs?"

"No." She smiled, understanding what he was trying to make her see. "He always tells me how much he loves spending time with me. It doesn't matter what we do or don't do."

"Then stop worrying that you're not holding up your end. Or, if you really feel that way, then ask him how he feels about it. Everything sounds fine between you, but if it's not, then you can ask him how you can fix it."

"Good idea." She took a sip of her coffee and a bite of her chocolate croissant.

He did the same, letting that part of the conversation go and giving Kate a moment to mentally prepare for the next topic.

"Okay." She bolstered herself with a deep breath. "You didn't come for relationship counseling. You want to know about the Rose Reaper and how this new killer is copying him so closely."

He raised a brow. "Any ideas on that?"

"I've thought about it so much, you'd think I'd come up with something that makes sense. I'm sure my guesses match yours and the police's and FBI's. Someone close to Freddy Poole knew what he was doing, and how, and now they're copying him."

"That does make the most sense. But why now?"

"Three years doesn't seem to be a significant anniversary. And the dates don't match up to the original abductions. The new killer is escalating much faster than the Rose Reaper's killings. He had a longer cooling-off period." Kate shrugged, appearing bewildered by it.

Ryan acknowledged that with a nod. "I know it's difficult and triggering, so we'll go slow, but let's talk about your time with him."

Kate took a calming breath and clasped her hands in her lap. "He took me from the driveway of the cottage I was renting at the time. The owners of the big house were out of town. No one saw anything."

"He knocked you out."

"Yes. A blow to the back of the head. I woke up bound, blindfolded, and gagged in a plastic box. I felt around and figured out from the slits in the sides and metal grate door that it was probably a dog crate. I tried to open the door, but he had it locked somehow. I'm guessing with rope, since I thought I could feel something rough against my fingers when I poked them through the metal."

"Did you hear anything?"

"Muffled music, like I was hearing it through a window or something. Which makes sense now that I think about it. He drove a truck to find me after I escaped."

Ryan nodded. "They found exactly what you described in the covered truck bed. A large dog crate and rope."

A thoughtful look came over Kate. "I can't believe I never pieced that together until now."

Mundane details got lost in the trauma. "What happened next keeps your mind busy enough."

Kate twisted her hands tightly together. "Yes. It does."

"We don't need to go into detail about those specifics. I want to focus more on where you were and what you could see and hear."

"Okay." That seemed to ease Kate. "We drove for a long time. At least, it felt that way. Other than the muffled music, I didn't hear anything but the sound of us driving on the road."

"Makes sense, you were found out in the country on a two-lane road. What did you see or hear when you finally stopped?"

Kate stared into the distance. "I heard him open and close the truck door, then walk to the back of the vehicle and open . . . well, I suppose it was the camper-shell window and tailgate. There were some other sounds. Him getting into the back, I suppose untying the ropes, and opening the crate. I tried to push into the back of it and kick him, but he just grabbed my ankles and dragged me out. My back got scraped up and my head swam from the blow I took earlier."

"Did you hear anything once he had you outside the truck?"

"I wasn't really paying attention. My head hurt. I was draped over his shoulder and could barely breathe. I was trying to struggle to get free, but he kept a tight hold on me." She went quiet for a moment, her breath coming in pants. "I remember feeling the cold. And maybe I can't remember hearing anything because it was quiet."

"Makes sense if you were in the deep woods."

"It had to be because the ride was so rough at the end. If felt like we bumped over ruts and turned this way and that a lot. I kept falling from side to side in the crate."

"Like maybe he was going around trees and obstacles, not on a road or clear path?" That made sense and helped explain why the cabin was so hard to find.

Kate held his gaze. "Yes. Exactly like that. In fact, when I escaped, I remember thinking there were so many trees around the place. They were right up close to the cabin."

"Which is probably why they never found it." The cabin was concealed in the forest with no driveway or road to it.

He needed to speak with Agent Chapman about property records for where Kate had been found and see if anything led them to Freddy Poole. And their new killer.

Ryan tried to spark more details from Kate. "Once he had you in the cabin, did he take the blindfold off?"

"Yes."

"Describe the place. Did it feel new or old?"

"Hard to say. It was a single large room with a kitchen area, a small table with two chairs, a woodstove in one corner, the bed up against a wall, and a bathtub and closet on another wall."

"So you walked in the door and straight into the main space."

"Yes. The bathtub and two large wardrobe cabinets on the right if you're facing into the cabin, the kitchen on the left and woodstove in the back corner, the bed straight ahead. On either side of the door, there was a window, but the other three walls didn't have any."

"So anyone coming toward the cabin would only be able to see in from the front."

"Yes. But like I said, there was nothing but trees out there."

"You said there was a tub."

"Right out in the open next to the bed." Kate sucked in a breath. "I forgot. There was an outhouse."

"So no running water." No public utility bills to find.

She shook her head.

"Did you see any other buildings when he took you to the outhouse?"

"I wasn't in a good headspace. I mostly just stumbled along as he dragged me. I think he only took me out there twice, maybe three times. Without anything to eat or drink, I didn't have to go." She sat quiet for a moment, a contemplative look on her face. "There were large store-bought containers of water in the kitchen. He drank from those and made coffee atop the woodstove. But at one point, he brought in a bucket of water to clean his dishes."

"So maybe there was a well with a pump outside."

"That would be my guess. Or he got it from the river."

Ryan perked up. "Could you hear the river?"

Kate's brows drew together as she thought about it. "No. That's just a guess because that's where he dumped the bodies. But the river might not have been close at all. He could have driven to it and disposed of the women miles from the cabin."

"Okay, this is good. Tell me more about the cabin."

Kate continued. "It was rustic. Everything was wood. He kept it clean. There was no garbage or debris left outside either. Just the cabin in the middle of nowhere."

"So anything he brought with him, he took away."

"There was only what he needed there. Nothing else. No decorations. Just a kerosene lamp on the table and one hanging from a hook above the bed. Another one he never lit on a low stool by the tub. No pictures on the walls. The kitchen had two shelves. There were a few plates, bowls, and mugs. A jar of silverware. By the woodstove there was a single cast-iron pan and an oversize kettle to boil water. That's it."

"He'd probably pump buckets of water from the well for the tub, then heat it with water from the kettle."

"I didn't get the feeling he liked being there. When he wasn't . . . with me, he sat in the doorway with his back to me."

"Maybe that place held bad memories for him."

Kate shrugged. "He never spoke. He didn't rage. He'd just come at me with purpose. And when he hurt me, when I begged him to stop, to let me go . . . he liked that. He'd stare at the rose he drew on my chest with contempt, and then I'd whimper or groan or try to buck him off me and he'd grin and give me this look like I deserved it."

Ryan gave Kate a minute to calm herself and let that horrible memory go.

She rubbed her hands up and down her thighs, then looked at him again. "I'm sorry. I'm not really helping, am I?"

"You're doing great. This is helping. Now I can talk to Agent Chapman about the search area they covered in the past and see if there's somewhere they missed. Maybe because they thought the trees too dense for there to be a cabin hidden among them."

Kate nodded. "Okay. That's a possibility. But do you really think this guy is using the same cabin?"

"If he knows what he knows about the Rose Reaper, maybe he also knows about the cabin."

"I suppose it would give him a thrill to kill where the Rose Reaper killed."

Ryan hated to admit it, but yes, it would be something the killer would relish. "Is there anything else about the place or him that you remember before we talk about how you escaped?"

"Not really. By then, I was pretty out of it. Hungry. Thirstier than I'd ever been. I could barely move, let alone put up a fight anymore. I think he was just about done with me."

He hated the look of desolation on Kate's face. "Are you okay to continue? If you want to take a break, or do this another day . . ."

She shook her head all through that. "No. I've remembered more of the details this time than any other. Let's keep going."

That was because they were talking about things that didn't bring forth the pain and trauma of what else she'd suffered there.

"Okay, I want you to think about the moments before you escaped." He didn't want her to talk about the rape, but after, so he prompted her. "He left you alone, right?" They'd covered this nearly four years ago when he interviewed her after she'd been taken to the hospital. He hoped to uncover new details now that she'd had years to let the initial overwhelming trauma ease and she could be as impartial as she was able as she remembered now.

"He left me, grabbed his smokes off the table, opened the cabin door, lit up, and stood there buck naked, not a care in the world." Kate fell back into the memory. Her face lax, eyes focused on what he couldn't see. "He had several scars on his back." She tilted her head again. "They went from the center of his back out. Like someone had raked their nails over his back and made him bleed." Kate met his gaze. "Maybe he liked that sort of thing."

Ryan didn't comment. He wanted Kate to feel free to talk about whatever observation came to her.

"He stepped out onto the little wood porch and leaned against a post." Kate's breathing increased, her face paled, then she spoke too quickly. "I suddenly had my hands and feet free and I ran for it."

Ryan leaned into her. "Wait, Kate. Take a slow breath."

She did. Once. Twice. A third time.

"Okay. That's good. Now you said he was outside smoking."

Her head bobbed up and down too fast. "Yes." Her breathing increased again.

"Kate, you are okay. You're safe here." He refrained from reaching out to touch her and offer comfort. Not now when she was in the grip of her nightmare.

She closed her eyes and nodded. "I know."

"Then unfold your fists."

Kate looked down at her balled hands and slowly released them, revealing the crescent marks from her fingernails digging into her palms.

"There you go. I know you're doing your best to remember what happened. I understand that the escape had to be really scary. The threat of getting caught was so high and you knew what would happen if he caught you."

"He was going to kill me. I knew that already. The dagger was right there on the bed beside me."

Ryan hated that ominous threat constantly at hand, yet out of her reach. "Just like before, I want you to try to see the cabin and him like a movie. You are safe here. He's still back there where he can't harm you anymore. You survived him, Kate. You got away."

She sucked in a ragged breath and tried again. "He was outside smoking." She paused. "It was quiet. Just a few night sounds filtered into the cabin. The sound of bugs. The breeze rustling leaves. Mostly just quiet. I remember wanting to hear something that would distract me. Even the fire had died down, leaving the cabin mostly in darkness, too."

"That's very good, Kate. You've described the scene very well. Now, he's standing outside on the porch, his shoulder against a post, right?"

"Yes. It's like time has paused. I want it to stay this way. I don't want what happens next."

"You're scared. I get that. I would be, too. But now you know you get away. You're safe. Does he finish the cigarette?"

Kate sat up straighter. "No. He tosses it and runs back inside."

Ryan leaned in. "Why?"

"I don't know. But he'd never thrown a cigarette butt like that before. He always brought them in and put them in the garbage." She blinked twice, really fast. "Why do I remember such stupid things?"

"Last time we talked about your kidnapping and escape, I only asked about what happened to you. Now, I'm asking you to remember the place and him in a different way. It's like turning the noise down on the traumatic events and focusing on the mundane. Those things don't evoke a strong response that sends your brain into fight or flight. He threw the cigarette butt. It seems like something most people would do. But you also remember that wasn't like him. When you're prey to a predator, you keep your eye on the danger. You track it, so you can anticipate. You stored all those little things away in case you needed them later because they might have signaled something coming, even if most of it was just throwaway information."

She shook her head, her eyes narrowed. "It's wild the way the mind works."

"It's instinct, Kate. You had good instincts. You paid attention to him. And when the opportunity presented itself, you knew when you had a shot at getting away. You found your strength and bravery and overcame your fear with your courage and you ran."

She tilted her head. "Because he heard something." She closed her eyes.

He gave her a moment to see whatever she remembered

"He rushed inside, grabbed his pants and shoes, put them on, took the knife, and ran out the door."

Ryan leaned in. "Did you hear anything?"

"No. Maybe he just sensed it. I'm not sure. But like you said, I thought now was my chance. I worked at the knot holding my wrists to the bedframe. I couldn't believe I got it free. I wanted to kick myself for not trying sooner. Though he never left me alone long enough to do it without him knowing."

"So you got free."

"Yes. I didn't think I had time to grab my clothes. They were mostly shredded anyway. But I grabbed my shoes, knowing they'd give me the best chance to run far and fast."

He gave her an approving look. "Smart. Good thinking."

A light of appreciation for the praise flickered in Kate's eyes before she continued. "I remember my heart pounding in my chest. I knew getting out the door would be the hardest part. So I just bolted as fast as I could." Her eyes went round with the echo of fear, then wider with another memory. "I stopped."

That shocked him. "Why?"

She held her breath for a moment. Her wide-eyed gaze met his. "Because I heard a strange voice."

He sat back, anticipating a revelation. "Not his?"

She stared at him. "No. Someone else's." She covered her mouth with her hand. "Why didn't I remember that until now?"

"Shock. Trauma. He was dead, the threat gone. So you didn't have to go back there and think about it." He put his hand on the table. "Did you see them?"

"No. They were around the other side of the cabin."

"Was it a man? A woman?"

"A man." Something in her eyes told him she was there, reevaluating what she remembered maybe, trying to make sense of it.

"Do you remember what they said?"

"I stopped because *he* said, 'You shouldn't be out here. This is none of your concern.' And then the strange voice said, 'I know why you're doing this, but you don't have to. You can stop.' And *he* yelled, 'I need this.'"

Kate shivered. "The words sent a chill through me and I ran." She rubbed her hands up and down her arms. "I ran as fast as I could because I knew those words to be true. He needed to kill me. He wouldn't be satisfied until he finished it. It had to be done." Kate wrapped her arms around her middle and hugged herself.

Ryan tried to think. Who could have been there trying to stop the Rose Reaper?

Someone who obviously knew what he'd been doing. Someone who knew not only where the cabin was but how to get there, even though it was not easy to find. The FBI had tried and failed. Of course, they gave up the search a couple of days in. They didn't need the place or any evidence there to make their case. They had Kate. The killer was dead.

"So after you ran, you only saw the killer again. No one else except for the couple who found you."

"He came in his truck. I didn't see anyone else." Kate ran a shaky hand over her hair. "There could have been someone else. Even another car. I just . . . I can't remember. It happened so fast. I was terrified he'd get me. My mind at that point . . . Everything felt lost. I didn't think I'd make it out of there. I remember feeling incredibly sad that he'd probably kill those two nice people who helped me." Kate wrapped her arms around her middle and sank in on herself.

"But they are okay. And you are safe." He kept reminding her because the past sucked her back into the pain and desperation and dread that her life was about to end. She'd believed that then. He needed her to remember and believe that she hadn't just survived, she was thriving again.

Kate pulled herself together and sat up straighter. "Do you think this will help with the investigation? I mean, someone else knew what *he* was doing. They were at the cabin basically asking him to stop. They were trying to save my life. Right?"

Maybe. Though he doubted the Rose Reaper would have left Kate alive even if he agreed to stop. He couldn't leave a witness alive. He'd go to prison for life. And if this someone who showed up there knew what he was doing, they could be charged as an accomplice.

But finding this person could help them identify the copycat killer.

"I don't think the person who confronted the Rose Reaper at the cabin is the same person killing now." It was a far stretch to think someone wanted him to stop then took up the very thing he wanted to end in some strange homage to Freddy Poole. And that made Ryan think it had to be family. Or maybe a very close, lifelong friend. Because he'd only trust someone with that secret who he knew he could count on not to betray him.

Though with the stakes so high and women dying, even family and friends would find it difficult to ignore their morals and allow it to keep happening.

Whoever went to see Freddy at that cabin was trying to get him to stop. Possibly, a last attempt before he went to the police and stopped the Rose Reaper himself.

"I'll talk to Agent Chapman and tell him what you remembered. Whoever showed up at the cabin had to know Freddy Poole well enough to know his hiding spot."

"And what he was doing and keep the secret for him," Kate pointed out.

"Exactly."

Kate gasped. "His brother." She bit her bottom lip. "I don't know why I didn't think of him before. I met him once."

Shocked again, Ryan asked, "You did?"

While many family members of people who commit terrible crimes sympathized with the victims and wished to offer their apologies, most didn't approach the victims directly, allowing them space to heal. That Freddy's brother had not only reached out but met with Kate in person surprised him.

"He wanted to apologize and tell me about the brother he knew before Freddy became a nightmare."

Freddy hadn't always been a monster. To those who loved him, Freddy had been more than just the worst things he'd ever done. He was a son, a brother, a friend. No one was all bad or all good.

"Was it difficult to talk to him?"

"Yes. At the time, I thought I was nuts for giving him the time of day. But . . ."

"You wanted to understand." Ryan would have been curious, too.

"Yes."

"Did it help?"

"In some ways, yes. In others . . . no." Kate sighed, her shoulders slumped. She'd had enough today.

He'd finished his coffee.

Hers sat nearly full and probably too cold to drink.

"You did well, Kate. I'm sorry we had to bring up all those bad memories."

"I wasn't looking forward to talking about it again. But talking with you about it, keeping the focus on the other stuff, it actually makes it feel more real, but also easier to understand." She eyed him. "Does that make sense?"

He thought he understood what she meant by real. To her, it was a living nightmare of horrors inflicted on her. "Now you have a sense of the place. Of him. The monster was a man who had someone in his life who knew what he was doing and wanted him to stop. You heard the man he was say he couldn't."

"I think he wanted to." Kate sighed again. "Something dark inside him wouldn't let him stop."

"And now you see him for who he really was. More than just a killer. A man who gave in to his demons and did terrible things."

"A pathetic man. He could have stopped. He could have turned himself in and asked for help if he didn't want to do those things. But he did want to do them." Anger filled her gaze. "Someone knew. They should have stopped him."

"Maybe they didn't get the chance because in the moment he knew he couldn't get away with you, he chose to stop himself."

Kate shook her head. "No. He didn't want to go to jail where he couldn't do the things he *needed* to do. Rather than a cage, he chose death and a legacy. The notorious Rose Reaper. And now someone wants a piece of that and to make a name for themselves. They want to use me to make a big splash. The seventh victim who survived the Rose Reaper is killed by his successor. It makes a great headline. It will get national attention."

A grave expression came over Kate's face. "I wonder what he'll do for an encore."

Chapter Sixteen

I wonder what he'll do for an encore.

That ominous thought echoed in Ryan's head as he joined Agent Chapman in the conference room at the FBI office. "I just came from seeing Kate. She remembered something new."

Agent Chapman sat up in his seat, a light of interest in his eyes. "What?"

"Someone else was at the cabin the night she escaped. It was the distraction she needed to get away."

"Did she identify the person?" Agent Chapman asked, eager for the answer.

"She never saw him. She heard his voice, telling Freddy to stop. He yelled back, 'I need this.'"

"Damn." Agent Chapman shook his head. "That's . . ."

"Chilling." Yeah. Ryan felt those words deep inside him. "Can you check the police report from the night they found Kate on the road? Were there any other cars there besides the Good Samaritans who stopped for her?"

Agent Chapman typed on his laptop and read through the information.

Ryan waited, impatient, hoping there was something there to find.

"The police report only states that Vivian and Jamal stopped to help Kate. I have both their statements taken at the scene. Neither witness reports seeing any other car besides the truck Freddy Poole was driving." Agent Chapman looked up at him. "So whoever was at the cabin didn't follow Freddy when he went after Kate."

Ryan thought about what Kate had described to him the first time they met. "It was a two-lane road. Freddy knew which way to go to catch up to Kate. He got there too quickly to think it was luck."

Agent Chapman consulted the case notes again. "Jamal states that the truck drove toward them slowly."

"He was looking for her along the road."

Agent Chapman met his gaze. "So whoever he'd been talking to at the cabin probably left and went the opposite direction from where Kate was found, otherwise he might have ended up being the one who found Kate first."

That sounded reasonable to Ryan.

Agent Chapman continued that line of thinking. "Freddy gets the other person to leave without them trying to save Kate. He walks back into the cabin and Kate's not there. He jumps in his truck and books it out of there, trying to find her before anyone else does. It's a safe bet that if Kate gets to the road, she'll either follow it or wave someone down for help. He wants to get to her first, but he's too late. She's been discovered. He tries to get her back in the truck, but she won't go, and the police show up. And we both know the ending to that."

"The person at the cabin had to be his brother," Agent Chapman supplied without hesitation.

"Kate and I both think so, too. That's a risky conversation. Freddy could have turned on him and killed him to keep his secret. If it was the brother, they must have been close for him to walk away."

Ryan hadn't known about a brother before today. He'd come in to the case only when Kate had been found. He'd gone in basically cold with a clear objective: find out from Kate how he took her, where he took her, what he did to her, and how she got away.

But a brother made the case even more interesting. Especially since he went there to stop Freddy but ultimately, Ryan presumed, left without trying to save Kate. "Tell me about him."

"I pulled the family information after we identified Freddy Poole. I made the death notification to the brother in person. I don't remember him being anything but devastated to hear how his brother died."

"Did you ask about whether or not his brother had been acting strange or not being in touch? Anything like that?"

"The guy was wrecked." Agent Chapman frowned. "But I followed up several days later and got some basic information, because it was clear Freddy had become a loner who didn't keep in close contact with anyone. Of course, the brother was covering for him. We had the killer. Kate identified Freddy as her abductor and rapist. He was dead. Case closed, pretty much."

Ryan understood. Why waste man-hours on getting the whys and hows when they had no one to prosecute. Kate gave them most of that in his interview with her. They had to be sure Freddy Poole was the Rose Reaper. She confirmed that for them sufficiently.

And the killings stopped.

Until now.

And since this killer changed the MO in slight ways, it made sense it was a copycat, not the Rose Reaper coming back after an extended cooling-off period if the Rose Reaper wasn't Freddy after all.

Why start over by killing women who looked like the original six victims, though they only had five right now, if you were continuing what you'd started? The Rose Reaper would have just abducted and killed Kate to finish what he started, then continued on.

No. It had to be a new guy.

Someone who thought he was so clever he could get away with all the murders even after bringing Kate into the game.

That thought made him think of Todd Lane. He'd gotten away with murder. So far.

There had to be a strong connection between the Rose Reaper and the new killer and none had been found between Todd and Freddy. But Todd could simply be a fan.

Ryan needed more information. "We should reinterview the brother."

"Can't," Agent Chapman said, opening a folder. "He died . . ." Agent Chapman looked thoughtful for a moment, then continued. "Eleven months ago. Suicide. I looked him up when the murders started happening, hoping to talk to him again, see if there was something there."

The new abductions and killings started after his death.

"How'd he do it?" Guilt was a powerful feeling that could drag some people down to the depths of despair and a land of recriminations.

"He hung himself in his garage."

Did Freddy's brother kill himself because he felt responsible in some way for what his brother did to his victims?

"Is there anyone else left in the family we can speak to?"

Agent Chapman ran his finger down the page in the file. "Henry Poole left behind a wife and son. Margo and Phillip. The kid is nine-teen." Agent Chapman shook his head. "Way too young to lose a parent, especially like that."

Ryan agreed and sympathized with the poor kid. He'd had a lot of tragedy in his life. He hoped he had people around him to help him through the devastating loss. "I'd love to talk to them about their impressions of Freddy, and if what he did, who he was, contributed to Henry taking his life. Maybe they can shed some light on who was in Freddy's and Henry's circle of friends. Maybe whoever is killing now reached out to Henry or someone in the family."

"I'll call the surviving Pooles and ask them if they'll help with the case."

"The sooner the better. Maybe we can stop a killer."

Agent Chapman sank back in his seat. "I've got the team digging deeper into Reed's life, seeing if there's anything that ties him to the victims."

If Kate's boyfriend was involved, it would crush Kate. He didn't know if she'd recover from something like that. She'd probably never trust another living soul in her life.

He hated that for her. She deserved better.

Ryan could only say, "We'll follow the evidence."

"I'll make the call to Margo Poole and see if she can see us today."

Chapter Seventeen

Ryan walked into Agent Chapman's office after lunch and checking in with Special Agent in Charge Booker. His boss was happy to have him on the case and hoped he could help Kate remember any other new information. Knowing someone else was at the cabin that night could lead them to their killer.

"Hey," Agent Chapman said the moment he stepped through the door. "I've done a deep dive on the Poole family. It's an interesting and sordid past."

"How so?"

"It's the question people wonder about. Are monsters born or made?" That gave Ryan pause, because he'd seen bad stuff and often found himself asking that very question. "Freddy and Henry Poole did not live a charmed life. From preschool on, they were in and out of foster homes due to neglect and abuse and then back with their mother multiple times. A few of the foster homes were no picnic either. They were moved a couple of times for the same horrible reasons they were taken from their mother. In too many cases, they were taken from one bad situation to another, never truly finding a safe place where they felt loved. Freddy had the most notes about his outbursts and bad temper. Henry seemed to be the quiet one, though I will give big brother Freddy credit. When he got in trouble, it was usually because he was protecting Henry."

Ryan could see a big brother doing just that in these circumstances. And though neglect and abuse were no excuse for abducting, raping, and killing women, it spoke to what made Freddy.

Hurt people, hurt people.

"So were they finally taken away from Mom for good?"

"Not exactly. When Freddy was sixteen, Henry thirteen, their house went up in flames. Mom died."

Ryan sat forward. "Was the fire ruled accidental?"

"Suspicious. But the fire department didn't have conclusive evidence to rule it arson."

Ryan considered the scenario. "Where was the mother found?"

"In bed under the collapsed roof debris. While the coroner did find evidence of smoke inhalation, it wasn't extensive."

"She died quickly after the fire started."

"Yes," Agent Chapman confirmed. "Even though the fire started in the kitchen."

Ryan read Agent Chapman's suspicious look. "Let me guess. Gas stove."

Agent Chapman nodded. "Freddy said he'd been cooking something to eat for him and Henry, since their mother had refused them food earlier. They waited for her to go to sleep before sneaking out of their rooms for food."

"So the grease fire starts, but they don't try to get their mother out of the house."

Abused boys out for revenge?

"They said the smoke was too thick, the fire spread too quickly. And when they went around the house to break the mother's window, the fire only swamped the room faster."

"Which means the mother's bedroom door had to be open."

Agent Chapman turned thoughtful. "Strange that they'd sneak out of their rooms to get food, but not close her door to keep her from hearing them."

Ryan nodded. "A lot of that story is suspicious. But it's not conclusive either."

Agent Chapman frowned. "No, it's not. And now both of them are gone, so we'll never know for sure."

"So did the boys end up in a foster home together after that?"

"Unfortunately, this was when they got separated. Henry went to live with a good family. By all reports his grades got better, he stopped missing days at school, and he graduated high school with honors. He went on to college with a scholarship."

"Let me guess. Freddy didn't have the same experience."

"He only stayed in foster care for two more years until he aged out. His record shows he was moved four times in two years. He ran away a lot, attended school little, and didn't graduate, though all the reports written by his advocates say he was smart, articulate, and not living up to his potential."

"How could he with all the turmoil in his life?"

"Exactly."

Ryan digested all that. "So we have a sense of who Freddy and Henry were and became based on their childhood."

"Henry went on to a career and family. Freddy had several run-ins with the law, nothing too serious, worked lots of different jobs, then turned serial killer. Both of them died young."

"What about their father? Where was he?"

"There's one report in the juvenile records. Dad was contacted to take the kids the first time they were placed in foster care. He declined to take them and told the agency not to ask again. He had a rap sheet for a bunch of petty crimes, mostly theft, drunk and disorderly, DUI, and a couple minor assaults."

"Bar fights?" Ryan guessed.

The agent confirmed that with a nod. "He died young, too. Fifty-three. Liver failure."

Chronic alcoholic, Ryan assumed based on the charges he'd racked up.

Agent Chapman stood. "Looks like Ms. Poole just arrived." He notched his chin toward the window behind Ryan.

He turned and caught the petite, dark-haired woman walking into the conference room across from the cubicles outside Agent Chapman's office on the other side of the building.

"Ready for this?"

Ryan stood and went ahead of Agent Chapman. He walked into the conference room just as the woman settled in a seat with a glass of water in front of her.

She stood to greet them. "Agent Chapman?"

The agent stepped forward, hand extended. "Thank you for coming in to see us today, Ms. Poole." They shook.

Ryan closed the distance and held out his hand. "I'm Ryan Strickland. I'm a psychologist. I consult with the FBI."

"It's nice to meet both of you. I have to say, I'm a bit confused about why you asked me here today."

Ryan took a seat across from Ms. Poole. "I assume Agent Chapman told you we're investigating the recent murders you've probably seen on the news."

"He did. But what does that have to do with me?" A light of understanding widened her eyes. "The murders must be similar to the Rose Reaper," she guessed.

Ryan glanced at the agent, who nodded for him to go ahead and take the lead. "We believe it is a copycat killer." Ryan gave Ms. Poole a moment to absorb that. "The killer has been reaching out to Kate Doyle."

She gasped. "The woman who survived?"

"Yes. The killer has been leaving her roses after he takes each new victim."

Ms. Poole laid her hands on the table. "I don't understand. What does this have to do with me?"

"Nothing directly. We've asked you here to talk about what you know about Freddy and your husband, Henry."

"Ex-husband." She sounded more sad than angry about the split.

"Of course. You divorced just after Freddy was exposed and died."

Her gaze dropped to her lap. "I couldn't take it anymore. Henry was always defending him. And then to find out Freddy had . . . done those terrible things." Ms. Poole gripped her hands together tightly on the table. "And Henry, he became less of himself without Freddy."

"Did Henry know what Freddy was doing?"

Ms. Poole kept her head down. "I guess it doesn't matter now if anyone knows. They're both gone."

Ryan shared a look with Agent Chapman, his anticipation that they were about to discover something important reflected back at him from Agent Chapman's eyes.

Ms. Poole glanced up at them, but then her gaze fell to her clenched hands. "I don't know if Henry knew about Freddy taking those women and killing them. Not for sure. Probably he did." She pressed her lips tight, glanced at them briefly, then looked away. "Freddy always came to Henry when he was in trouble. Mostly it was minor things. But there was always something." She met their gazes. "And I sympathized for the most part. I mean, the life they had as children. No kid should grow up like that."

"Can you tell us what you mean by that?" Ryan hoped she'd fill in the details the sparse reports they read didn't include.

Ms. Poole scrunched her lips, anger and disgust filling her eyes. "Their mother wasn't a mother at all. She hurt them. She starved them. She punished them. And worse . . ." The last word was said on a barely there whisper.

Though his mind didn't want to go there, Ryan wondered, what could be worse? What he came up with as the possibilities based on his experience on other cases made him cringe. "What do you know that's not in their social services files?"

She sighed. "I learned it by accident. He was usually so careful about how much he consumed. But every once in a while, when he was under a lot of stress, or something came up with Freddy, Henry would drink. A lot. He always got it back under control after a bad night. But this one time, early in our marriage . . ."

When Ms. Poole lost herself in the past and didn't say more, Ryan prompted her. "What did he tell you?"

"Everything. The whole sordid mess. His mother didn't just mistreat them, she abused them. Freddy, mostly. Because he tried to keep their mother from Henry. But it didn't always work. For Henry, it happened when he was ten. His mother beat Freddy badly, saying he wasn't going to stop her from teaching her son how to treat a woman."

Agent Chapman swore under his breath.

Ryan remained focused on Ms. Poole and stated the blunt truth. "She sexually molested and raped both boys."

Ms. Poole nodded her head several times, her gaze still down, her hands clenched. But then she looked at him. "Freddy tried to spare Henry, but the older Freddy got, the more she wanted Henry."

Ryan imagined Freddy had grown. He had more strength. He could fight, though he probably gave in so his mother didn't abuse Henry. She probably played the boys, one against the other, to get what she wanted. But as the boys got older, the manipulation didn't work as well.

"Freddy hated that he couldn't spare Henry, so he took matters into his own hands."

"What did he do?" Ryan had a good idea, but wanted Ms. Poole to tell the story.

"He killed her." Ms. Poole held his gaze, approval in her eyes. "Henry said he planned it for a week. Freddy knew exactly how he'd do it. And the next time she forced him into her bed, he did what he always did and stared at the rose until she was distracted, then he pulled the knife from beneath her pillow and drove it right up under her ribs and into her black heart."

Ryan fell back in his seat and took that in.

Ms. Poole gave them the final piece of the puzzle of how Freddy got away with it. "Freddy knew the fire wouldn't cover up the knife wound, so he broke the glass lamp attached to the overhead ceiling fan and shoved a piece into her."

"The ceiling collapse due to the fire did the rest," Ryan guessed and felt Agent Chapman's stare but didn't look away from Ms. Poole. "Why didn't you report Freddy for the murder?" He knew the answer, but if he didn't ask it, Agent Chapman was required to as law enforcement.

Ms. Poole didn't hesitate or mince words. "She deserved it."

"Did Henry feel guilty about it?" Agent Chapman asked.

"No." She frowned. "Not about her. He felt guilty that Freddy had endured so much protecting him. That's why Henry tried so hard to help Freddy when they were adults. He wanted to make up for what he'd caused Freddy."

"But it was their mother who hurt them," Agent Chapman pointed out.

"And Freddy took Henry's turn time and time again. That evil woman used Henry to get Freddy to comply. Over and over and over again. Did Freddy end up doing terrible things? Yes. I can't dispute that. But do I understand, in some small way, how he turned into that? Yes. She made him a rapist and a killer."

"Did your husband know the whole time that it was Freddy taking and killing those women?"

"I don't know for sure." She shrugged, but it didn't seem as if she believed her own words. "The last couple years of our marriage were very rocky. But probably. Henry made it a point to keep track of Freddy in case Freddy needed him. I think more often than not, Henry kept Freddy on the straight and narrow until Freddy's demons took hold and he did something he shouldn't." Ms. Poole frowned and narrowed her gaze on her hands. "I've thought a lot about Freddy over the past almost four years. He was in a lot of pain. If you can't find a way to heal it, if you're not willing to talk about it, then all you're left with is trying to get rid of it. Freddy inflicted it on others, probably hoping it would make him feel better. Maybe hurting those women did in the moment. Maybe killing his mother over and over again eased him in some way for a brief time."

Ryan was impressed she'd thought it through and come to many of the same conclusions he now had about Freddy Poole, a.k.a. the Rose Reaper. "You said something about him staring at the rose. What did you mean?"

"I know Freddy left roses where he took his victims from. I think he wanted to leave a gift so someone who knew those women would know they'd been taken. I don't know if it was an apology or simply a means for him to tell on himself."

"You think he regretted what he was doing?"

She tilted her head and frowned. "He was really messed up."

"And the part about staring at the rose?" Agent Chapman reminded her.

"Oh. I learned that later in another drunken mumbled confession. Freddy used to tell Henry to just look at the rose, focus on that and not what she was making him do. The bedroom had rose wallpaper. I think that's why Freddy burned the house down. He didn't want to look at her or that wallpaper ever again."

"Do you know if Freddy or Henry ever talked about the rose thing with anyone? Did they draw it?"

She shrugged. "I doubt they'd share that with anyone."

"What about your son, Phillip? Does he know any of this?" Agent Chapman asked.

"Of course not. We tried to raise Phillip with love and understanding and fill the house with happiness. Henry wanted Phillip to have the carefree life he never had, so he did everything with Phillip. Sports. Camping. Fishing."

"Did they have a favorite spot?" the agent asked, taking notes like usual, though the conversation was being recorded.

"All over the place. Local lakes and reservoirs. The river, of course. Phillip played lots of sports, but ultimately liked football the best. He's very competitive and likes to win. And like all kids, he loved video games, would play them for hours. That's why Henry pushed him to outdoor activities, too. Why?"

"It sounds like Henry was a great father."

"He tried to be, even though he worried that he wasn't up to the task because he didn't have a good example. At least, not until the Miller family fostered him after his mother died. By then, he'd seen the worst in so many people. They were good to him right up until his death."

"How did he feel when Freddy died?"

"He was devastated. But also, strangely relieved."

Ryan could believe it, but asked, "Why, do you think?"

"Because Freddy didn't have to hurt anymore. He was finally free of this life and all the pain it had brought him." Henry looked at things from Freddy's perspective. Just like Ms. Poole was doing now, explaining her husband and how he spiraled and why and ended up hanging himself when it all became too much to bear.

That made a lot of sense to Ryan. "Did Henry ever mention seeing Freddy the day he died?"

"No. Not specifically."

Ryan leaned in. "What did he say?"

"That he was sorry he couldn't talk Freddy into getting help."

I need this. Freddy's words, overheard by Kate, rang in Ryan's head.

Ryan took it a step further. "Did Henry blame himself for Freddy's death?"

"I believe Henry blamed himself for everything that ever happened to Freddy, that he was either too young or too powerless to stop. I think he felt guilty for every success in his life, for every good thing he had that Freddy didn't. And when Freddy died, leaving Henry alone with all the pain and nightmares they'd shared, he couldn't take it anymore." Tears gathered in Ms. Poole's eyes and ran down her cheeks.

Ryan got up and went to the coffee station at the end of the room and grabbed a napkin. He took it to Ms. Poole and handed it to her.

She dabbed at her wet cheeks and eyes. "I'm sorry. I thought I had put all this behind me."

Ryan squeezed her shoulder before taking his seat again. "I'm sorry we have to dig up such painful memories."

"I just want Henry to rest in peace now. I want my son to be able to live his life without his uncle's misdeeds making everyone suspect Phillip's like him."

"I guess your son endured some taunts and accusations when Freddy's identity was released publicly?"

"It was terrible. People who had known us for years thought we knew about it and did nothing. They didn't want to associate with us. A few were sympathetic. I guess you really learn who your friends are when someone in the family is revealed to be a serial killer."

Ryan knew that to be true. "I've worked enough cases to say for sure that serial killers are good at hiding who they are around the people closest to them."

"It's a strange thing. I know I saw Freddy a time or two during the time frame he was killing those women. I mean, he always seemed a bit off, but I thought I knew why. But it was so much worse."

"How did Phillip handle it?"

"Teens are strange creatures," she admitted. "A lot of his friends thought it was cool in a creepy sort of way. They'd ask macabre questions like, *Did he stare at you like he wanted to kill you? Did you ever see blood on his clothes? Did you ever see him kill anything?*"

"Did Freddy, Henry, and Phillip hunt?"

Ms. Poole shook her head. "Just fishing. At least, that's all they ever told me. I don't think after what Henry went through as a child he wanted anything to do with guns or knives or hurting anything.

He even said they threw back the fish they caught. Phillip adored his father. His loss hit Phillip hard. But my boy, he's strong. He's doing well in school. I think working through his grief and settling into a more independent life matured him. I just wish he kept in touch more."

"Is there a reason you two don't keep in close contact?" Ryan wondered if it had to do with Henry's suicide or if there had been something else that tore a rift in their relationship.

Ms. Poole waved that off. "He's focused on school and being with his friends. He wants to be treated like an adult and live his own life. But he's my son. I want to know how he is, so maybe I call and fuss too much."

Ryan understood. He had a loving mom, too. "I should probably call my mother. She'd love to hear from me more often." He wanted to put Ms. Poole at ease.

Agent Chapman continued with the interview. "Did your son inherit all of your late husband's things?"

"Yes. As far as we know, there are no other family members, at least none that Henry would have wanted in his life."

Agent Chapman continued with that line of questioning. "Were any of Freddy's possessions included in the things Henry left to your son?"

"Yes. Though Freddy didn't have a lot. Henry took the furniture from Freddy's apartment to the dump. It wasn't worth keeping. But the personal things—mementos, pictures, stuff like that—he kept."

Ryan wondered if Phillip would show them some of Freddy's things. Maybe that would help them identify any other friends or associates. Maybe there was a clue they didn't even know they needed to solve this case.

Agent Chapman tapped a pen on the table. "What happened after the house burned down? To the property, I mean."

Ms. Poole frowned. "You know, I'm not sure. I believe the property belonged to their mother and had been in the family for quite some time. Once the house was gone, and the boys were put back in foster care, I suppose Freddy and Henry inherited the property. Henry never said anything about it, though. I doubt he'd ever want to go back to it. Maybe they sold it. Maybe it was part of what went to Phillip."

Agent Chapman raised a brow. "You don't know exactly what Phillip received?"

"Not specifically. Aside from Henry's condo, his bank accounts, and possessions, I don't know what else there would be. Maybe some investments and retirement funds. Phillip is young, but an adult. He wanted to speak to the lawyer and handle it himself. I offered to help him navigate everything, but . . ."

Phillip didn't want his mother butting into his business.

"I really don't think there's anything else I can tell you." Ms. Poole bit her bottom lip, then met Agent Chapman's gaze. "Am I in trouble for not telling the authorities that Freddy killed his mother?"

"Since Henry told you that, it's hearsay. I can't prove or disprove that's what he told you, or even if it's true, because Henry isn't here for me to question. And what would I do with the information anyway. All the people involved are dead now. So don't worry about revealing the secret. I bet it felt good to get it off your chest."

"I wish Freddy and Henry hadn't had to carry that burden, too."

"Does your son know about it?" Agent Chapman asked.

Ms. Poole shook her head. "No. Of course not. I wish he didn't know about his uncle either, but I couldn't help that with all the press. Henry wanted to keep all the bad from Phillip. He wanted our son to have a normal life. I hope he can still do that even with all this other stuff coming back up again."

Ryan thought that was a good place to end things. "Thank you for coming in to see us today."

Ms. Poole stood and took a step away from the table, but turned back to him. "Do you have any idea who is killing these women and harassing the poor woman who survived?"

"No." He went with the simple truth. "But we're working hard to find out."

"I wish I knew something that would help you." The sincerity in her words matched the look in her eyes.

"You helped us a lot by filling in the blanks of Freddy's past and why he did what he did. We can use that information to maybe find a connection between Freddy and who is killing now. For all we know, it's just someone who wants the same kind of attention the Rose Reaper received for what he did."

Ms. Poole rolled her eyes. "All this death and hurt and pain for the families so he can have his fifteen minutes of fame. It's vile. I hope you catch him soon. I hope he spends the rest of his life in jail. Freddy did terrible things. But maybe he earned the easy out he took after what had been done to him." Ms. Poole still had compassion for Henry's brother. Maybe because Freddy had protected Henry and Henry had been able to love her, she found it easier to find a little love for the goodness buried deep inside the monster.

Chapter Eighteen

Ryan and Agent Chapman went over everything Ms. Poole told them. It didn't lead them to the copycat killer, but it did help them understand the Rose Reaper better.

Maybe understanding him would give them some insight into the new killer.

Probably not.

They were simply two very different people.

Freddy had been spurred on by his hatred for his mother and his need to kill her over and over again.

Ryan imagined there was some sort of distorted sexual component mixed in with Freddy unable to forge real relationships with women but needing the sexual gratification that maybe only came when he hurt them, the way he'd always wanted to hurt his mother.

The new killer wanted the notoriety of the Rose Reaper.

Ryan wondered what would happen after he finished his quest to kill seven victims and finish what the Rose Reaper started. If he successfully kidnapped and killed Kate, would he change his MO? Would her death release him from the Rose Reaper's bonds and allow him to explore new ways of killing?

Ryan wondered if he got the same sense of satisfaction in raping and killing the women as the Rose Reaper had, or if it fell flat because his motivation differed from Freddy's.

Maybe he'd get a chance to find out if they caught the man doing this.

He hoped they did so before Kate suffered any more harm.

Ryan had called and checked in on Kate before he left Agent Chapman's office. All was well and quiet at her place. She and Reed were having dinner together at home.

He still had some reservations about Reed and didn't know why.

Kate seemed happy with him. She trusted him.

Letting it go for now, Ryan headed back to his hotel for the night, stopping off for dinner on his way. He didn't want the restaurant noise and opted for takeout so he could kick back in his room and think. But the moment he got into his room and set the pizza on the coffee table, all he wanted to do was call Molly.

She was probably at work, but maybe he'd get lucky and catch her on break or when they were slow.

He got her voice mail. "You know what to do, but it's probably better if you just text me."

He chuckled and left a message. "Hey, it's me. I'm still out of town. No idea when I'll be back, but I . . . miss you. Yeah. Anyway. Call me on your break or something." He hung up, let his head drop so he was staring at his shoes, then shook his head over what a lame-ass message that was and pulled a slice of pizza from the box.

His phone pinged with a text.

MOLLY: Miss you 2

MOLLY: I find myself wondering what ur doing there and hoping it's not bad

MOLLY: Or sad

It touched him that she'd think about that and his job and know that it took a toll on him.

RYAN: Lots of information gathering today.

RYAN: I'd love a break on the case. But I also don't want anyone else to get hurt.

MOLLY: Totally

MOLLY: Send me a selfie of what you're doing right now

RYAN: You send me one too

He snapped a pic of him biting into a slice of sausage and black olive pizza and sent it to her.

She sent him a pic of her standing at the bar, her back to the shelves of booze, smiling with one hand up showing him the universal sign for *rock on*.

It made him smile.

He bet her customers were enjoying her banter and drinks.

MOLLY: I don't know which looks better u or the pizza

He laughed again.

RYAN: You're beautiful. I want to take you out when I get home.

MOLLY: It's a date.

MOLLY: Gotta go. Big crowd tonight. There's a couple in a booth making out. He kind of looks like you. She's practically in his lap, her hand on his jaw, her lips locked with his. I'm thinking that could be us.

So was he now.

MOLLY: Sweet dreams.

Ryan grinned. She'd done that on purpose, leaving him wanting her.

RYAN: I'll be dreaming of you.

Because he'd much rather be thinking about her than the case.

The Rose Reaper's Journal Entry

I hum that silly tune all the time now.

It used to seem ominous.

Now it is the theme song to my every delight.

I think about my roses, the ones I plucked from the weeds, the ones who gave me such comfort, the ones who made me, me.

Each one is the same and different.

Each one special and a part of me now.

Only one knows my secret. Only one knows my pain. Only one understands I can't ignore the need growing inside me.

He wants me to stop.

I wish I could for him.

At first I found relief in their pain. Now I find myself almost able to delight in their surrender and quietness.

It is an odd feeling.

I wonder if I am changing.

I wonder if they are changing me as they yield and accept the inevitable.

Now when I watch the life burn out in their eyes, I feel it is a gift. One they give to me. The last thing they ever do is just for me.

And so I hum my silly tune and watch and wait to find the next rose among the weeds. The next to give me, with her last breath, the last spark of her life.

Chapter Nineteen

The body hit the water with a whoosh and a splash, then disappeared as the current pulled it under and downriver. The river would wash her clean.

Her death had bathed him in joy.

He hummed the silly tune, his death anthem, on the way back to the cabin.

Everything was going to plan. It wouldn't be long now.

Kate.

Just thinking about her made him yearn.

Five down. One to go.

His sixth rose needed to be perfect. She needed to do what none of the others had done: leave Kate vulnerable.

Kate remained his biggest temptation. He loved watching her go about her day, knowing he was coming for her.

At first, she didn't believe it. The first rose upset her, but didn't convince her of what he had in store. But with each new rose, she understood. She knew what was happening. What was coming.

Now, when he saw her, she acted like someone who knew they were being stalked.

She felt him closing in.

Little did she know he was so close.

Of course, now the FBI was on the case and the police and feds were watching Kate's house. Whatever.

He expected them and the increased surveillance. They were abuzz with catching him.

And because of that, he was all over the news.

They hadn't given him a name yet. Annoying bastards.

He didn't worry. He'd get his due.

He'd make Kate come to him.

That idea held a lot of appeal.

But first, he was going to put Kate on notice.

Nothing and no one was going to keep him from her.

Chapter Twenty

Ryan called Phillip Poole first thing in the morning, hoping to catch him before he headed to class on the nearby college campus. Ms. Poole had supplied her son's cell phone number as well as where he went to school and worked. Phillip didn't pick up, so Ryan identified himself as a consultant with the FBI, asking for a meeting to talk about his uncle Freddy.

He hoped the message didn't spook or upset the nineteen-year-old.

The hotel's buffet breakfast gave him time to think about the questions he wanted to ask. Phillip had been in elementary school when the Rose Reaper started killing and high school when Freddy Poole died after Kate's escape. He wasn't sure Phillip knew anything beyond what news reports detailed on TV and online. He suspected Phillip's parents would have shielded him as much as possible, even though Ms. Poole made it clear the kids at school had certainly let Phillip know what was happening.

An hour later, he still hadn't heard from Phillip. Maybe he liked having early classes and the rest of the day to study and work and time for his friends at night. In college, those had been Ryan's priorities as well.

On a whim, he drove to the college, hoping to find Phillip at his dorm. Ryan checked in at the school office, then headed over to see Phillip. Getting into the dorm required a badge, but the office had given him a temporary one. He stood outside Phillip's second-floor door with a sign on it that read You're *NOT* Welcome. He knocked anyway.

No one answered.

He didn't hear any sounds coming from inside the room, but just as he was about to leave, someone called out from down the hall, "Hey, what are you doing at my door?"

Ryan met the young man's suspicious gaze. "Phillip Poole?"

The kid held eye contact with confidence. "Who's asking?"

"Ryan Strickland. I'm a consultant with the FBI."

The two guys following Phillip grabbed on to his shoulders, grinning and shaking him. "No fucking way," one of them said. The other smacked him on the back. "You weren't lying."

Phillip nearly dropped the to-go cups in the holder he was carrying, but managed to keep them upright. "Told you," he said to his friends, looking smug.

Ryan wasn't exactly sure what was going on, but it appeared that Phillip liked being connected to his serial killer uncle. "Do you have a few minutes to talk?"

"About the Rose Reaper?" the blond kid asked.

Ryan didn't say anything, just held Phillip's gaze.

Phillip tried not to look so pleased and like a big shot, but it came through. "Sure, I've got time for the FBI."

Ryan understood the ego behind the words. Phillip wanted his friends to think he was cool and had an in with the FBI and the case.

"I bet he wants to know about the new murders," the other kid announced.

Of course they knew about the new serial killer. It was all over the news.

Phillip unlocked his door, enthusiastic grin still in place. "Sorry, guys, gotta do my civic duty and help the FBI catch a killer."

The blond grabbed his coffee, smirking and eyeing Ryan.

The dark-haired guy took his cup, shaking his head. "Whatever. We'll catch you later."

The blond's jolly demeanor dimmed as his gaze narrowed. "Don't disappoint. You better call and tell all."

Phillip notched his chin up. "I'll see you in bio class."

The dark-haired guy started walking away. "You better show."

Ryan remembered his college days and hanging with his buddies just like this, each of them always trying to one-up each other. He stepped into the dorm room behind Phillip, pleasantly surprised to find the place neat but lived in.

Phillip set his coffee and the holder on one of the two desks and pulled his messenger bag over his head and dropped it on the bed next to him.

Ryan dove into the conversation. "So I'm here to talk to you about your father and uncle. While I work for the FBI, I am not an agent. I'm a psychologist who consults on cases. My specialty is working with victims and witnesses."

Phillip leaned back against the desk. "I'm neither, so what brought you to me?"

Ryan held up his phone. "Do you mind if I record our conversation so that I can provide it to the agent in charge of the case?"

Phillip shrugged a shoulder. "Sure. Why not? It's not like I have anything to hide."

Ryan tapped his phone to start the recording, then looked at the printed-out pages on Phillip's desk. "I see you're following the case."

Phillip had photos and news stories of all the victims. "You hear about a murder and you don't really think anything more than *That sucks* and move on because it doesn't have anything to do with you. But then there's another and another and you hear reports that maybe there's a link to the Rose Reaper."

"And then it does have something to do with you," Ryan finished for him.

Phillip folded his arms over his chest. "It feels that way, because of my uncle. I knew the guy, but never suspected he was . . . doing what he was doing."

"He abducted and raped seven women. He killed six of them."

Phillip didn't really react to that statement. Maybe because he'd grown accustomed to people being so blunt about something so brutal. Maybe he kept his reaction to himself so that people didn't read anything into it. "Why are you here?"

"I spoke to your mother about Freddy and your father."

"Did she tell you the truth or just tell you she didn't know anything about what Freddy was doing and why?" Though he tried to hide it, Ryan sensed Phillip's anger and resentment that he'd been coddled by his parents and not given the full story.

Kids were often left in the dark when it came to grown-ups explaining things without any real detail or insight to spare the kids. All it did was leave them with questions and feeling like they were missing out on something that affected them, no matter how hard adults tried to shield them.

"She was very forthcoming with what she knew. Especially because your uncle and father have passed. There's no reason to hide the truth anymore to spare them."

"Or put my father in jeopardy of being arrested for knowing about Freddy's needs."

Ryan raised a brow at how Phillip described Freddy's criminal activity. "You sound like you know about Freddy's reasons for doing what he did."

"I do. I took a couple psych classes my first year of college. When something like that hits so close to home and no one will give you a straight answer, you go looking for them yourself. My friends thought it was cool or weird or fucked up to have a serial killer in the family. I wanted to know how the man who took me fishing and treated me like a son could do something like that. I wanted to know how my father could just ignore his responsibility and let Freddy kill all those women."

"And did you find those answers in a textbook?"

"Between that and pieced-together conversations I overheard growing up, I knew my dad and uncle had a shit childhood. I knew that my uncle often took a beating or the blame to protect my dad. I knew because of that my dad felt like he owed my uncle his life. I knew my uncle's troubles were a result of his fucked-up past." Phillip's insight showed maturity and thought.

Ryan wondered if he knew more. "Did your father ever speak to you about your grandmother and being placed in foster care growing up?"

"No. He talked a lot and often about wanting me to have a good childhood. He wanted me to just be normal." Phillip shrugged. "Whatever that actually means, because normal for me may not be the same for someone else. My dad's normal was not mine, that's for sure."

Phillip had a point.

"Do you miss your dad?"

Sadness softened his eyes. "I wish I'd known what I know now back then. Maybe he could have given me the answers I needed to feel like this all made sense. Instead, I was left to make sense of it on my own."

Ryan dove into the real reason he'd come. "Your mother told me you inherited your father's estate."

Phillip shrugged. "Since they're divorced, he left it all to me."

"I understand it included Freddy's things."

"It did. Though he didn't have much."

"Would you be willing to show me and the agent in charge of the case his things?"

Phillip took a second to respond. "Sure. Why not?" Phillip checked the time on his phone. "But it will have to be some other time. I've got a class in fifteen across campus. All the stuff is in a storage unit about twenty minutes from here."

Ryan pulled out his card. "Here's my number. Call or text me with a time and the address and we'll meet you there."

"Sure." Phillip took a long sip of his coffee, then met Ryan's gaze again. "What do you guys know about this new serial killer? Is he really like my uncle?"

Ryan evaded the question. "Thank you for your time."

One side of Phillip's mouth drew back. "Yeah, I didn't think you'd give me an answer." He hadn't gotten one from his family either, at least not a direct one.

Ryan threw him a bone. "Just like your uncle, this one will make a mistake. They always do."

"Maybe. My uncle got away with it for a long time. This new guy hasn't made a mistake yet. You guys have no leads. At least that's what the news reports say. It must be frustrating." Something in Phillip's tone pricked Ryan's annoyance.

"Just because a killer is careful doesn't mean he's infallible. The FBI and local law enforcement are working the case. They want to catch this guy before he kills again. That's the job."

"And yours is to talk to victims and witnesses, yet there aren't any in this case. So what brought you into it?" Genuine interest lit his eyes.

"That I can't discuss."

"If you're looking into the Rose Reaper, then I have to wonder if you've spoken to Kate Doyle. She survived him. She'd know the most about him and what he did to the other women."

Ryan's curiosity about Phillip grew. "What's your major?"

"Pharmacology."

Ryan glanced at the computer screen filled with icons for different popular video games. Several trophies and certificates for gaming tournaments lined the shelf above the desk. "Why not computer gaming?"

"That's for fun. This is . . . practical." Phillip quickly changed the subject. "Do you like it?"

Ryan caught on. "Working for the FBI? Yes. Most of the time." His job was sometimes overwhelming and it took a toll on him personally.

Phillip shook his head. "No. I mean getting into the heads of the victims and killers."

"Helping victims is rewarding. Putting bad guys away is, too. Getting justice for the victims and their families even more so. But it's difficult work, putting yourself in that dark world."

Phillip shrugged once again. "It feels like that world has always been a part of my life now. It's my new normal."

"It doesn't have to be. Your uncle is gone. You can have whatever life you want."

"And yet, here you are bringing my uncle back front and center. Or at least this new killer has done so. Will there be others who emulate him?"

"I hope not."

Phillip gave him a *Me too* look that came with a lot of skepticism.

"Don't forget to call or text me with a good time to go through your uncle's things." Ryan left the room and dorm, walking out into the bright sunlight. He took a second to allow his eyes to adjust before he headed for his car.

His phone rang. He glanced at the caller ID and answered the call. "Good morning, Agent Chapman."

"Yes, it is. We have something very interesting on Reed. We're bringing him in now. Care to sit in with me and question him?"

"Yes. Absolutely." Finally, maybe they had a break in the case.

"Great. I'll fill you in on everything as soon as you arrive. I think we've got him." The excitement and anticipation in Agent Chapman's voice infected Ryan as well.

"You think it's him?" Admittedly, Ryan had suspicions about the timing of Reed coming into Kate's life and the first murders happening close to that time frame, but he'd held out hope that he was wrong. For Kate's sake.

"It's one too many coincidences adding up to look like a pattern. You'll see."

"I'm on my way." Ryan slipped into the driver's seat of his rental car and started it. "I'm about twenty minutes out. I stopped by Phillip Poole's college campus to see him. He's going to contact me with a time and place to meet him to go through the Rose Reaper's things." Ryan backed out of the parking spot and headed toward the exit.

"Well, we may not need to do that if Reed turns out to be our guy."

"Is whatever you have on Reed enough to clear Todd Lane and Ed Silva as potential suspects?"

"If we're lucky." Agent Chapman ended the call.

Ryan still wanted to see if there was anything in the Rose Reaper's personal effects that gave them any more insight or clues about why he did what he did. And where.

For all they knew about Freddy Poole, they'd never found his cabin in the woods.

Ryan wondered if it held even more secrets.

Chapter Twenty-One

Ryan had just pulled into the FBI building's parking lot when his phone rang. He checked the caller ID, grinned, then accepted the call from his sister. "Hey, Thea, what's up?"

"Did you forget something?" His sister's tone alerted him that, yes, he had. But what?

"Uh. Maybe?"

"Lunch. With me."

He swore. "Thea, I'm sorry. I got called away on a case."

"Where are you?"

"Maine. Someone I helped a few years ago is in trouble. She asked for my help."

"Why didn't you tell me you were going back to work early? Are you sure you're ready?" Her concern touched him deeply.

"Yes." He didn't hesitate to say that because being back at work, feeling like he was helping Kate, gave him a purpose. One that helped him climb his way out of his grief about finding his sister Lisa's body and his last case. Helping others helped him see that life went on. And though this case echoed with the brutality and inhumanity of his last case, it also gave him a chance to help a victim who needed to know that the terrible things that happen in life can be overcome.

Kate had done it once. She could do it again.

She knew he'd help her through this, so she could get to the other side and be happy again.

He gave Thea a better answer. "I can't wallow in the past and keep thinking that I failed Olivia." She'd been a victim and witness to the Copeland County Killer's murders. She'd taken Ryan to his sister's body. He'd tried to help Olivia. He regretted not being able to help her more. "I have to move forward, knowing there are other victims out there I can help."

"Olivia made her choice. You didn't fail her. You told her story. That's what she needed you to do for her."

Yes, he'd done that, but he hadn't saved her from herself.

"I'm sorry I forgot about our lunch. I'm not sure when I'll be home, but as soon as I am, we'll catch up."

"Okay, but you owe me."

"Fine. I'm buying."

"Great. I'll pick the place."

He rolled his eyes even though she couldn't see him. Thea was going to put a dent in his checking account. He didn't really mind. No doubt the food would be good. But being with his sister would be even better. "I'll see you soon."

"Take care, Ry. Call if you need me. Or if you just want someone to hang with, even if it is long distance."

He immediately thought of Molly. "I did that the other night with someone."

Thea went dead silent for a second. "Who? What's her name?"

"Molly. I met her at a bar. We're . . . keeping things uncomplicated and fun."

"But it's a thing, right?" She sounded so hopeful.

He chuckled under his breath. "It's something. I like her. Though we've barely been in the same room together."

"Does she mind that you're away for work?"

"So far, not really." But it could definitely become a problem.

"Well, something is better than nothing, and if you're happy with uncomplicated and fun and actually sharing this news with me, then I'm happy for you. I hope you have a hell of a lot of fun. You need it. You deserve it."

"Thanks. How's Jake?"

"Perfect. And seriously overworked. Like you. We have a dinner date tonight. He promised."

Jake was an emergency physician and often on call. Thea adored him. He treated his sister like she deserved to be treated when he wasn't overworked and away from her for all those long hours.

"Do something nice for him, because you know he's got something planned for you."

"He always does." The suggestive tone was so not necessary.

"Gross. I have to go now. I've got an interview with a potential suspect."

"You have your fun, I have mine," she teased. "Love you."

"Love you." He hung up with her and headed in to find Agent Chapman and learn whatever he'd discovered about Reed.

Chapter Twenty-Two

The FBI offices were abuzz with anticipation and a vibrant energy that came with the feeling a case was about to break.

Ryan made his way to the conference room.

"You're here. Great." Agent Chapman stood and went to a new board that had been added to the other five used for each of the new victims. The new board had a picture of Reed, along with dozens of copies of what looked like bank and credit card statements. "So after you and I spoke about Reed, I had the team dig a little into his past, his whereabouts when the victims went missing, and when he met Kate. And guess what? We have a timeline that puts him in the same places as our victims within days of their abductions."

The surprise of it sent a wave of urgency through Ryan, but then he thought twice. "So what you're saying is that his credit or debit card charges show him in the exact same place as one of the victims before they were kidnapped?"

"Yes. Coffee shops. Restaurants. Even a movie theater. We put Todd Lane close to a couple of victims, but never anything like this." Agent Chapman slid a stack of printouts closer to Ryan, then held up two photos. "Reed at a coffee shop six days before victim number two, Kelly Russell, was kidnapped. Another of him getting lunch at a taqueria with victim number four, Cathy Evans, there at the same time. They appear to be having a conversation."

Ryan couldn't doubt the evidence. But if a picture said a thousand words, were these two pictures saying what they wanted them to say, or were these simply coincidences, albeit very suspicious chance encounters? "Don't you find this rather convenient and . . . sloppy? Todd seems more adept at covering his tracks than this. If Reed is our guy, he'd have to know if you dug into his whereabouts you'd find this surveillance footage."

Agent Chapman's excitement waned. "True. In this day and age, you can't go anywhere that doesn't have cameras watching you. Maybe he was counting on the places not storing the information long enough for us to find it."

"What about the first, third, and last victims?"

"While we connected Reed to the victims via staff statements for victims three and five, the respective movie theater or restaurant had already deleted the video footage."

Most places probably kept the recordings for only a week, maybe two at most. Some places might even turn it over in a matter of a couple of days. That was a lot of data to store. And if there were no complaints or thefts identified the same day or within a few days, why keep it.

And the victims weren't found in the river for several days, even weeks, from the time they were abducted. They weren't even reported as missing for at least a day or two. By the time the police started looking for them, the videos could have been erased or recorded over. Plus, without a suspect, the cops wouldn't know who they were looking for anyway. Reed wasn't the only person in the shop with the two victims they had surveillance videos on.

Still, to place him with four of the five victims . . .

"What about victim one?"

"We can't tie him to her at all yet. But we're still looking."

There could be any number of reasons why. Maybe the killer picked her out of a crowd. Maybe he saw her somewhere other than a place where you'd make a purchase. A park. An office of some sort.

Like when Todd Lane was out on a job.

Later, he found the women in places he frequented. Though that seemed riskier with the transaction recorded and shop surveillance.

Ryan wondered about the latest victim. "Has the body of Anne Murphy been found yet?"

"No. But maybe he'll tell us where she is?"

Ryan doubted it, but it was worth a shot. And he wanted to hear everything Reed had to say about the case, the missing women, and especially Kate.

Ryan and Agent Chapman left their floor and headed down one to where the interview rooms were set up. They entered the room next to where Reed waited for them. They stared at the monitor showing him sitting in the interview room alone. For the most part, he looked relaxed, his gaze moving from staring at the table to the door. He didn't fidget or fuss with his hands or clothes. Dressed for work in jeans, a company polo shirt, and work boots, he didn't appear to be anything but what anyone would see.

Was the facade hiding a killer instinct and cruel heart?

If so, Reed had learned to mimic the behavior of a caring boyfriend well enough to trick Kate into believing that was what he was, despite her innate mistrust of others after her kidnapping and rape.

Seriously an amazing feat if true.

"Did he ask for a lawyer?"

Agent Chapman shook his head. "He said he was happy to help in any way he could."

"He's either confident we don't have enough evidence to charge him, or he's actually innocent." Ryan could think of a few other reasons why he didn't hire an attorney. The cost. He didn't think he needed one for a simple conversation about his girlfriend and a serial killer. He thought he was smart enough to handle this himself. It could be one of those reasons or something else.

Still, Reed should have a lawyer present because you never knew when you needed one—until you did.

"Let's go find out if he's who he says he is." Agent Chapman walked out of the room and right into the other.

Ryan studied Reed's face as the agent dropped the file folder on the table and stared down at him.

Reed looked up expectantly at the agent, but he still didn't look nervous. "Ask your questions. The sooner you clear me, the sooner you can get back to looking for the real killer."

Ryan had to hand it to Reed. That sounded like a man who knew he was being looked at and understood why and wanted to be helpful, while also wanting the focus to be back on Kate's tormentor.

Agent Chapman covered the preliminaries. "I want to reiterate that you are here voluntarily and have declined to have a lawyer present. You are not being charged with a crime. We just want to ask you some questions about your relationship with Kate Doyle and about the ongoing investigation into the kidnapping, rape, and murder of five women."

"Ask what you want to ask," Reed prompted, looking ready for anything.

"Why do you think we're focusing on you?" Agent Chapman asked.

"Because I'm the person closest to Kate. But I didn't do this. It's not me. The sooner you know that, the sooner we can all get back to protecting Kate and looking for the real asshole who is doing this."

Agent Chapman took his seat and settled in.

Ryan left the adjoining room, walked into the other, and took a seat beside Agent Chapman, keeping a steady gaze on Reed, who leaned forward, arms on the table, and waited for the questions to begin.

Agent Chapman laid his hand on the folder in front of him. "How did you and Kate meet?"

"The construction company I work for is building her law firm's new office building. Kate is the go-between for me and the partners. I liked her efficiency and insight into what the employees needed in their spaces and how to lay out the offices and cubicle space. Her intelligence, the shyness beneath her confidence, her smile, all of it appealed to me, along with her beauty. She kept things all business. Polite. But I also noticed her caution around others. I wondered why. And though I don't normally ask out people I'm working with on a project until it's over, I couldn't help but want to get to know Kate better. She declined several dates before she said yes."

That all matched Kate's description.

Agent Chapman opened a booklet and made notes. "Why did you persist when she'd made it clear she wasn't interested?"

Reed shrugged and a slight grin tugged at his lips. "Because I kept catching her staring at me like she couldn't help herself. When I'd look back at her, she'd quickly turn away. I thought it was cute. I took it as a sign that she was shy but interested, and something was holding her back. I asked her outright if she was seeing someone. She said she never dated anymore. I figured that meant she'd been burned in the past. I hoped that if I showed her I was a good guy, she'd say yes to a date."

"So you finally wore her down."

Reed's gaze narrowed and he frowned, a sense of affront coming off him. "I gave her the time and space she needed to make up her mind about me, while also letting her know I still wanted that date. The first time we met for coffee, she was so nervous she bailed on me after barely touching her drink. It was then I knew some guy hadn't just dumped her and made her wary of men. She was frightened."

Ryan held Reed's gaze. "After realizing that, you continued to pursue her."

Reed didn't hesitate to look Ryan in the eye. "It made me angry to think someone had hurt and scared her so badly that she was afraid of strangers. Of me." Reed made it seem like Ryan would understand.

He did. He also wondered if Reed's insight into Kate came from already knowing what she'd been through with the Rose Reaper, or if it was born out of his interest in her as a potential partner.

"I didn't like her fear. We had to work together. And while I could go back to being the guy she had to deal with on the project and keep it casual and all business, I still wanted her to like me." Reed shook his head. "No. That's not right. I wanted her to trust me. I wanted her to know that I wouldn't do whatever it was that had been done to her. I would never hurt her. In any way."

Reed shifted his gaze to Agent Chapman. "So you see, that's why there's no possible way you can think I had anything to do with the kidnapping and killing of those women. I am not messing with Kate. I don't want to hurt her. I love her."

Ryan believed that.

Reed made it sound so real.

But was it?

It was Ryan's and Agent Chapman's job to find out.

Agent Chapman's face and demeanor remained passive.

Reed sat back and sighed. "I'm telling the truth. If you don't believe me, then I don't know what else to say. I would never hurt Kate."

But would he hurt all those other women?

Agent Chapman tapped the folder with his index finger. "Denise Simmons went missing not that long after you and Kate started dating."

Reed stared at the agent but didn't comment.

"Kelly Russell went missing after you and Kate were together."

Reed nodded his agreement and pointed out, "So did three more women. Anne Murphy still hasn't been found."

Agent Chapman didn't hesitate to ask, "Do you know where she is?"

Reed sighed. "No. But I have no doubt you'll find her in the river, like all the others."

"How do you know that?"

Reed shook his head. "I didn't do this."

"Tell me about the time you met and had a conversation with Cathy Evans."

Reed cocked a brow. "I don't know what you're talking about."

Ryan read the lie just as well as Agent Chapman did.

Agent Chapman shook his head. "Here I thought you wanted to help."

"I do. But this is getting you nowhere. I did not do this."

"That's what you say, but—" Agent Chapman slid a photo out of the folder and placed it in front of Reed. "That's you, right?"

Reed nodded.

Agent Chapman tapped on the woman he was facing. "And that is Cathy Evans."

Reed met the agent's gaze again, but this time his was resigned. "I didn't know who she was at the time. When I saw her face on the news later, I remembered her. I thought it was just a chance encounter with a stranger, a weird coincidence at a place I go to all the time. I eat there at least once a week. I don't even really remember what we said to each other. Something insignificant about us ordering the same thing and going up to the counter to grab the food when it was called out, not knowing if it was hers or mine."

"Sounds like you do remember the encounter," Ryan pointed out.

He shifted nervously in the seat. "Just because I was in the same place as her on that day doesn't mean I kidnapped and killed her."

Agent Chapman nodded. "You're right. It doesn't."

"It's just a coincidence." Reed sounded sure of that.

"And yet . . ." Agent Chapman took out another photo of Reed at a coffee shop standing behind a woman. "Here you are with victim number two, Kelly Russell, just days before she went missing."

Reed sat up and leaned forward, staring at the picture. "No way. That can't be. I don't remember her at all."

"We have evidence that puts you in the same place with four of the five victims days before they were abducted."

Reed's eyes went wide, surprise and horror filling them. "No. It's not me. I did not do this! You can't tell Kate. I'm not the one who kidnapped and killed those women."

Agent Chapman pressed his lips tight. "Having a conversation with someone in a taqueria, then they go missing is a coincidence. Putting you in the same place at the same time as four of the victims is a pattern."

Reed smacked his hand on the table. "I'm being set up. Whoever is doing this is setting me up. That's the only explanation."

"Why?" Agent Chapman leaned on his arms on the table.

"So that Kate will think it's me. So that she won't see who is really coming for her."

"Because you're right in front of her," Agent Chapman suggested. "You have been all this time. You met all these women, or at least saw them, while you were grabbing something to eat, ordering coffee, just running an errand, then you stalked them, took them, raped them, and killed them."

Reed shook his head over and over. "No. NO!" He smacked his hand on the table again. "There's video of the killer leaving the roses at Kate's house. That's not me."

"You're the same size and shape as the person captured on the video. You set up the cameras. You were at the house at least once when the video was taken."

"Yes." Reed sat up taller. "Asleep with Kate. In her bed. In the house. She'd have known if I got up and left, then came back."

"Maybe." Agent Chapman shrugged one shoulder. "Maybe not. If you were careful—and let's face it, this killer is very careful—you could have done it."

"*Could have* and *did* are not the same." Reed glared daggers. "But what you're saying is that I kidnapped all these women without leaving any evidence behind, never being seen or caught doing it, but I'm stupid enough to leave a trail of evidence that puts me with each victim at some point before they're abducted?" One side of his mouth drew back and he shook his head.

"It's circumstantial," Agent Chapman admitted. "Maybe you thought you'd get away with it."

Maybe Todd Lane and his superficial proximity to a couple of the victims made more sense.

"I made it this easy for you to connect me to the victims? I made sure I was on video talking to one of them? I made it so that you'd look at me as the killer and hinder myself from being able to do it again, because you'll be watching me? That makes no sense."

"It's cocky is what it is," Agent Chapman snapped.

Reed huffed out his frustration and fell back in his seat. "It's a distraction. You're looking at me while this guy is out there with another victim. Can't you see? *He's* orchestrating this and you're playing to his tune."

Ryan wondered if maybe that was true. He didn't have enough evidence to discount it. What they had wasn't concrete. They'd need more.

Agent Chapman leaned forward again, pinning Reed in his gaze. "Is Anne Murphy alive or already dead?"

Reed shrugged. "How would I know? I didn't kidnap her."

"But you were both at the same grocery store hours before she went missing."

One side of Reed's mouth drew back in a half frown. "Let me guess, there's video or a picture."

Agent Chapman pulled out the photo taken from the video feed. "There is indeed."

"So very convenient for you." Reed looked at the picture of him standing two customers behind Anne Murphy at the quick checkout for customers with fifteen items or less. "I don't remember seeing her at all."

"And yet, it appears that you're staring right at her."

"Since you pulled this all together, have you looked to see if there is anyone else who also appears in all these surveillance images with us? Because it seems to me that I'm being followed, and then your killer is picking a target that I encounter in some insignificant way so he can pin this on me."

Ryan wondered the same thing. Were they too focused on Reed to see the bigger picture? Was there even something else to see?

It was Agent Chapman's job to find out.

"That's the story you're sticking to?" the agent asked.

"It's the only thing that makes sense. I did not do this. I am not the killer. I would never hurt Kate." Reed sounded not only assured but resigned. "All this so-called evidence against me shows is that this guy has been watching Kate and thinks I'm a threat and an easy target to pin this on. I'm an obstacle between him and Kate. And if you arrest me for this, you're playing right into his hands. Kate will be left alone."

"We'll protect her."

"Maybe. But I have a feeling this guy has a plan to take Kate, even with her in protective custody. Either way, without me in the picture, she's more vulnerable." Reed looked to Ryan. "You know I'm right."

"She relies on you to help her feel safe and protected. She leans on you for support."

"Take that away and . . ." Reed left the rest for Ryan to fill in just how quickly Kate's anxiety and trauma could crumble her resolve to stand strong against this threat.

Agent Chapman played devil's advocate. "Maybe that's been your plan all along, to make Kate feel safe and secure so you could get close to her, then you take her as your seventh victim. You get to taunt her that she's been fucking a killer, the very predator who's going to kill her and finish what the Reaper started."

"Or maybe this killer is using me to taunt her because she's the one who got away from the Rose Reaper, but she won't get away from him. Not if you make it this easy for him to get me out of the way so he can take her," Reed snapped.

"You think you can protect her?" Ryan asked.

Reed met his gaze. "I would lay down my life to save hers in a heartbeat."

Ryan wanted to believe him for Kate's sake.

"About those cameras you set up at Kate's house . . ." Agent Chapman brought them back to the investigation. "You installed them yourself, right?"

"Yes."

"Were they hard to set up?"

"No. The instructions are easy to follow. A child could probably do it."

Agent Chapman nodded. "So why did you leave such a wide swath of the back and side of the house uncovered?"

Reed eyed the agent. "The guy keeps leaving the roses on the front path. I wanted to catch him doing it. And I did."

"But you also made it easy for someone to go through the backyard, along the side of the house, come out on the sidewalk out front, and put the flowers on the path. I mean, you could have done that." The agent pointed out the very thing Reed denied doing and how he could have accomplished it easily.

Reed rolled his eyes. "Which only makes the story the killer is getting you to buy more plausible."

"And since you set up those cameras," Agent Chapman went on, "it's not a stretch of the imagination that you set up the one in the tree facing Kate's house. And the one behind her place."

So Ryan's suggestion that they check out the area around Kate's property had yielded them some valuable information about how the killer kept watch on her.

Surprise and shock lit Reed's eyes. "What cameras? Where?"

"They weren't easy to find. I don't imagine they were easy to place and conceal, especially with the solar panels powering each of them.

The password protection kept us from seeing the actual video feed. You wouldn't want some neighbor randomly finding the open feed and seeing what you'd done."

Reed shook his head. "I didn't do that. Why would I when I was already in the house and in Kate's life? I didn't need a camera to keep track of her. I could just call her, or show up at her door anytime I wanted."

Ryan had to admit, the cameras didn't make a lot of sense for all the reasons Reed pointed out and more. If Reed really wanted to keep a close eye on Kate, he could put cameras *in* her house without her knowing.

"But if this guy wanted to keep track of me coming and going from Kate's place . . . and now the FBI protective detail . . . Well, that's a great way to do it without being seen in the neighborhood."

"Except the range on the cameras isn't very far. You'd have to be close to use it. And it would be convenient, as you say, to keep track of any law enforcement in the neighborhood, both marked and unmarked. You'd be able to determine who belongs and who doesn't and use that so you could, say . . . leave roses on Kate's walkway."

Reed momentarily closed his eyes and shook his head. "We can twist this back and forth to suit our narratives, but the simple fact is that I didn't do any of this and you have no proof that I did."

"I'm working on that as we speak," Agent Chapman assured Reed.

Reed stood, ready to walk out. "I'm assuming I'm free to leave."

Ryan guessed Reed was smart enough to know he didn't have to stay and finish the interview if he didn't want to without them charging him with something.

Agent Chapman looked up at him. "You don't want to talk about where you took these women?"

Reed stared at Agent Chapman. "I hope your focus on me doesn't blind you to the fact the killer is still out there and Anne Murphy is waiting for you to find him and her before it's too late." Reed walked out.

Agent Chapman rose and went to the door. "Will you walk him out?" he asked a fellow agent, then came back into the room.

The agent paced from one side of the room to the other across from Ryan. "What do you think?"

Ryan took a second to collect his thoughts and analyze his impressions of Reed. "He doesn't come off as being deceptive. In fact, his declaration that he'd never hurt Kate and that he loves her rings true to me. Is that because he's obsessed with her?" Ryan shrugged one shoulder. "I don't know for sure."

"What about him being in proximity to each of the victims before their abductions?"

"It's too convenient to be coincidence. And his assertion that the killer could be following him and picking his victims from people connected to Reed, even in this perfunctory way . . . You need to look into that. Have the team scour the tapes again to see if there's anyone else who is also in all of them." Once they found the connection to Reed, had they zeroed in on him and missed someone else on the videos?

"You think if this guy went to all the trouble of setting Reed up, he'd be on the surveillance, too?"

"It's worth a look. Because a lawyer will poke holes in the flimsy connection."

Agent Chapman pressed his lips tight. "Todd Lane shops at the same grocery store as Anne Murphy, the one where we have video of her and Reed in line at the same time."

"If it's Todd, he could have seen Anne there and picked her as a target. Or he could be watching Reed and used their proximity to pick her for that reason."

Agent Chapman leaned against the wall. "We can put Reed with four of the victims before their abductions."

Ryan met the agent's disbelieving gaze. "That's not enough to say he raped and killed them."

Agent Chapman gripped the back of the chair Reed had been sitting in. "I want this guy."

"You want the killer. You need to be sure Reed is the guy. Otherwise, you've done what Reed said is happening, taking him out of Kate's life and leaving her vulnerable."

"We need to tell her we're looking at Reed."

"I will," Ryan volunteered. "Maybe she's got some insight into his behavior or activities that will shed some light on whether he's everything he seems to be, or a wolf in sheep's clothing."

"If it's him, he's too careful to give himself away."

Ryan tilted his head. "And yet we connected him to the victims so easily."

Agent Chapman swore under his breath. "It's too damn easy. I mean, people get caught all the time for stupid mistakes, but this seems like it was handed to us. If you're looking for a victim, why leave a digital trail linking you to that person? If he'd used cash, we wouldn't have been able to track him so easily and connect his activity to the victims."

"So what he's saying makes sense." Ryan wanted to be sure the agent was keeping an open mind.

"But is it true, or is he just playing a game, not only with Kate, but the cops, too?"

"We need more information. Go back to the videos. See if there's someone else at some or all of the places."

"I've got someone looking into where the bodies were found, backtracking the river's currents to see where they might have been dumped and if those locations tie to Reed in any way. Or the woman Todd is suspected of killing. It's got to be one of them."

"With the victims being taken from different towns along the river, their bodies found in other locations, it's difficult to pinpoint where this guy is keeping them before he kills them," Ryan indicated.

"Based on what Kate told us about the Rose Reaper and where he held her, we're assuming remote cabin, heavily wooded, along the river."

"That makes the most sense," Ryan agreed.

"Did this killer find the Reaper's cabin?" Agent Chapman shrugged. "Reed manages several construction projects at a time. It's possible he's using one, or several, of those locations, or something he discovered while on the job to use that's not in his name."

"Like an abandoned property?"

"I bet he comes across a lot of properties customers are looking at for residential or commercial reasons. He goes in and assesses them for renovation or new builds. Depending on the customer's needs, they take it or leave it. Maybe he steers them away from a place he finds suits him for his dark deeds."

As speculations go, that one had some merit. "The same could be said about Todd with the commercial properties he works at for his heating and air-conditioning job. He could run across buildings or properties that aren't in use, too."

Agent Chapman's forehead creased with his amped frustration.

Ryan tried to keep things in perspective. "So we continue looking into both of them, but also keep an open mind that this could be a distraction the killer wants us focused on so we're not looking for him."

Agent Chapman gave a firm but short nod. "I'm not saying Reed's definitely our guy. But it doesn't look good for him if the evidence starts piling up."

"Yeah, but so far all we've got is him in casual contact with the victims. That's not enough to convince a jury he's guilty." It wasn't enough to convince Ryan that either Todd or Reed had committed the murders.

"Then we find more dots to connect to him and get a warrant. Or we find something that points us away from him and follow those dots. That's the job." Agent Chapman raked his fingers through his hair. "Though this one is starting to feel more like a game. And I don't want to be on the losing team who gets it wrong and more women lose their lives."

Neither did Ryan. "Send me the recording of Reed's interview. I want to show it to Kate and get her take on it. I want her prepared."

"For what? That he's a target or a killer?"

"I have a feeling we're going to find out soon."

Chapter Twenty-Three

Ryan sat across from Kate at her breakfast table while she watched the recorded interview they'd had with Reed earlier. He didn't like how quiet she was or how remote she seemed as Reed's words flowed over her.

The recording ended and silence filled the room.

Kate stared at the screen, but he knew she was in her head, trying to comprehend and second-guessing every interaction she'd had with Reed, analyzing every word they'd ever said to each other.

He gave her the time and space she needed to sort it out well enough that she could speak to him about it.

It started with a headshake. "No. I don't believe he's the one doing all this. It can't be him."

"Why?"

The simple question sat between them.

Kate squared her shoulders, a resolved look coming into her eyes. "He's a good man. He's kind. He's thoughtful." She met his gaze with a directness he'd never seen from her. "He's genuine. I have to believe that, Ryan."

He knew exactly what she meant by that, because if Reed wasn't who she thought he was, then their whole relationship was a lie. And how could Kate trust herself to know the difference in anyone else ever again?

"Does it feel right to you?" he asked.

"Yes." Confidence and a deep need filled that simple answer. "In my bones I know he didn't do this."

"What about him being at all the places the victims were prior to their abductions?"

"I'll admit, that's too much coincidence to dismiss. It feels too easy to find." She gave him a questioning look.

"I think so, too. Why be careful about everything else and not that you could be tracked to the women through their records and yours?"

She shrugged. "Then again, if that's the only thing that connects you to the women . . ."

It's too circumstantial to stick and you get to make the cops look bad for not being able to find any solid evidence.

He asked about another aspect Reed could manipulate. "What about the cameras on the house catching the killer leaving the roses?"

She pressed her lips tight. This one wasn't so easily explained away. "Why disguise yourself so completely to do that? You know there's a camera, so why come at all? But also, if you know there are cameras in those places you met or saw the women, why not try to conceal yourself then, too? If you're worried about getting caught, wouldn't you look for the cameras, avoid them, or at least make sure they never got a clear shot of you? Especially with the women. If you found the woman you wanted to take, why not watch from afar? It's less risky and even more probable you'd not be connected to them so easily."

All very good points.

Which led Ryan to think of Todd and how he'd already gotten away with one murder without leaving conclusive evidence, while Reed linked himself to four victims on video.

Coincidence? Purposeful? Targeted by the real killer?

"And for that matter, why would Reed, if he is the killer, get so close to me and act like he's protecting me? Because he'd want the thrill of watching me suffer wondering about what he's doing to all those women." She answered her own question. "Reed has been kind and loving. He distracts me from what's going on. He doesn't ask about the murders, or what happened to me in the past. He doesn't rehash the news reports or try to get me to talk about the cases. Wouldn't the killer want to revel in what he'd done and get a thrill out of torturing me with it by talking about it all the time?"

"Possibly." Most likely, probably. "But he could also enjoy knowing something you don't. That he's right here in front of you, so close he can touch you." And has, Ryan thought. "Maybe it's enough seeing you receive his roses, agonizing over the victims, and reliving your past each and every time he takes a new victim."

Kate covered her face, then rubbed her hands down her cheeks and looked directly at him. "It can't be him. It's not him. I just don't believe the man I've known for months, the one who is so patient and nice, could do something like this to me. I don't believe he raped and killed those women. Not like that." She shook her head. "No. It can't be him." She needed more to convict Reed in her mind.

It surprised Ryan that she'd sound so convinced when her past trauma could cloud her judgment. Reed had certainly made an impression on Kate. He'd gotten past her defenses and made her trust him.

That trust wasn't shaken, even though they'd tied Reed to the victims.

Was he that good of an actor? Was he that good at mimicking emotions and pretending to be a kind and loving partner that he'd fooled Kate?

If Reed was the killer, it would shatter Kate. She'd have an even harder time trusting anyone again.

He really hoped Reed turned out to be the man Kate knew him to be. For Kate's sake.

"Until we clear Reed, I think you should stay away from him."

Kate looked him in the eye. "He said the same thing."

Ryan raised a brow.

"After you called to ask to come over to show me the interview, he called to tell me that you or Agent Chapman would probably contact me about it. I didn't tell him you already had."

"What else did he say?"

"He explained what you had discovered about him and the victims. He swore he wasn't the killer and that he'd been set up. He said we were right about feeling like the killer could be watching us. It's why he sometimes left his car at home and sneaked over to see me, so that if I was being watched, then the killer would think I was home alone when I wasn't and Reed would be here if he came for me while he thought I was vulnerable. Now, he thinks it's best if he stays away so the killer believes that his plan is working to set up Reed while the police look into it more and clear him."

Ryan couldn't believe Reed had told her everything and still had faith in law enforcement to clear him instead of just pursue him. "How did that make you feel?"

"Scared. Confused. Also angry that the police would think he'd had anything to do with this."

"Based on the way you feel about him, I can see why."

"He told me he hated to be away from me, but that as soon as he's cleared he'd be right back by my side. He told me to stay home and let the FBI protect me. He said if I needed him, he'd be there for me always, anytime." Her brows drew together. "That's what he always says to me. And I believe it. He said he loves me and he'll hate every moment we're apart."

"Having someone like that in your life is really special, Kate."

"For the longest time, it felt unreal. But he made me believe in it and him while all this was going on. It can't be fake, Ryan. No one is that good at pretending and lying."

Ryan hated to admit that there were people in this world who could lie like that and others who believed it even when confronted with inconsistencies and outright evidence of the lies.

But he didn't think Kate was doing that. At least, it didn't seem to be the case. Because Kate would be looking for the holes and the lies. She'd be looking for all the times something felt off and she dismissed it.

But she wasn't doing that right now.

She held fast to her belief in Reed and backed that up with not just his words but his actions toward her.

Which left Ryan wondering if Reed was the good guy or a killer who could convince Kate he loved her even as he terrorized her.

Chapter Twenty-Four

"The body of Anne Murphy was found this afternoon along the river's shore. Anne had been missing for three days. This is the fastest a body has been found since the killer started leaving the bodies in the river. Authorities say Anne Murphy was wrapped in plastic. Her remains have been taken by the coroner for autopsy to determine her cause of death, though authorities have confirmed she had a single penetrating wound to the chest and ligature marks on her wrists and ankles.

"This is the first time a body has been found so far upriver, while the other four victims' bodies were found miles downriver in separate locations and jurisdictions on both sides of the river. The killings have escalated in the last many months, making the authorities anxious to catch him before he strikes again."

Kate turned off the TV news, knowing it wasn't going to be today. There were no roses left on her path.

She was glad Anne had been found. She hoped it gave her family some peace of mind to have her back.

Still, another woman had endured hell and not lived to tell the tale. Or see whoever was doing this behind bars.

It had to stop.

When would the authorities find the person responsible?

Had they already?

Could it really be Reed?

He hadn't been detained by the police or FBI. He was out there, free to do as he pleased.

Had he gone to wherever he'd been holding Anne and dumped her in the river last night?

No. She didn't want to believe it was him. She still had hope that this would be resolved. But it would be another day at home, away from work, her friends, watched by the FBI, alone without Reed to be here to cheer her up and distract her from the reality she faced.

Had the killer taken Reed from her to torment her more?

It sure felt that way.

She'd lost so much at the Rose Reaper's hands.

Now this new killer wanted to tear her life apart, too.

He was doing a good job.

She didn't want to be his victim. Not like this. Not if he actually accomplished his ultimate goal of taking her.

But what could she do? Nothing but wait.

Chapter Twenty-Five

Ryan had learned a long time ago that investigations took time. He spent most of that time waiting for more information. Today was no different.

Anne Murphy's body had been found yesterday afternoon. The media couldn't stop talking about it.

He'd checked in with Kate yesterday evening to give her an update, but it was mostly him telling her they only knew the basics so far and they'd know more today. He hated how she sounded. Alone. Isolated. She asked if they'd found anything to tie Anne to Reed, other than the fact he'd been seen with her in the grocery store.

Kate held out hope Reed was innocent.

Agent Chapman joined him in the conference room. He dropped several files on the table, then practically fell into a chair.

Ryan eyed the agent. "You look like you've been up most of the night."

Agent Chapman's bloodshot and weary eyes met Ryan's. "Try all of it. But we've got some new information to go on and let's hope it all sticks to Reed."

That got Ryan's attention. "What do you know?"

Agent Chapman pulled the map at the center of the table closer to him. "Remember the Xs mark where our victims lived, where they worked, and where they were found?"

"Right. There's no rhyme or reason to it, other than it's purposefully arbitrary. He hunts in different locations—the bodies aren't even found in the same town the victims live in."

Agent Chapman scrubbed his hands over his face. "Because he's smart. By doing that, he makes it harder for law enforcement to track him and his victims until we actually expand the geographical hunting ground and go looking to tie them together. Now . . ." Agent Chapman marked a red X on the river where Anne's body was found. "What do you see?"

"The same thing the news reported yesterday. Her body was found way upriver from the rest."

Agent Chapman nodded, then pulled the plastic overlay from beneath the map and laid it on top. "Based on river currents and the number of days the coroner has estimated for each victim being in the water, we believe the bodies are being dumped in this general area." Agent Chapman indicated a large rectangular area above all but Anne's red X.

"He changed the location of where he dumped the body in the river?"

"It appears so."

"Why change it now? Is law enforcement watching this portion of the river?"

"It's about five to ten miles of river with banks on both sides that are mostly forested and rocky and unnavigable unless you're on the water or on foot. And on foot, you'd be a hell of a distance from any road. To carry a body that far . . ." Agent Chapman shrugged, like it wasn't a task he'd undertake. "Why not just bury the body in the woods if you're out there?"

"Because then who would find it?" Ryan answered. "The water could serve many purposes. Washing the body clean. Both literally and figuratively for the killer. Maybe he wants to return them to their families and knows this is a way to do it. So far, all the bodies of those we know about have been found. And the obvious reason. He wants people to know what he did. Because he wants to be stopped? Maybe. Most likely, he loves the attention. He wants credit. Knowing what we know now about the Rose Reaper, I think he knew he'd never stop unless he got caught. This new killer, he wants the fame. He's telling the world what he's doing. He wants everyone to know that he's going to finish what the Reaper started. Hell, he's even told Kate. He's counting down to her. He wants law enforcement to know he's smarter than them. He's getting away with it, just like the Reaper did until Kate escaped."

"Do you think he's also pinning this on Reed to show us just how cunning he can be?"

"Maybe. But while Reed looks good for all this, it's a bit too conveniently laid out for us. Even that could be the killer taunting law enforcement, leading us by the nose to Reed and making it look so obvious. Yet it's taken us five victims to suspect him."

Agent Chapman scratched at his beard-stubbled jaw. "You really know how to make a guy feel like he's good at his job," he teased. "Todd Lane, heating and air-conditioning repairman, doesn't seem cunning enough to pull off the murders without anything leading to him and at the same time setting up Reed. I just don't see it. Especially since I questioned him an hour ago and he had a solid alibi for the time we suspect Anne Murphy was kidnapped. So right now, I'm following the evidence that points to Reed. In fact, I just had him picked up and brought in for questioning again."

"Do you have something new?"

Agent Chapman pulled a second plastic overlay out from under the map and set it atop the other. This time orange *X*s marked the spots.

"What is this telling me?" Ryan asked.

"Those are the official properties along the river where Reed has worked in the last five years according to his company's records."

Ryan focused on two properties. One several inches above the suspected dumping ground of the killer. The other right on the edge of the bottom of the area. The one above was right where Anne's body had been found. The other would be a good spot to put the other four bodies in the river so they'd end up down the way where they'd later been found. "Was Anne's body ravaged at all by debris and rocks in the water?"

Agent Chapman shook his head. "There were some rips and tears in the plastic and abrasions to the body, but nothing like the other bodies. In fact, most of what the coroner noted on the preliminary autopsy were antemortem and perimortem, not postmortem."

"What did the coroner conclude from that?" Ryan could guess that the victim hadn't been in the river that long.

"He suspects based on where and how she was found that she was placed in the river and didn't actually move down the river."

"Do you have the photos of the crime scene?"

Agent Chapman tossed a file across the table in front of him. "I thought you might like to see them."

Ryan didn't really want to look, but they might help him understand why this was different from all the others. The second he opened the file and looked at a shot of Anne's body in the water, close to the bank, tangled in some tree limbs, a chill ran through him. "Were you at the scene?"

"Yes."

"Did it appear that he put her there because she would stay put, or at least not get far? Because it seems odd that there's no real current along this edge, and getting her out far enough to be taken by the current away from the trees and bank would put you in jeopardy of being taken downriver with her."

"Unless he was in a boat."

"Yes. But then why not dump her in the swifter current?" Ryan turned the picture to the agent. "Look at how the current is flowing way out toward the center. But along the bank, it's quiet, almost placid.

She didn't end up on the bank because the current pushed her there. She was placed there."

Agent Chapman nodded. "That's what we believe."

"Did you find footprints, drag marks, anything to indicate he brought her down from land?"

"Yes, though the mud and wet vegetation obscured most of it, so no shoe imprints. Just the *wink, wink, nod* that Anne was found practically on one of Reed's worksites."

Ryan eyed the agent. "You don't buy it."

"I find it yet another very convenient arrow pointing to him. On the other hand, if it is him, it pisses me off that he's telling us it's him and still not giving us enough to hang him," the agent grumbled.

Ryan could relate. "I guess we'll have to talk to him again and see what he has to say about all this."

"That's the other thing. Since he left the last interview, we've had him under surveillance. He's gone about doing his job and living his life like he's got nothing to hide."

"So how did he dump a body?"

"Just because we're watching him doesn't mean he didn't sneak out and do this right under our noses. We don't have his place surrounded. Still . . ."

"It doesn't make sense."

"Unless you want it to look like it's him and ignore the fact that circumstantial evidence won't hold up in court and any real proof is near impossible to come by because of how he disposes of the bodies. So unless he's a hell of a lot cockier today about getting away with all this, I'm wondering if the killer really is fucking with us."

"It wouldn't be the first time a killer thought he was smarter than the cops and found out he wasn't."

"Yeah, well, I'd like him to get tripped up on something and make one mistake that I can use to nail him."

They all did.

Agent Chapman grabbed his files. "Let's go see if Reed is interested in talking to us today, or if his lawyer keeps him quiet."

"He got a lawyer?"

Agent Chapman nodded. "We got one freebie interview. Now, he's being smart and probably not going to say anything other than what his lawyer lets him say."

Either way, they still didn't have enough to hold or charge him.

And they didn't have time to waste. The killer was probably already hunting for victim number six, so he could get to Kate.

Chapter Twenty-Six

Ryan shouldn't be surprised Reed hired a female attorney, but he was for the simple fact he wouldn't think a man who'd raped and killed five women would trust a woman with his freedom. And his life. But maybe Reed wanted to use the attorney to his benefit, to show that she supported him, so they should, too.

The attorney stood—as did Reed out of politeness to her—and held her hand out to Ryan. "Hi. I'm Emily Bell."

"Ryan Strickland."

Emily nodded. "Reed told me that you've been a great comfort and help to Kate."

Reed caught Ryan's eye. "How is she?"

"I checked in on her this morning. She's coping."

Reed frowned. "Can we please wrap this up so I can get back to her?"

Emily touched Reed's arm. "Agent Chapman, you called this meeting. What can my client help with today?"

They all sat and Agent Chapman took the lead with Reed. "I'm sure you've heard that the body of Anne Murphy was recovered from the river."

"My client saw the news reports and contacted me, anticipating this very meeting," Emily replied for Reed.

"Why is that?" the agent asked.

"After your previous conversation with Reed, and the fact that you're focused on him as a potential suspect, though you haven't named him directly as a person of interest or a suspect, which we appreciate with such flimsy evidence, my client felt it best to have representation." Emily pressed her lips tight, then added, "Reed knew I'd assist him because of our past relationship."

Ryan found that very interesting. And telling. If an ex would stand up for him and help him like this, they'd obviously parted on amiable terms. It backed up Kate's assessment that Reed was a good guy. So much so that he remained in good enough standing with his ex to ask for help.

Agent Chapman caught on to what wasn't said. "It's good to have friends with skills you need."

"It's good to have friends who know you so well, they'll defend you against ridiculous accusations." Emily held the agent's gaze, hers direct and serene.

Agent Chapman conceded that with a slight nod. "Still . . . Don't you find it odd that not only can we connect Reed to four of the five victims prior to their disappearance, we also discovered Anne's body near one of his recent jobsites?"

Reed's eyes went wide.

Emily took it in stride. "I'd say that's another very convenient coincidence that adds merit to Reed's assertion that someone is setting him up."

"Maybe he's setting up himself," Agent Chapman suggested, eyeing Reed.

Emily laughed under her breath. "Maybe the tooth fairy did it." As ridiculous statements went, she proved her point.

Agent Chapman went with it. "Maybe he gets off on telling us he did it without us being able to actually arrest him."

Emily shook her head. "That would be difficult to prove. Unless you found some actual evidence that tied my client to the kidnapping, rape, or murder of these women. What you have is him in proximity to them for a short period of time. Tell me, have your analysts gone over the surveillance more thoroughly, looking for other individuals who appear in one or more of the videos who could also be called into question due to their proximity to the victims?"

"I'm not at liberty to discuss an ongoing investigation," Agent Chapman evaded.

"And we're here, which means you're still hoping the simplest answer is the truth, even though my client had nothing to do with these crimes." Emily reached down to her bag and pulled out several sheets of paper. "To assist with your ongoing investigation, Reed has put together, as best he could based on his recorded work schedule, his whereabouts for the past ten months. Obviously the further back he went to the first abduction, his recollection of his whereabouts is difficult to remember as he has fluid plans most days when it comes to lunch and breaks and errands he runs between meetings and driving to worksites for his company."

"He's a busy man." Agent Chapman glanced through the pages.

"He is. Which would make it difficult to stalk these women prior to their abductions. As news reports are vague with actual details about what time these women were abducted, we were unable to highlight specific alibis. I'm sure you'll be able to do that. Though I do know by most accounts made public, the window in which the women were abducted is many hours."

"Yes," Agent Chapman agreed. "Overnight hours. When your client probably can't account for his time either."

"Well, except for those nights where he was with Kate." Emily scored that point.

Reed leaned in and held Ryan's gaze. "You know human behavior. That's your specialty. So tell me, what kind of fucked-up asshole would I be to do this to Kate?"

Agent Chapman answered, "The kind that kidnaps, rapes, and kills women, then dumps them in the river."

Resignation softened Reed's gaze, but then resolve returned and he pinned Agent Chapman in a hard stare. "I'm not that kind of asshole."

Emily put her hand on Reed's arm as if to warn him to stop talking and let her handle this. "Do you have any pertinent and specific questions for my client?"

Agent Chapman pulled out his own papers and set them on the table.

Ryan recognized the printouts as map sections of the river.

Agent Chapman pointed to the first location. "Do you recognize this place?"

"My company is in the middle of construction on a multi-unit apartment complex on that property."

"How are you associated with the project?"

"That project has another site manager, however I have more experience and manage several of the other site managers, so when there's a problem, I help out. In this case, there was a small electrical fire at the build that took out one unit. I came in to supervise and assist with the investigation into the fire, insurance, and getting the site up and running again in a timely manner."

Agent Chapman took Reed through two other sites and got mostly the same answers. In each case, Reed was on location at different times in a supervisory role and to assist with some problem that came up to help keep things on schedule and on budget.

To Ryan, it sounded like he was smart and good at his job. More than that, he enjoyed his job and that it offered him diversity in his day-to-day work. He never quite knew what was going to come up, and solving issues seemed to keep things interesting and challenging.

Agent Chapman flipped over the last page. "And this site?"

Reed stared at the map and turned it toward him. "I own this portion of land." He used his finger to circle an area right on the river.

"How did you come by this piece of property?"

Reed didn't answer the agent immediately, but glanced at Emily.

She nodded for him to answer. "I bought it a year ago after a deal went south with one of our clients who wanted to build a warehouse. For some odd reason, there's a swath of land cut through two commercial-zone areas marked for residential. I thought it a good investment opportunity and bought part of the residential land."

"Who owns the other portion?"

"I don't know. Only this piece was up for sale. The man who owned it inherited it from a great-uncle, who at some point lived on the property and worked as a fisherman. The man selling the property needed the money to send his twins to college, so he put it on the market. I snatched it up."

"In fact, you own three other pieces of land."

Reed turned to Emily, then answered at her nod. "I do. Being in construction has taught me a great deal. Owning land is a good investment for the future."

Agent Chapman tapped his finger on the map. "An isolated piece of land like yours is also a great place to hide someone, then dump their body."

Reed sighed. "There's nothing out there. Not even the original house that the great-uncle lived in years ago."

"Then you wouldn't mind if we searched the property." Agent Chapman sat back, relaxed but still totally focused on Reed.

"For what, exactly?" Emily asked.

Agent Chapman raised both brows. "Maybe a cabin in the woods. A secret place only he knows about. As an experienced builder, it would be easy for him to construct a simple cabin by himself."

Ryan hadn't seen that coming. Not that he expected the agent to give him every detail of the case. But this could really break the case wide open if they found something.

Emily held up her finger. "Let me confer with my client a moment."

Agent Chapman sat back and waved his hand. "Take your time."

Emily and Reed stood and went to the far corner of the room. Not that it gave them much privacy in the small space, but it did allow for her and Reed's whispers to be unintelligible.

Ryan watched the scene play out with Emily saying something close to Reed's ear as he leaned down to hear her. Then he'd lean in and speak to her. The back and forth went on for only four exchanges like that before they both came back to the table.

Emily spoke for Reed. "While my client would like to grant you access to the property, he is going to heed my counsel and decline at this time without a search warrant."

"That's what I thought," Agent Chapman said.

"My client has nothing to hide, however he hasn't been to the property in many months. And with the circumstantial evidence mounting and our belief that he is being set up, it isn't prudent to allow law enforcement onto the property without proof that you've found something to warrant the search."

"But let me guess," Agent Chapman went on, "your client is going to search that property now that it's been brought to his attention that Anne's body was found suspiciously close to it."

Emily tilted her head. "That sounds awfully close to you admitting that you, too, suspect my client is being set up."

Agent Chapman gave her a questioning look.

Reed answered that look. "Why would I need to search my property if I'm the killer?" Reed held up his hand to stop the agent from saying anything. "I have to cover my ass. You know that. That's why I got a lawyer and am following her advice. But you also know that if I am being set up and there is something on that property, then I want to know about it first. I'll let you know if I find anything."

Agent Chapman pressed his lips tight, knowing he'd misspoken, showed his hand, and couldn't stop Reed from going to his property. Searching it, or destroying any evidence he'd left behind if he was the killer.

Ryan decided to try to salvage this in some way. "Do you think someone could have gotten onto the property and built something without you or others in the area knowing?"

Reed took a second to think about it. "The thing about the property is that whatever dirt track or road used to exist years ago has been overgrown. I assume that the great-uncle used the river for the most part back in the day for work and errands. The crumbled foundation for the house is close to the water. Whatever dock he had is gone, too. It's just an overgrown piece of land with nothing on it but potential. I thought to one day build a house, maybe several and parcel the land, but that would require building a road, bringing in utilities, that sort of thing. It's a project I thought I might take on in my retirement. The income would mean I didn't have to worry about money in my old age."

A good plan. Something he'd obviously thought a lot about.

Would a killer think beyond their obsession and need to kill? Would a killer who thought about those things consider his future sound if he made himself a target of the investigation?

Reed leaned in and spoke to Ryan directly. "The plans I have for the future include Kate. While I bought the property before I met her, it became an even more important part of what I wanted for me and her down the road. Kate wants to travel, though she hasn't had the opportunity or confidence to do so. I thought we could do that together. Now . . . I know it's going to take Kate time to get past this and learn to live without being scared every second of the day again." Reed talked like this would be over and Kate would be free again.

Ryan wanted that for Kate.

Reed seemed to be holding on to the belief that they'd get past this and have that future he planned for them.

Agent Chapman scooped up the pages from the table and stuffed them into a folder. "If I was you, I'd start keeping track of every second of my day."

Reed sighed. "Don't you have any other leads you can follow? Something, anything, that will lead you to the person who is really doing this?"

Agent Chapman stood. "We're working on getting the person who did this. Until next time . . ." The agent held his hand out toward the door. "You're free to go."

Reed walked out looking dejected and resigned that this probably wasn't the last time he'd be in the FBI offices.

Emily went to follow him, but stopped at the door and turned back. "You know he didn't do this. He's a good man."

Agent Chapman eyed the attorney. "That sounds a lot like what all those neighbors say about the serial killer next door. He was so nice. Kept to himself. Quiet. A good guy. But let's not forget that Reed is tied to four of the five women. Anne's body was just found nearly on his property. As for tormenting Kate . . . Maybe he gets off on seeing it up close and personal. You think you know him. But do you really?"

Emily walked out and slammed the door behind her.

Agent Chapman looked at him. "Something I said?"

Ryan didn't respond to the sarcasm. "You make a valid point, but we also have nothing solid on Reed."

"Just because we don't have it yet doesn't mean he didn't do it. We had nothing on the Rose Reaper when Kate escaped and he was killed either. Just because everyone *thinks* he's a good guy doesn't mean he is. It's my job to look past that and follow the evidence. And what little we have points us to him. But that doesn't mean I'm not looking beyond him. We are reviewing the surveillance footage again. We are still keeping Todd Lane in the suspect pool, because though he has *one* solid alibi, it doesn't mean he didn't have help to cover his tracks."

Ryan understood the agent's frustration and that he was doing the best he could with this case.

"I want to get this guy before he takes another woman. Now, I have to meet the medical examiner to go over Anne Murphy's autopsy. Care to join?" Agent Chapman didn't wait for an answer and left the room, leaving Ryan to think about what they knew and if it added up to Reed being a cunning, coldhearted killer.

Maybe Anne Murphy could tell them that.

They say the body speaks for the victim. He wondered what Anne's had to say.

Chapter Twenty-Seven

Ryan didn't usually get this involved in a case. The last thing he wanted to do was see one of the victims up close and personal. But he thought this time maybe he'd gain some insight into the killer, something that would help him see Reed as a murderer, or tell Ryan it had to be someone else.

He wanted it to be someone else for Kate's sake. And maybe that was clouding his judgment and Agent Chapman's impartiality and dogged investigating leading to the right person. So far, the investigation led in only one direction.

On an academic level, Reed hoped to gain some insight into how this killer operated. What he did to his victims would speak to the kind of gratification he needed or strived to achieve.

How alike was this new killer to the Rose Reaper? Was this purely an act of copying what had been done before, or was the new killer evolving into who he would become once he finished what the Reaper started?

Ryan walked into the morgue behind Agent Chapman and Dr. Tom—*just call me Tom*—Hodum. Ryan liked the older gentleman immediately. His easy manner and experience were a huge plus in this case.

Tom stopped at the table where Anne's nude body lay on the stainless steel.

Ryan took a few seconds to study her bloated and discolored body. The river had distorted her figure and face from the bright and vibrant woman she'd been in life. He tried not to gag from the smell and focused on something else. His gaze immediately went to the marks and abrasions around her wrists and ankles. The rose branding above her left breast stood out on her pale skin. So did the single slit in her chest. All that was exactly as he expected, but there was more and that raised a red flag for Ryan, because this kill looked aggressive where all the others, including the Rose Reaper's, had seemed almost merciful, the ending of the pain and sending the victim on. Not so in this case.

"Okay . . ." Tom's voice filled the quiet room. "We have victim number five. Anne Murphy. Twenty-four, five-foot-four-inches tall. Weight, one hundred and eighteen pounds. In comparison to the other four, she's by far the most . . . injured prior to being killed. While the others felt methodical, for lack of a better term, this one feels more ruthless."

"He slit her throat." Agent Chapman cringed.

"He broke her wrist, most likely from holding her arm so forcefully it left that bruising and snapped her bone because of the restraints. Also during that . . . struggle, he dislocated her shoulder."

"She had to be in a great deal of pain," Ryan pointed out. "While the other victims by no means had an easy time of it, they weren't hurt like this."

"No. He followed the . . . plan, I guess you'd say. But with this one . . ." Tom shook his head in dismay.

Ryan studied the wounds. "This is a sign he's losing control. Copying the Reaper isn't giving him enough of what he wants. It's too rigid. The Reaper used his victims to feel in control. *He* raped *them*. *He* wasn't the one being used. But he never hurt them beyond the restraints and showing his dominance. He left bruises to subdue them, but never broke bones. He dispatched them with a quick, nearly painless death. Maybe he even hoped he wouldn't have to do it again to ease his pain, but then it would build and he would do it once more. But always the same, because he didn't get off on causing them pain. He got off on being in control." Ryan looked at Anne's body. "This is not control. This is someone who likes hurting them and gets a thrill from killing them."

Tom gave a solemn nod. "He only kept her for about a day, maybe a little into day two. No food found in her stomach, but she wasn't dehydrated. Which speaks to your point. No control. He wanted the kill, not the time with her."

"Any drugs found in her system?" Agent Chapman asked.

"None. But some drugs metabolize quickly, so it can't be ruled out. Just like all the others." Tom pointed to the rose branded into her chest right above her left breast. "Compared to the first few, this is nicely done. He didn't use unnecessary force. The image is clean. No shifting or overlapping of the lines."

"Do you think she was unconscious when he did it?" the agent asked.

"That or he doesn't use the brand to torture them, it's simply to mark them as his."

Ryan found the doctor's insight interesting. "Maybe that explains the difference in how they're marked. The Rose Reaper drew on them. This guy brands them. The fact that they are the exact same image despite how they are put on the victims led us to believe we had a copycat. Though how he knows that closely held information is for you to discover. My feeling is he's telling us something. The marks are the same, but different. Those were his. These are mine."

Agent Chapman stared at the rose. "The brand is also more brutal. The Rose Reaper maybe used the drawing to fixate on while he raped them. Like what Ms. Poole told us about him staring at the wallpaper. It was a means for him to distance himself."

Ryan nodded, going along with that scenario. "For our new killer, he's got no attachment to the rose symbol, other than it belonged to the Reaper."

The doctor added, "I've gone over the Rose Reaper autopsy reports for all his victims. He liked to hit them. In the ribs, mostly. A jab to keep them still or quiet them, whatever. He smacked them in the face, leaving bruising, cut lips, superficial abrasions.

"This killer likes to hold them by the neck, leaving minor bruising. He's not strangling them per se, but definitely holding them. But with Anne, he probably strangled her to near or even fainting before he released her and let her breathe again."

"Showing his dominance with the first four and trying out something new with Anne," Ryan suggested. "He's figuring out what he likes. What gets him off."

Tom notched his chin toward Anne. "This was brutal. He also didn't just rape her. He sodomized her."

Ryan stuffed his hands in his pockets. "He's tired of the restraint and confinement of the Rose Reaper's MO. At first, he enjoyed taking his time with them, mimicking the Rose Reaper. Now . . . He's anxious to get to Kate."

Tom agreed. "The first victim's body showed he'd been unsure in some things like the brand. It was sloppy with overlaps and it was unnecessarily deep. He was forceful in others, like the rape and stabbing."

"Adrenaline," Agent Chapman pointed out. "He got excited. Now, it's rote. The thrill is gone. He's been confined to the Rose Reaper's MO."

"And he's getting impatient to finish it so he can move on to his desires." Ryan wondered what the killer would do if he finished the Reaper's seven and had the freedom to act out all his twisted fantasies. "Does Anne tell us anything else about what happened to her, or about him?"

Tom shook his head. "Not really." He paused, then added, "I don't think she pleased him."

Ryan cocked his head. "Why do you say that?"

"Because he didn't hold on to her longer. Maybe she didn't have the fight the others had. Maybe she simply succumbed to his control."

"More than likely, the kill is what he really gets off on. The other stuff is just to wind him up," Ryan suggested.

"The ligature marks are consistent but different from the Rose Reaper's victims. Our killer always ties them tight. Two wraps around the wrist or ankle, once around both limbs, then knotted."

Agent Chapman stepped closer to look more closely at Anne's ankles and wrists. "How can you tell that?"

Tom pulled a pen from his white coat pocket and pointed to Anne's wrist and the darker lines going around it. "See here? Though the bruising and abrasions look like a solid line, there are actually two on the inside of the wrists and three on the outside."

"Huh." Agent Chapman studied them. "And it's the same each time?"

"Yes," Tom confirmed. "The Rose Reaper used a different kind of rope. Thicker. More fibrous, creating more friction and abrasions. This guy is using nylon or cotton, something smoother and thinner."

Agent Chapman took that in, then asked, "Anything else found on the body? Fibers? Biologicals?"

"The river did its job in washing the body clean despite the fact she was found more quickly than the others."

"Thank you, Doctor." Agent Chapman put his hands in his pockets and stepped back from the body. "If you get anything else from the samples you sent to the lab, let me know."

"Will do." Tom gave them a nod goodbye, then pulled a sheet from a drawer and began to drape it over Anne's body.

Ryan followed Agent Chapman out of the room where they both took a deep breath in the hallway, away from the scent of death.

"I hate having to see them like that," Agent Chapman admitted. "But it helped. I think it's clear our killer is getting anxious to end this."

"Which means he'll be hunting for his next victim soon."

"And my guys will keep close tabs on Todd and Reed. Maybe we can catch the killer before he puts another woman on a cold slab."

Ryan's phone pinged with an incoming text. He pulled out his phone, intrigued to see who it was from. "We've been invited to a storage facility tomorrow at ten a.m."

Agent Chapman raised a brow. "Phillip Poole?"

"Yes. Do you think there's something in his father's or uncle's belongings that will tell us anything?"

"I guess we'll find out in the morning."

Ryan held up his phone. "I'll forward the address to you and meet you there."

"Sounds good. Do you want to grab a drink, maybe dinner?"

Ryan wanted to check in with Kate, then see if he could get a few minutes with Molly on the phone, though she was probably at work again this evening. "Rain check. I'm going to stop by Kate's before I head to my hotel for the night."

Agent Chapman looked thoughtful, then nodded like he'd come to a decision. "I didn't want to do this until it was absolutely necessary because I know she's cautious and mistrustful of strangers, especially men. But it's time."

Ryan understood exactly what the agent was telling him. They'd discussed it in the past. "You're putting an agent in her house."

"We're down to one more victim before he goes for her. We can't keep expecting him to do one and then the other. We can't assume he'll keep to the same MO of kidnapping a woman, holding her for a few days, dumping the body, then going for Kate. He could take a woman at any moment, stash her wherever he's taken all of them, then get Kate and take her there, too. It could be a two-for-one kind of thing so he can move on to whatever he has planned next. Hell, maybe he's simply going to surpass the Rose Reaper's record and he'll just keep doing this over and over again."

"But, like me, you think he's going to escalate to something more. Something more in line with his fantasy, not the Rose Reaper's."

"That's how I feel about it, but we can't know. Not for sure. What I do know is that I don't want to make her an easy target. She's wanted to stay in her place for now. I know that's where she feels safe, in an odd way."

"She's holding her ground. That's a powerful thing for her. She's a fighter. She doesn't want him to think she's weak. But he's wearing her down." Ryan considered that for a moment. "Maybe that's what all this has been about. Him putting her back in the position of being a victim. If she's scared and reacting emotionally instead of logically, then he has the advantage."

"He's also giving her time to plan, to fortify her resolve. That works against him."

"He thinks women are weak. They're nothing more than a means to an end for him. They serve his purpose."

Agent Chapman's eyes filled with disgust. "Yeah, well, I'm not going to be the stupid agent who doesn't use the available resources to protect a potential victim."

"I'll tell Kate to expect company."

"Tell her I'll see if there's a female agent available first, but I can't make any promises."

"She'll appreciate that you tried."

They walked out of the building to the parking lot.

"I'll have the agent there in the next hour or so. Catch you later." Agent Chapman split off from him and headed to his car.

Ryan got behind the wheel of his rental and texted Phillip back.

RYAN: See you tomorrow at 10

RYAN: Thanks for indulging our curiosity about your uncle and letting us go through his things.

PHILLIP: It's been a while since I looked at that stuff. It will be interesting to see it again.

Tomorrow would be a journey into the past for both of them and maybe the discovery of something that led from the Rose Reaper to their copycat.

Chapter Twenty-Eight

Ryan knocked on Kate's door, hoping to find her in good spirits and ease her mind at the same time that things were moving forward with the investigation.

She answered with a relieved sigh and an inquisitive expression. "I'm happy to see you. I've been anxious here all alone. My friends and coworkers call to check up on me, but mostly I think they just want to know details about the investigation. And probably if I'm still alive."

Ryan touched Kate's shoulder. "Curiosity is human nature. But don't mistake that as they don't care."

Kate sighed. "Of course they do. I know that. It's just . . . Reed had this way of making me forget. Or at least not to focus on it. He helped me keep living my life and not get stuck in obsessing over this asshole who is ruining everything." Kate's quick fury dissipated. "Sorry. See. I'm strung tight." She seemed to realize she was also blocking him from coming inside and stepped back. "Sorry. Please come in."

Ryan entered the house, noting how quickly Kate locked the door, bolted it, then reset the alarm system. "Kate."

She looked up at him.

"Breathe."

"I think I need to leave. I need to go somewhere he can't find me."

Ryan didn't disagree. "You're safe here with the surveillance team outside. And while I came here to check on you, I also wanted to prepare you for company. Agent Chapman is assigning agents to protect you in the house."

She shook her head, then stopped herself. "I didn't want to live like a prisoner in my own home. But that's stupid. Being alone here without a guard gives him the advantage."

"If it helps, Agent Chapman hopes one of the female agents is available."

Kate waved that away. "At this point, I can't be picky or sensitive about who comes to protect me."

"You are absolutely in your right and deserve to feel comfortable in your home and with the people you surround yourself with. If whoever arrives makes you uncomfortable, you can ask for someone new. No one will take it personally. Your safety is what's important."

"Yes. That takes priority over my comfort."

"No, Kate. It doesn't have to be that way."

"Well, I can't have it my way," she snapped, immediately putting her fingers to her lips. "I'm sorry."

"Don't apologize. You're under a great deal of stress."

"I just . . . Why can't things go back to the way they were when I had finally started living my life again instead of just existing through it? Why can't Reed be the man I thought he was?"

"Who says he isn't?"

"The FBI. The evidence." She clasped her hands tight. "But not my heart."

"The FBI is looking into Reed because of suspicion, not hard evidence. The same way they're looking at two other suspects."

"That may be so, but let's face it—so much of what the FBI does know points to Reed. They found Anne's body near his property. A place I knew nothing about."

"Do you know everything about his investments and money?" Ryan asked, hoping to show her that just because she didn't know didn't mean Reed was hiding it.

Why he was playing devil's advocate, he didn't know. Maybe because Kate needed some hope. But was it wise of him to give her some, then have it all vanish if Reed really was the killer?

Kate bit her bottom lip. "No. Reed and I shared a lot about our lives, but we've never talked about money. Mine or his. It just never came up. I figured he made a better-than-decent living, owned his own house, and never seemed to be worried about picking up the bill when we went out, no matter how often we did or didn't." Kate's gaze fell to the floor. "I guess I don't know him as well as I thought I did."

"You were taking things slow. It's not like you'd joined your lives or were living together."

"He stayed here a lot more than he didn't recently."

"That's not the same, Kate. You weren't sharing the expenses. He wasn't moving his stuff here."

"It doesn't matter now, does it? Even if it's not him, how do we go back to what we were when he knows I think he could have done this?"

"You don't want to believe that. But you have to be cautious and consider that it is him and act accordingly. If it's not him, he'll understand that because he cares about you. He knows you and what you've been through. And if it is him . . . Maybe he'll give you a reason for why he's doing this."

"Do you think there's anything he could say that would adequately explain this?"

"No. And while you already know the person doing this is fulfilling his need and acting out his desires and that really has nothing to do with you, you know that he's targeted you for a very specific reason."

"I'm the one who got away."

"And you learned to thrive again. I have no doubt you can do that again."

"I just want this to be over."

Someone knocked on the front door.

"My babysitter is here." Kate went to the door and answered it.

"Hi. I'm Agent Kincaid." The agent held up her badge and credentials.

Kate held the door open wide. "Thank you for coming."

The agent stepped in. "My pleasure." She turned to him. "You must be Mr. Strickland. Agent Chapman said you'd be here."

Ryan shook the agent's hand. "Nice to meet you. Kate and I were just talking about the case and the necessity of keeping her as safe as possible."

The agent met Kate's gaze. "I understand this isn't easy for you. I'll try to be as unobtrusive as possible. I'll be working with another agent. We'll work in shifts. She'll be here in a couple of hours."

Kate's shoulders loosened with what appeared to be relief at hearing the other agent would also be a woman.

He'd let Agent Chapman know the gesture helped ease Kate.

"The two of us will go over the logistics and plans. I want you to know up front that we understand you want to remain in your home where you feel comfortable, however, there may come a time when we have to move you."

"I understand. As much as I'm a lure, I really don't want him to actually get me."

Ryan wanted to reassure her. "Kate. You say the word, and you will be taken to an undisclosed location and kept safe until we catch this guy."

She shook her head. "I'm aware of the risks and willing to take them to get this killer."

Agent Kincaid smiled. "You and I are going to get along just fine. I won't keep things from you, so long as you want to know what's happening. If it becomes too much and you simply want me to let you go about your business while I go about mine protecting you, we can do that, too."

"I'd rather know what to expect. It will help with my anxiety. Routine is helpful to me, though I know there will be some spur-of-the-moment decisions that have to be made."

"I'll do my best to keep you updated and informed, while also giving you as much time as I can to prepare for what's to come. And in that vein, one of the first things I'd like you to do is pack a bag with enough clothes and toiletries, plus any medications you take, to last a few days. If we have to leave in a hurry, I want you to be prepared."

Kate put her hand to her chest. "Okay. I can do that."

"Great. I'm going to walk through the house, check out your security, and get myself acquainted with your home."

"Sounds good. And please, help yourself to anything in the kitchen."

"I appreciate that. My partner will also be bringing in groceries, so if there's anything you need from the store, please give me a list and I'll see that she brings it."

Ryan liked the agent's efficiency and how she put Kate at ease with her up-front attitude. "Kate, if you're okay, I'll leave you in Agent Kincaid's capable hands."

"Yes. Of course. You must be as ready as I am to relax and end this day."

"I'll be in touch tomorrow."

"What's happening tomorrow?" she asked.

He didn't want to overwhelm her with a reminder of the Rose Reaper by telling her he'd be talking to Phillip and going through the Reaper's things, looking for any kind of connection between him and anyone else who could be their killer. "Agent Chapman and I will be looking through everything we have on the case, trying to find new leads to follow."

Kate nodded. "Thank you for coming."

"Of course. I didn't want you to be alone all day here without a visit from a friendly face."

She smiled at him. "I appreciate it. But I meant that you came at all. I know this is sort of outside your scope of work."

"I know this case. I know you. As long as I'm useful, I'll be here."

"You've been a great help and comfort to me."

"This will end, Kate. I wish I could tell you when, but it will be over and you'll be okay, even if your life will look different again."

"I know. It's just, I thought things were looking really good there for a moment. Then he stole it from me."

"I hope you'll have the chance to take it back very soon, because you deserve happiness and peace of mind." He wanted to squeeze her hand, or offer comfort in some other gesture, but refrained and gave her a simple smile. "Good night, Kate. I'll see you tomorrow."

"Good night, Ryan. See you tomorrow." She closed and locked the door behind him.

He heard the beep of the alarm being set yet again.

And then his phone pinged with a text.

MOLLY: Waterboy is on HBO in twenty. Can you make it?

Dinner and another Adam Sandler movie with her sounded like a great way to end his night. Though he'd rather be with her in person for it.

RYAN: I can't wait. Headed to my hotel now.

RYAN: I'll call you when I get there.

MOLLY: I hope you had a good day.

MOLLY: Or at least a productive one.

He didn't know how to answer that, because while they'd found Anne's body and learned a few new things about the killer, they hadn't arrested the bastard and ended this.

There was always tomorrow.

He climbed behind the wheel of his rental and started the car.

RYAN: Productive, yes. Good : . . . TBD.

RYAN: Dinner and a movie with you will make my night.

MOLLY: I could do better than that if we were together.

MOLLY: Just saying . . .

He grinned, thinking of all the ways she could make his night.

RYAN: I would love to make your night but I'm here and you're there.

RYAN: But a couple hours on the phone with you will still be the best part of my day.

MOLLY: You don't know how much I appreciate that.

MOLLY: How can I miss you like this when I barely know you?

RYAN: I miss you, too. Because we miss the good things in our life when they aren't there.

He pulled away from the curb and headed for his hotel, anticipating his call with Molly and the evening ahead, even if in the back of his mind he was wondering if the killer was out there watching Kate's house. And him.

Chapter Twenty-Nine

They knew about his cameras and had taken them down. He didn't care. They missed one. And he'd managed to place a second. So he saw everything at Kate's house.

She had company. And not just that psychologist she'd called.

He wondered what the specialist knew about his predecessor and what he had to say about him.

He'd love to have a conversation about how one becomes a killer.

His predecessor had been made.

He'd been born.

And once he finished his quest, he'd be reborn again. Free to be his true self once he'd paid his respects to the past and set right that which had been done wrong because of her.

He expected the babysitters outside her home and in it. He actually thought they'd move Kate and try to hide her from him. Not that they could. He had the tech to track her, even if she didn't know just how close he'd gotten to her.

None of them did.

They were trying to find and stop him, but you couldn't stop a force like him. It was like trying to stop the ocean's waves.

He would take her. He would kill her.

It was just a matter of time.

He hummed his favorite tune and thought about just how close he was to finishing this.

One more to go.

He better get on that.

He touched his finger to the monitor and the picture on the screen of Kate's home.

"Soon, my rose."

Chapter Thirty

Ryan pulled into the storage place just after 10:00 a.m., using the code to get through the gate that Phillip texted him. He was feeling good after a great night. He and Molly had eaten dinner together but separately again. They talked about their day and watched *The Waterboy*. They shared some laughs and flirted a lot. And she ended the night with another flirty innuendo about how if they'd been together he'd need his own water boy after she got through with him, then wished him sweet dreams and hung up.

He didn't think she was out to sexually frustrate him, but that's how he felt before he got in the shower and took the edge off last night with thoughts of how she'd wear him out.

He really couldn't wait to get home and see her.

Though he enjoyed this thing they had going on because she kept it fun and never made him feel like he was letting her down because he was out of town working a case.

He hoped that lasted.

But right now, he had to get his head in the game and focus on work.

He pulled in behind Agent Chapman's vehicle and the open storage locker across the way where Phillip and the agent shook hands in greeting. He got out of the car and headed toward them. "Good morning."

"Morning," Agent Chapman said.

"Hey." Phillip held his hand out to indicate the stuff packed into the small room. "Everything at the back came from my dad's house. The boxes on the right were what my dad packed up and kept of Uncle Freddy's. There's also some stuff on the shelves."

Ryan immediately scoped out the metal shelving rack and the items on them. Most of it was tools, gardening stuff, a couple of lamps, some mismatched shades, and camping gear. A sleeping bag, cooler, lanterns, a camp stove, some bottles of propane.

Next to the shelving unit several fishing poles leaned against the wall.

Ryan checked them out. "Do you still fish?"

Phillip shook his head. "Not since before my dad died. I think the last time we went, it was with Uncle Freddy. I was like ten or eleven."

Ryan thought about the time frame. Freddy might not have started killing yet. Though they knew about his seven victims because of the roses he left behind, he could have started earlier and they'd never found the connection.

Phillip offered more information. "He seemed fine. At least that's how I remember it. Just a day out on the river."

"Did you use a boat? Or fish from shore?" Agent Chapman asked.

"Both. But that time we were on shore."

"At a park?" the agent asked.

"Sometimes. Other times, we'd drive down some back road, park in some cutout, and hike it to the riverbank. That's what we did the last time we went. We'd been to that spot before, so I knew we were going to catch a lot that day."

"Did you guys camp out, too?"

"Mostly when I was really little. I loved being out in the wild under all those stars. My dad said I spent too much time watching TV and playing video games. He wanted me to enjoy the outdoors like he did. He said being outside was an escape for him as a kid."

Ryan could understand why Henry, and probably Freddy, didn't want to be locked up in the house with their mother. Or with the unfortunately bad foster parents who'd mistreated them.

Agent Chapman read the labels on the boxes at the back of the unit. "Your dad kept journals."

Phillip pulled the box closer and opened the lid. "Since he was a kid. I asked him why, once. He told me that the social worker who helped him and my uncle told him it was a way for him to get out all those things in his head he couldn't talk about." Phillip picked up one of the books and flipped through it.

Ryan caught the lines and lines of handwritten text. "He had a lot to say."

"It's a lot of free-flowing thoughts. After he died and I found all these, I went through some of them. Especially the ones during the years when my uncle was killing. While it's clear if you know what Uncle Freddy was doing that my father knew and struggled with whether he should reveal Uncle Freddy's secret or not, he's very careful to never say that outright, or give any details or hints about the killings."

"What did you make of that?" Ryan was curious if Phillip thought his father should have done something or stood by his brother because Freddy had tried to protect Henry when they were young.

"I'm not sure if keeping the secret, that it was revealed, or losing his brother was what ultimately made him take his life. I think all those deaths weighed on him. Maybe it was all of it that finally overwhelmed him."

"It could have been something else," Ryan suggested.

Phillip cocked his head. "What do you mean? That wasn't enough?"

Ryan shook his head. "That was more than most people could take. But I think something else might have been even harder for your father to handle."

"It's clear he loved my uncle. He believed Freddy saved him and felt guilty about it daily." Phillip flipped the pages of the book again to indicate that's what filled the pages.

"Did your father ever talk to you about Freddy and what he did after Freddy died?"

"Some. He wanted me to know that Freddy's actions weren't my responsibility to carry through my life like I owed everyone an apology. He didn't want people to look at me and see him. He even suggested I change my last name to my mother's maiden name so people wouldn't make the connection."

Henry wanted to protect his child from the stigma of being related to a serial killer.

"But you didn't."

Phillip shrugged. "At the time, most of the attention I received was because of a macabre cool factor."

Ryan understood that. "You were in high school. Teens would be fascinated by death and a serial killer that closely linked to them."

"The story and Uncle Freddy were sensational. And though I knew nothing about what he was doing and couldn't give any details the press didn't already spread far and wide, I was still the blood relative of a killer."

"There had to be those who looked at you sideways after that," Agent Chapman said.

"Of course. Some girls were leery of me. Others . . . not so much." The chagrined look on Phillip's face said he didn't care why the girls were interested, just that they were into him.

Ryan made the decision to reveal one of Henry's secrets. "We can't prove that it was your father, but someone was at the cabin talking to your father, begging him to stop, the night Kate escaped."

Phillip's eyes went wide. "No shit! I didn't know that."

Ryan shook his head. "If it was your father, then perhaps what he couldn't live with was that Kate got away because he distracted your uncle and your uncle took his own life because he couldn't face life in prison."

"Who wants to be locked in a cage?" Phillip went quiet, his focus turned inward. "I mean, it makes sense that my dad would blame himself for Kate's escape. In his mind, he probably just wanted my uncle to stop and for no one to find out."

Phillip went to the box of journals and pulled out a folded piece of paper. "My mom doesn't know I have this. She's never seen it. In fact, no one has. I took it when I found my father's body."

"You found him." Ryan wondered what that did to a kid to find his father hanging in the garage after he'd discovered his uncle was a serial killer.

"Yeah. My dad and I spoke on the phone before . . . he did it."

"What did he say to you?" Agent Chapman asked the very same thing Ryan wanted to know.

"He said he was sorry he couldn't be more for me." Phillip went quiet, then gave a little shrug again. "But the letter said more." He unfolded the paper. "I'll just read the part that I think is relevant. *'I can't do it anymore. I've tried so hard to forget the past but it keeps coming back. I tried to steer things in the right direction but I've found myself right back where I started and ended. I thought it was over. But I fear it only inspired instead of deterred. I can't stay and feel what's left of my heart ravished with this darkness that is a living thing I can't stop or destroy. I am helpless. I am complicit. I am responsible. I need it to end so I can escape the torment that is coming.'"* Phillip frowned and sucked in a breath. "He was lost. He thought he could change Freddy, or make him stop. But you can't stop something like that. It is a living, breathing thing." Phillip looked up and pinned Ryan in his earnest gaze. "Don't you think so?"

Ryan knew Phillip wanted to be validated that his uncle couldn't control his desire, that it controlled him and therefore it wasn't his father's fault. "In some cases, there is only one thing that will stop someone like your uncle."

"Death." Phillip's definitive answer seemed to come with an understanding of his uncle, and maybe his father's suicide, too.

"I'd settle for our latest killer in a cell." Agent Chapman scanned all the labels on Freddy's boxes. "Did your uncle keep a journal, too?"

Phillip shook his head. "I didn't find any in these boxes."

"So all this stuff was at your father's place?" Agent Chapman asked.

"Yes. It's my understanding that my uncle rented an apartment or something before he died, though it sounds like he often didn't pay his rent, so he moved around a lot from one place to another." Phillip looked at the much smaller stack of boxes for his uncle than his father. "He didn't hold on to much. Most of the stuff is just clothes, kitchen stuff, random knickknacks. There is one thing that might interest you." Phillip went to a box marked CHRISTMAS and opened the lid. He pulled out a wooden box with a rose in full bloom burned into the lid.

"Was this your uncle's?" Ryan asked.

"He made it in woodshop in high school. He taught me how to do it when I was little." Phillip dipped his hand into the box and pulled out a round wood ornament with a dove burned into it hanging from a red ribbon. "He was a much better artist than me."

"How old were you when you made that?" Agent Chapman asked.

"Six. Maybe seven." Phillip opened the lid and showed them the glass paperweight inside with a rose encased in the glass. "I don't know why the fascination with roses," Phillip admitted, "but he made and kept this for a reason, I guess."

The box was the exact size to hold the round paperweight. It was as if Freddy had found the glass rose and made the box for it.

Maybe the glass rose belonged to his mother.

Ryan held his hand out. "Do you mind?"

Phillip handed the box over to Ryan.

He turned the box over, dropping the glass rose into his palm. He examined it up close.

"Ryan." Agent Chapman sharply said his name.

He looked at the agent, who notched his chin toward the open, and now empty, box.

Ryan stared at the bottom of the box and the rosebud with two leaves on one side burned into it.

"What is it? What's wrong?" Phillip looked from one of them to the other.

"Nothing," Ryan said, putting the glass rose back in the box, covering the Reaper's signature rose design.

"Come on, you can tell me."

Law enforcement had never released the information about the Rose Reaper drawing the rose on his victims. They'd never released that the same rose was being branded onto the new victims.

Ryan gave Phillip a banal answer. "It's just that the red rose is exactly like the ones he left where he took the victims from."

"Is it the same as the ones Kate's receiving?"

"Yes."

"You're lying," Phillip accused. "Or holding something back. Why am I even trying to help you if you're not going to tell me what's going on?"

"There are things we can't share because this is an ongoing investigation."

"Freddy is dead. That case is over. You can tell me what that rose had to do with him." Phillip sounded like a petulant child denied what he wanted.

"You should ask your mother." Ryan wasn't about to spill the family secret that Freddy and Henry had been abused by their own mother.

"Like she'd tell me anything. All she wants to do is forget all of this ever happened. She left my father and me." Phillip stuffed one hand in his pocket and lifted the other with the suicide note still in his grasp. "It's complicated."

Ryan wondered what more the letter might reveal. "Do you mind if I take a picture of the letter? It might help us see something different in the past and give us some insight into what's happening now."

Phillip handed it over. "Sure. Why not? I don't know why I'm keeping it. It's not like I want to be reminded of why my dad killed himself."

Ryan snapped the photo quickly and folded the letter again and handed it back. "Maybe you should talk to someone about your grief and experience with your father. It might also help you process what happened with your uncle and how it's affected your life."

"Now you sound like my dad. He thought I needed to talk to someone, too. I think he's the one who needed a therapist." Phillip gave that nonchalant shrug that said so much about how he didn't want to talk about it anymore.

Ryan probed a little deeper. "Did you see your uncle a lot?"

Phillip shook his head. "A few times a year. Though he'd come by to see my dad when no one else was home."

"How do you know?"

"My dad would tell my mom. She'd ask why he stopped by. My dad would confess to giving him food, money, whatever he needed."

"What was your impression of your uncle? Was he nice? Mean? Angry?"

Another shrug. "Quiet, mostly. But intense. He and my dad seemed to communicate with nothing but a look most of the time. When he spoke, it was with efficiency. He said what he needed to say and that's all. He had this air about him that he didn't want to be around others." Phillip turned thoughtful. "He didn't like being touched. I remember being little and putting a hand on him to steady myself on the boat or something equally harmless. He'd push me away, or my dad would pull me away. My dad would say, 'Give him some space.'"

Ryan understood that came from being abused by his mother and others who had fostered him. Freddy didn't find comfort in human contact. It reminded him of all the pain he'd suffered.

It also helped explain why he restrained his victims in the way he did. So they couldn't touch him. When they fought back, he hit them. Maybe not to hurt them, but to get them to be still so they weren't touching him. He took from them. He held control. They didn't get to do anything he didn't allow them to do.

"When I was little, he seemed odd. Different from my dad and others. Now, I guess it makes sense. Anyway, have at it." Phillip did that little shrug thing again and waved his hand out toward the boxes. "Go through those if you want to. I need to check my class portal to see how I did on a test." Phillip took a seat on the floor by the boxes stacked to the ceiling nearby at the back of the room.

Agent Chapman opened one box after another, taking a picture, riffling through the contents, then closing the box again.

Ryan did the same with other boxes.

Nothing struck either of them as significant.

Agent Chapman's phone rang. "What do you have?" he asked without a greeting, probably anticipating something on the case.

The agent locked eyes with Ryan, spared a glance for Phillip, then walked out of the unit and far enough away that they couldn't hear the conversation.

Phillip rose from the floor and walked to the opening below the rollup door. "What do you suppose that's all about?"

Ryan gave the obvious answer. "Probably the case."

"Is he keeping the news from you, or just me?"

"If it's important and he thinks I need to know about it to be of help on the case, he'll tell me."

"I wonder how long it will take them to catch this guy. I mean, he's not making it easy."

"They hardly ever do." Ryan studied Phillip watching the agent. "Investigations are mostly slow, especially when there's little evidence and no clear suspect."

"You're not looking at anyone right now?" Phillip eyed him like he didn't believe that.

"We're looking at the past and the present to see where Freddy and this killer are the same, different, and how they collide."

"You want to know why this guy is copying the Rose Reaper."

"Any guesses?" Ryan imagined that Phillip spent a great deal of time thinking about his uncle and the new killer, even if he kept it to himself.

"Maybe it's just a game to win."

Interesting take on it.

For someone of Phillip's generation, who grew up in front of a screen playing video games, maybe life looked very much like something you played to win.

And if your goal was to become a serial killer and you lived in this area, then maybe you'd want to beat the one who had the most notoriety.

Agent Chapman ended the call and came back to them and walked right up to Phillip. "Why didn't you tell us you inherited a piece of property from your father along the river?"

Phillip raised a brow. "You never asked. Why does it matter?"

"I think you're smart enough to know why it matters. The property was left by your grandmother to her two sons. It was her grandparents' farm a long time ago."

Phillip squared off with the agent. "Yeah. And now it's acres of overgrown land with nothing on it."

"Are you sure?" Agent Chapman asked.

Phillip shrugged. "I mean, I haven't been there since I was a very young child. I drove out there after I learned about the property to take a look. It's nothing but trees and overgrown fields."

Agent Chapman narrowed his gaze. "I asked about your fishing trips. You didn't mention going there."

"I don't remember if we ever did. All the places we went along the river looked the same to me."

"Is there a house, a cabin, some sort of structure on the property then or now?"

"I barely remember being there at all." Phillip frowned. "I don't know."

Agent Chapman didn't back down. "Can I have your permission to search the property?"

"Why?"

"We never found the cabin where your uncle took his victims. Maybe it's there."

Phillip raised a brow. "Why would you think that?"

"Because it is very close to where Kate was found after she escaped."

"For real?" Phillip's eyes went wide with surprise and interest.

Agent Chapman held Phillip's gaze, waiting for permission.

Phillip did that shrug thing again. "Sure. Let's go."

"You don't need to be there."

"It's my property. If there's something there, I want to see it."

Agent Chapman sighed. "Suit yourself." The agent glanced at Ryan. "While he closes up here, let's talk about where we're going."

Ryan didn't think the agent would include him in the search of the property, and wondered what else the agent had to say that he didn't want Phillip to overhear.

They walked to the back of the agent's car and stood close.

Agent Chapman leaned in and whispered, "Phillip's property isn't the only one we're searching."

"What else did you find?"

"We're issuing a search warrant on Reed's property. Because guess what? A piece of Phillip's property touches Reed's down by the river. The analyst who pulled the land records went back through the land titles and discovered that Reed's property was originally part of Phillip's maternal great-grandparents' land. They sold off two pieces. One to the fisherman who Reed purchased the land from through his grandson, and another piece bisects part of the property between the fisherman's purchase and the original piece of land."

"Do you think Reed purchased the land because it was part of Freddy Poole's inheritance? He's so obsessed with the Rose Reaper, he wanted to own something that once belonged to his family?"

Agent Chapman shrugged. "It seems that way. Reed bought the property about a year and a half ago."

"The new killings started about ten months ago," Ryan pointed out.

"He needed to plan, pick a victim, figure out how to connect with Kate. Her company puts out a request for bids on their new building project. Reed makes sure his company wins the bid. Now he's working with Kate. He's close to her. And he sets the rest of his plans in motion."

"But how does that tie to the property?"

"The Rose Reaper killed on his property. Now Reed has his own little hideaway on his." Agent Chapman shrugged, guessing like Ryan how this all could make sense.

If it even did.

Because right now, they didn't have any proof Reed knew the land had once belonged to Freddy's family. Of course, in his line of work, it would be easy for him to pull land records. He'd know what he was looking for and how to get it.

If he was the copycat, he'd need a place to hide the women, some-place no one would see them or hear their screams.

Both properties were on the river where the bodies were dumped.

It made sense.

And maybe they'd finally have their killer and Kate would be safe. If they found the cabin on either property, or one on both, explaining the two sets of killings, they could end this before the killer came for Kate.

Agent Chapman opened the car door. "Let's go catch a killer."

Chapter Thirty-One

Ryan wasn't sure what to expect of the search, but because the land was mostly open overgrown fields and large areas of forested land, they didn't search on foot. Most of the searching was done by drones and with agents on ATVs. Hours went by with nothing to report, except to mark the map laid out in the command center tent that had been set up. So far, most of Phillip's property was marked off as showing nothing significant. The only signs of life found were the foundation and chimneys for the old farmhouse that had collapsed from years of neglect, water damage, and rot, along with the bones of a couple of barns, their rotted wood and overgrown weeds covering rusted farm equipment.

Like the search of Phillip's property, the team searching Reed's place started at the top from the road, working their way down to the river.

Since it was taking so long, Ryan had driven up to the road with one of the team members to scout the place where Kate had been found.

He was standing with the agent next to the SUV looking at a tablet zoomed in on a map of the area. The agent circled the part of the road where they were parked, indicating they were exactly where Kate had been rescued. Ryan waited for him to zoom out so they could see the larger picture of the two pieces of land they were searching, the river, and the road.

"Any idea how long she ran through the woods to get here?" the agent asked.

"No. When I spoke to her in the hospital afterward, she said it felt like she ran forever."

"But she was hurt, dehydrated, cold, and unsure of where she was going. She'd have to dodge tree limbs, brush, other obstacles . . . So we're not talking a straight path."

"And with limited energy, even with an adrenaline rush, I don't think she could have run far and also get up this hill."

"I don't know . . ." The agent looked out across the sea of trees bordering the road. "If I knew my life was on the line, I'd run as far and as fast as I could."

Ryan looked down the road and something occurred to him. "We came from that way." Ryan pointed in front of them. "That's Reed's land. Behind us is Freddy's property." Now Phillip's land.

"Yeah."

"And when Freddy Poole came after Kate, his car came from Reed's direction."

The agent's head snapped up from the tablet in his hands and he looked down the road toward Reed's place, then back the other way toward Phillip's place. "That's odd."

"I mean . . ." Yeah. It was. "Maybe he cut across the land somewhere to get to here?"

The agent held the tablet out. "It's possible where the two pieces of property connect that he could have come across in a four-wheel-drive vehicle way down here by the river. But we searched the Rose Reaper's side of the property and didn't find a cabin like Kate described."

"Maybe because it's on Reed's side and we haven't gotten down that far in the search."

The agent studied the map again, then got on the radio. "Welch to base, come in."

"Base, go ahead."

"Ryan and I have identified a possible area that is of interest. Let's get the team to focus on areas nine and ten."

"Why there?"

"Because of their proximity to the river, forest, Phillip's land, and the possible path Kate took to the road."

There was a pause. "On it. Agent Chapman would like you to return and brief him."

"On our way." Agent Welch started for the driver's door.

Ryan went around to the passenger side, hoping they found something soon, knowing this could be the break they needed.

Chapter Thirty-Two

Ryan saw the increased activity in the base tent and walked faster to hear what Agent Chapman was conveying to the group of forensic techs who'd been assembled but until now had nothing to really collect evidence from or search.

He immediately recognized one of those assembled. "Sylvie, it's good to see you again."

"Sorry we keep meeting under such circumstances." She bumped her shoulder to his. "That last case . . . that was a doozy." The Copeland County Killer case had taken a personal toll on him. Sylvie and her team had uncovered the killer's well-hidden secrets at his farm and returned the remains of his many victims to their families, along with some unexpected victims they hadn't known about until Olivia had helped him find his sister and uncover the truth. "How are you?"

"Good. And you?"

Sylvie held up her forensic kit. "Ready to stop another killer. They found the cabin in the woods."

A blast of adrenaline shot through Ryan. His heart beat faster as his mind filled with questions. He wanted to see it up close and hoped it held the answers they were all looking for. "You're on your way there now."

Sylvie nodded. "Let's hope it gives up its secrets easier than the Copeland County Killer's farm did."

Reed rushed over to him, his attorney on his heels. "I didn't know about the cabin."

Ryan met the man's determined gaze. "It's on your property."

"Someplace I've never been since I bought the place. I was more interested in the riverfront than the woods."

"They've found a half-decent trail to follow to the cabin," Agent Chapman called out to the team. "Get ready to move."

Agent Chapman walked over to them. "Ryan, what do you think about bringing Kate here to see the place? She can confirm this is it."

"No fucking way in hell," Reed snapped. "You're not bringing her here."

"Why not? You don't want her to see we were right about you all along?" Agent Chapman stared down Reed.

"My client hasn't done anything but cooperate with your investigation," Emily intervened. "If this cabin is where the Rose Reaper took his victims, my client had no knowledge of that fact. He didn't even own the property at the time."

"And what about bringing his five victims here?" Agent Chapman asked.

"My client did not abduct, rape, or kill anyone. Here or anywhere else." Emily defended her client.

Reed gripped Ryan's arm. "You can't let them bring her here. You know that's the worst thing for her. It will traumatize her. Isn't it bad enough this guy is threatening her, now they want to bring her to the place where she was held and worse? No. That's not happening."

Ryan glanced down at Reed's hand on him, then met the man's gaze. "Let go."

Reed realized what he'd done and released Ryan immediately. "Sorry. It's just . . ." He raked his fingers through his hair, his distress clear.

"Until we know more about this place they found, there's no reason to tell Kate anything. If it is determined that this cabin is where the

Rose Reaper, or the copycat killer, took their victims, then I'll talk to Kate. As it has always been when it comes to this investigation, Kate decides what she wants to do." Ryan wanted that to be clear to Reed and Agent Chapman.

"She's going to want to help. But this . . ." Reed shook his head. "This won't help her. This will take her back. And she's come so far."

Ryan appreciated the depth of emotion and Reed's determination to advocate for Kate's well-being and mental health. "I understand how you feel. But right now, you don't have a say, or even an opinion that she'll listen to, so trust me that I have Kate's best interests in mind. I will be by her side through whatever comes next."

Though his words didn't seem to ease Reed, he nodded his agreement anyway.

"Can I come?" Phillip asked.

Agent Chapman and Ryan both turned to the man behind them.

"What are you doing here?" Agent Chapman asked, surprised like Ryan to see him.

"I overheard the agents searching my place say they were coming to help with the search here since my place turned up nothing. I wanted to see if you found my uncle's killing cabin."

The term shocked Ryan.

Phillip seemed nonchalant about the reason they were here, like finding the place where his uncle raped seven women and killed six of them was like visiting a museum or something.

He guessed in this day of serial killer documentaries and true crime podcasts people had become desensitized to the horrors of murder and mayhem. It was something to talk about over coffee and sensationalize for entertainment value.

Agent Chapman shrugged. "You're not supposed to be here. This is a federal investigation."

Phillip raised his shoulders, his hands deep in his hoodie's pockets. "I cooperated with your search of my place and my dad's and uncle's stuff." His shoulders dropped. "This is about my family, too, not just whoever is killing these women now."

Agent Chapman looked resigned. "Fine. Just stay back and out of the way of the investigators doing their jobs."

They loaded into the SUVs. Agent Chapman rode up front with another agent. Both of them quiet and ready to solve this case. Phillip took the middle seat between Emily and Reed. And despite his size, Ryan managed to climb in the third-row seat. Anticipation filled the vehicle as they followed others through the tall grass along a barely there track that led into the woods. Ryan remembered Kate's description of being in the back of the Reaper's truck and feeling like they were turning and swerving around trees. Experiencing it firsthand felt disorienting.

But then, just when he thought they were lost or would get stuck in a spot where the trees were too close together to pass, he saw the cabin hidden in the shadows of the tall trees, the roof mostly covered by thick limbs.

Reed leaned to the side, practically over his attorney, and forward to get a look at the place.

Without the suspicion hanging over Reed's head, Ryan would believe the man had never seen this place. But Ryan held on to his doubts and wondered if Reed was just making a good show of it.

The car stopped. All the others lined up behind them.

Agent Chapman was the first person out of the vehicle. He immediately walked to the four other agents who were already at the cabin—the ones who had found it first.

Reed, Emily, and Phillip jumped out.

Ryan was the last to exit. He stood looking at the cabin wall facing him. No windows. He walked in a wide arc to see the other side. The second he spotted the narrow porch with the railing and posts that led to the door with a window on each side, chills ran up his spine.

He kept walking around until he could look through the open door and see the metal-framed bed with a bare mattress directly in front of him against the back wall where there were no windows. To the left of the bed stood a potbelly woodstove. On the right, the bathtub Kate described with the stool and a lantern.

"This is the place, isn't it?" Reed asked from five feet away from him. "I can see it on your face. Kate described this place to you."

Ryan turned to Reed and realized that would be the way toward the river, the way that Henry probably came in to plead with Freddy to stop, on the other side where Kate couldn't see them. Ryan looked behind himself and knew that's the way Kate ran, the path that led to the road.

"Is this it?" Reed asked again, his question an order for an answer he needed.

"Yes." Ryan watched the blood drain from Reed's face.

Reed hung his head and shook it. "I didn't know." He looked up at Ryan. "I'll burn it to the ground. There will be nothing left of it or this place when I'm done."

A line of forensic techs walked past the two of them and into the cabin.

Ryan held Reed's steady gaze. "You don't get a say in what happens next. This is a crime scene. And you are a suspect in this case."

"Do you have any idea how incredibly frustrating it is for no one to believe you? Even worse, the one person I need to believe me thinks I'm capable of this." He held his hand out toward the cabin. "I would endure the pain of a lifetime without Kate before I ever hurt her." Reed shook his head. "But you probably don't believe that either. That is the fucking hell I'm living right now, knowing she's facing all of this without me there to protect and hold her. She's alone. And knowing that, for me, is agony." Reed walked away, back to his attorney, who had just finished a conversation with Agent Chapman.

Ryan guessed the agent was going to go after Reed hard now with more warrants for his home and work and whatever else he wanted to search.

God help Reed if they found any shred of evidence in the cabin that put him or one of the new victims in that place.

"So he's the number one suspect?" Phillip asked, bringing Ryan out of his thoughts again.

Ryan didn't confirm or deny. Obviously the kid had overheard their conversation. So Ryan asked his own question. "Was there anything in your father's journals about this cabin?"

"I didn't read all of them. They go back to before I was born. I was only really interested in the time frame when my uncle was killing. Like I said, he was careful about what he wrote about my uncle."

"Did he write about you?" Ryan didn't know why he asked, just that he had a sense that Phillip and his father had a close but complicated relationship.

"Sure. But that got boring. You know, like I'd heard it all before. It's a strange thing to read that someone knows you that well but still doesn't get you." Phillip shrugged.

Ryan was getting used to the way Phillip used the repetitive gesture before, during, and after he spoke. "Did he not get you because his dream for you didn't match the dream you had for yourself?"

Phillip smiled.

The first one Ryan had ever seen from him.

"You must be really good at your job with insights like that."

Ryan raised a brow. "Am I right?"

"Yeah. I just never saw it like that. Now that I do . . . It's a perspective shift. He wanted me to live the life he thought was safe and respectable. I know what I want and will make me happy. Those two things didn't always align."

"The dilemma everyone faces as they grow older. Their parents' expectations versus them stretching their wings and taking risks to figure out what they want."

"Exactly." Phillip shrugged. "I'm not in jail or dead, so I must be doing something right."

"Especially if the line for failure is jail or death." It struck Ryan suddenly that the Rose Reaper had faced those very things at the end. Kate had escaped. The Reaper hadn't finished her off and dispatched her like all the rest. He'd failed and faced jail or death. He chose death.

Ryan eyed Phillip.

"What?" he asked.

Ryan shook it off. "Nothing. Just a random thought."

Sylvie walked out of the cabin and waved him over.

"Excuse me." Ryan walked away from Phillip to the forensic lead. "What's up?"

"You're working with Kate Doyle, the victim who survived, right?"

"Yes."

Sylvie frowned. "There's nothing here." Sylvie looked back at the cabin, then at him again. "And yet, there's something here."

He narrowed his gaze. "I don't follow."

"Remember the Copeland County Killer barn? No fingerprints, no blood, no DNA, nothing out of place, everything clean and organized, looking like just what you'd see in a barn."

"I remember." He also remembered what those ordinary things could do to a human being. "And here?"

"Just a one-room cabin with the bare necessities. Cleaned spotless."

Ryan tilted his head, looking past Sylvie into the cabin. "Out here in the woods, this rustic place, not a spiderweb, dust, critters of any kind?"

Sylvie nodded. "Spotless."

"I want to ask, *How can that be?* but I know the answer. Do you think someone's been here recently?"

Sylvie looked at the ground around them. "We have one single partial shoe tread in the dirt outside the cabin door. We'll run it, see if we get anything."

"How can there only be one tread?" He looked down at where he was standing and behind Sylvie to see her clear path of footprints in the moist dirt back to the cabin.

Sylvie looked up at the trees. "They keep the dirt moist and also provide a means for brushing the tracks away."

"So he comes out here and uses a broken-off tree limb to wipe away his path when he leaves."

"Simple. Effective. Something a hunter or survivalist would know. And in these parts . . ." Sylvie didn't have to finish that sentence. Not when hunting and fishing were a way of life for so many of the people who lived here.

"Were there any tire tracks leading in here that you could see?"

Sylvie shook her head. "Nothing usable. Wet leaves and debris litter most of the forest floor. There's been rain in the past couple of weeks. Unless he was out here in the last four days, we missed our window to find anything."

It hadn't rained since Ryan arrived in town.

Sylvie dropped her voice. "I overheard Agent Chapman say he wants to bring Kate out here. I know you're the expert and all, but I don't think it's a good idea. There's nothing here she can point us to that will break the case. The only thing she can do is confirm this is where he held her. Other than that, this is just her nightmare."

He was about to agree with her when he spotted Kate coming forward with a female agent beside her. "Shit."

Sylvie turned and swore, too. "Not good, Ryan. Not good." With that, she turned and headed back to the cabin, probably to tell her team that Kate had arrived.

To her nightmare.

Chapter Thirty-Three

Kate felt everyone's eyes on her. All the agents'. Ryan's as he walked toward her, a look of concern on his face. Reed's familiar and compassionate gaze, tinged with worry and a desperate plea she couldn't answer now.

Whoever that lady was with him gave Kate a speculative look.

Who the hell was she?

What was she doing with Reed?

Agent Chapman stepped in front of her. "Thank you for coming."

She nodded, unsure why. Her brain couldn't seem to focus on one thing. Her gaze kept going to the cabin just twenty feet away, though it felt like it was engulfing her, making it hard for her to breathe.

"Kate." Ryan said her name like he'd said it at least once before and she hadn't heard him.

"What?"

"Look at me."

She turned her head and met his calm gaze.

"Just keep looking at me. Now take a slow breath."

She glanced over at Reed with that woman.

"Not at him," Ryan demanded. "Look at me, Kate."

She turned back to Ryan, letting her eyes and mind focus on him. She took a breath, then another.

"That's it. Good. Did you come because Agent Chapman asked you to, or because you wanted to be here?"

"I . . ." She wasn't exactly sure how to answer that. When Agent Kincaid told her they'd found the cabin and Agent Chapman wanted her to come to confirm this was where she'd been held, it seemed so easy to say yes to the request. They were protecting her and trying to find the new killer, so of course she wanted to do her part and participate. But now, it felt like the world was closing in on her. It felt like the past and present converged and the fear she felt then was real in the here and now.

She'd spent nearly four years trying to forget this place and what happened to her here. Did she really need to see it again? To bring back all that pain?

"Kate, you are not the same person who escaped here. You survived. You rebuilt your life. This place is nothing but your past. You are strong and capable and not his victim anymore. You don't need to be here. You don't owe anyone anything. Walk away."

She looked up at him, so appreciative to have him here with her. "I can't. I need to just see it, to know that it's real. It exists."

Ryan's eyes pleaded with her. "You already know that. You lived through it."

"Now I need to stand in front of it again as me. The me I am now."

"Please, don't do this, Kate," Reed implored without coming any closer to her.

She turned on him. "Why not? Is this why you bought this place? Because you knew he held me here. Raped me here! Wanted to kill me here!"

Tears welled in Reed's eyes. "No. I didn't know it was here. It was just a piece of land. They told me nothing was on it. Just the land."

She turned her back on him and walked toward the cabin.

"Kate, don't," Reed pleaded again.

Ryan walked up next to her as she rounded to the front of the cabin. She stood in the dappled light filtering through the trees and closed her eyes, listening to the quiet, remembering it like it was yesterday she was lying in that bed, bound and helpless to *his* whims. She could almost smell the smoke from the fire. The rustling leaves of the trees had been a constant whisper as it was now.

Ryan didn't say a word. He simply stood close. Not touching her, but close enough that she could feel him there.

"I feel him here, too. He was a part of the quiet. He was a part of this place." She opened her eyes and stared in through the front door at the bed that had felt like her final resting place. "He was the monster in the woods. The evil in the cabin. Death awaiting my final breath. I could feel him anticipating it. I can feel it now in the pit of my stomach." She pressed her hand to her belly. "I can taste the fear." She swallowed back the bile rising in her throat. "I can feel time, the way it crawls and runs. How it stops when he looks at me the way he did as he decided my next fate."

She stared into the maw of her undoing, choking on the fear and nightmares that assailed her.

She fell to her knees and gave in to the overwhelming emotions without a clear thought but a jumble of them. She sobbed for the women who lost their lives here, for who she used to be, for all the terrible things she endured here. She let it all out. She hadn't cried like this in a long time. And knew that there were new things to cry about. Her peaceful life had been disrupted again. She lost the one man she thought she'd spend the rest of her life with. She hated that she didn't have faith in others anymore. She cried because her foundation had been shaken and cracked again.

She cried because she hated this.

She cried over the injustice of it all.

And then she got mad. How could someone do this to her? How could he be so arrogant and heartless and ruthless and hurt and kill all those women? How could he drag her back into her nightmares?

Just like in the past, it was Ryan's steady, calm voice that pulled her free of the pain and anger. "It is wood and metal and stone, constructed to conceal what he did here. He took the bad with him. This is just a thing in a place. There is nothing of you left in there. You are out here. Free. Alive. Safe."

She wiped her tears, stood, and turned her back on the cabin and her nightmares. "I'm not meant to be here. This part of my life is over. No matter what the new killer wants me to think, no matter how hard he tries to make me what I was then, I'm different now." She believed that and it strengthened her conviction and resolve.

"Yes, you are. And whatever it is he wants from you, you don't have to give it to him."

She took that in and held it close. "I want this to all be over." She could feel the end coming and knew she had a part to play. She didn't know if she was strong enough to survive again. "I want the good back and the bad banished to nothing but a memory."

"Then start by leaving this place. Go back to the home you made, the friends you know, the life you worked so hard to build. Don't leave any of yourself here. Don't take any of this place with you." Ryan's plea sank deep into her heart.

She met his earnest gaze. "You have no idea how much I appreciate you."

"You have no idea how much I admire you for your strength and determination and courage. You inspire, Kate, with your ability to live through this."

"Even after I leave this place for the last time, this still isn't over."

Ryan conceded that point with a nod. "But you can be over it. Say the word, and the FBI will take you away from this. He won't know where you are. He won't be able to get to you again."

She sighed. "Maybe that's best."

"Go home. Settle your mind. Think about it. If it's truly what you want and you can live with it, then tomorrow we'll make it happen."

"Thank you, Ryan, for knowing how important it's been for me to stand my ground. But I've made my point when it comes to this killer walking in and out of my life at will. I know I'm strong enough to stand up to him. I'm not his victim. He's cast his shadow in my life for too long. Maybe now is the time to step away from it."

"Agent Chapman will need a little time to set it up. If the killer is watching you and the house, he'll need to figure out a way to get you out of there and to a safe place without you being followed."

"I'll tell Agent Kincaid I'm ready to be moved and let her and Agent Chapman make the arrangements."

"I'll stay until you're safely away."

"Thank you for coming the way you did. I appreciate it so much." Kate couldn't help herself and hugged him.

Ryan held her close and whispered in her ear, "You're going to be okay, Kate. I knew it when we met the first time. I know it now."

She stepped back from him. "I will be. This time, it's a whole different kind of loss and trauma." She glanced at Reed, feeling that pit of regret and sadness, but finding it hard to be angry when she still had doubts that he'd done this to her.

"Even after all this, you're still not sure it's him," Ryan said.

"What more do I need to be convinced? Am I so afraid of being alone that I'll deny all of this and still believe in him?"

"All we know for sure right now is that he bought a piece of property that happens to have the cabin you were held in on his land. Did he know it was here? He says no. Was it easy to find? No. Is this the coincidence that makes all those others fact? I'm not so sure. But maybe."

"Are you just saying that because you feel for me and my situation and you don't want it to be Reed either?"

"Yes. And no. The FBI deals in hard facts. Right now, there's a hell of a lot of speculation and possibilities. Those don't convict people."

"But they can convince you one way or the other."

"Are you convinced he raped, killed, and dumped five women in the river like they meant nothing to him? Because I'm not." Ryan's candor and directness was exactly what she needed, when so many others would hint or change the subject or tell her that it had to be him. Some would even tell her she was out of her mind for not believing it.

But Ryan was right. She believed there was a possibility it could be Reed, but she wasn't wholly convinced.

And she needed to be so that her heart would accept that the man she loved, who had been nothing but good to her, was not the man she thought him to be.

Ryan touched her arm. "Agent Chapman is waving me over to talk to him. You okay?"

"Yes. I'm fine. Thank you again for everything. I'll have Agent Kincaid drive me home now."

Ryan walked with her toward the line of vehicles. He broke off from her just as they passed Reed and the woman he was with, whoever she was, and Kate headed toward where Agent Kincaid was watching her approach while she spoke to one of the other agents on scene.

"You're Kate, right?"

Kate halted and turned toward the young man in a hoodie she was sure she'd never met but who seemed familiar. "I'm sorry. Do I know you?"

He shook his head, his gaze direct on her. "No. I hope this doesn't upset you, but I just wanted to say that I'm sorry about what happened to you here."

She didn't really know how to respond to that. "Thank you. Um . . . are you working here or something?" He didn't look like an agent. Too young. Maybe a member of the forensic team.

"No. The feds searched my property nearby. I came over to see if they found what they were looking for here."

Something niggled at the back of her mind. "Why did they search your property?"

"Oh, uh, yeah, I didn't introduce myself. I'm Phillip. Phillip Poole."

Kate gasped and stepped back. "You're *his* . . . What?"

"Nephew," he supplied quickly. "My dad was his brother."

Kate swallowed her surprise and gathered herself and her thoughts. "I'm so sorry. I heard about your father's passing." She didn't blame the family for what happened, but found it surreal to be standing here talking to this young man who did in fact resemble Freddy Poole. It sent a chill up her spine.

"Yeah. A lot of people suffered because of my uncle. So, yeah, sorry. That's all I wanted to say." He started backing away from her.

She didn't have anything else to say either, took the out, and headed back toward Agent Kincaid when she heard the strangest humming. The hairs on the back of her neck stood up. She spun around, only to find Reed walking up behind her with the woman. "What were you humming?"

Reed stopped in his tracks and eyed her. "Are you okay?"

She spun around and ran for Agent Kincaid, ready to be away from here and back home where she didn't have to confront monsters anymore.

But would she ever be free of them again?

Not yet. Not until this killer was locked up.

Chapter Thirty-Four

Ryan joined Agent Chapman by the SUV and stared at the paper he held up in his hand.

"We have a new search warrant."

Finally, they were getting somewhere. "For Reed?"

"Any and all vehicles he owns, plus his shoes."

Ryan knew the print by the cabin would be looked at closely. If they matched it to a pair of Reed's shoes, they'd finally have some solid proof against him. He glanced over just as Kate rushed away from Reed and over to Agent Kincaid. He glanced at the guy's boots and wondered if he'd be brazen enough to wear them here today.

Phillip walked out from between the two SUVs as Ryan turned back to Agent Chapman. "Oh hey. I was just going to tell you both that I'm headed back to school. Big bio test coming up."

Agent Chapman went to him and shook his hand. "Thank you for your cooperation."

Phillip did the shrug thing he always did. "Sure. No problem. I guess I won't be seeing you anytime soon."

"If you're lucky," Agent Chapman teased.

Phillip shrugged again and grinned. "If I see you, it's because I've made a grave mistake."

"Don't," Agent Chapman warned.

Phillip walked away, leaving Ryan with the agent. "Listen, Kate is going to talk to Agent Kincaid tonight, but I'll give you the heads-up. She's done. She wants to leave before this guy gets a chance to come after her."

Agent Chapman sighed out his relief. "I was going to talk to her again about it. This makes it so much easier. I'll get the ball rolling." Agent Chapman looked past him to where Reed stood nearby with his attorney. "But first . . . Miss Bell, I have something for you and your client." He handed Emily the search warrant. "I'll be keeping your client's truck and his boots. I have a team at his house taking his other shoes as we speak."

Emily read the search warrant, her lips pressed tight, then looked up at Reed. "Please remove your boots and hand them over to the agent."

"Just set them on the SUV hood for me." Agent Chapman indicated the SUV next to them. "Thank you."

Reed didn't say a word, just did as he was told.

"I'll just drive you, Miss Bell, and Ryan back to your vehicles. Miss Bell, I assume you will drive your client home."

"Yes," she said, climbing into the back seat of the car.

A forensic tech retrieved the boots from the hood, and Agent Chapman climbed into the driver's seat as Ryan took the front passenger side and Reed climbed in the rear seat with Emily.

The ride back through the trees and overgrown field was twisty and bumpy and fraught with tense silence.

Ryan couldn't wait to get back to his hotel.

Tomorrow he'd book a flight home and maybe be there in time to see Molly before she went on shift at the bar.

But first, he'd make sure Kate was away from the killer, safe and secure where no one could find her.

Chapter Thirty-Five

Kate was beyond anxious at home, wondering how she could be so stupid about Reed and alternating back to being positive he hadn't done what the FBI suspected him of doing. It couldn't be. Or he did do it and she'd been too blinded by her desire to have a normal life that she'd dismissed or not seen what was right in front of her.

She felt like she was spinning out of control, thinking about every tiny little detail of the past ten months she'd been seeing Reed. Every interaction, every conversation, it all seemed so normal. Nothing seemed off to her. She couldn't think of a single time she second-guessed the reason behind something he said or did.

It didn't make sense.

He couldn't have done this.

He wouldn't have taunted her this way, then acted like nothing had happened.

He couldn't have been that concerned about her, her safety, her mental health, then turned around, killed another woman, and left her those roses, bringing back the nightmare from her past over and over again.

But if not him, then who?

Why? Why would someone do all this?

Why go after Reed? To get him out of her life? To make her mistrust him and everyone else around her?

Because right now, she had a hard time focusing and seeing what was real and what wasn't.

Did she have confidence in herself to know the difference between the truth and lies coming out of Reed's mouth, or anyone's for that matter at this point?

Could she trust the FBI and Ryan to uncover the truth?

She needed to speak to Reed. She had to know. Over the phone wouldn't do. She needed to see his face, hear his voice, and assess his body language to be sure. She needed that certainty to stop the wild thoughts circling her head. And there was one way to ensure he didn't play any tricks, try to harm her, or try to lie.

She grabbed what she needed and put it in her bag. Before she left, she pulled out her phone and ordered an Uber to pick her up down the street. She had three minutes before the car arrived and went into her bathroom, opened the high window, and pushed out the screen. She dropped her bag out the window, stood on the wood stool she kept in the shower to shave her legs, then lifted her upper body through the window. It was only about four feet to the ground with her body hanging down over the windowsill. Still, it took some effort with her hands planted on the wall to shimmy her backside over the ledge until her weight and momentum did the rest of the job and she landed on her hands and tumbled over, hitting her hip on her bag. Her wrists ached from the sudden impact, but she rubbed both of them and ignored the pain, hoping it subsided soon.

And Agent Kincaid hadn't heard her daring escape.

She took her bag and pulled the strap over her head and across her body. The agent watching over her in the house didn't come running to stop her. She thanked her lucky stars, knowing this was probably a stupid move but also something she had to do for her own peace of mind.

The shadows from the bushes and trees, along with her black clothes, kept her hidden for the most part. She made her way along the side of the house until the privacy fence between the houses ended and she crossed over to her neighbor's yard, where she dashed across the front of their house and onto the sidewalk down the street. She walked to the next block and spotted the headlights of a car coming her way. She waited for it to stop and checked the license plate number and driver to be sure they matched her app. Then she climbed into the back seat.

"How is your night, Kate?" the driver asked.

"Good. Yours?"

"Kind of slow. I'll have you to your destination in less than ten minutes."

Kate settled in, her hand on her bag, her thoughts on what she planned to do next.

Chapter Thirty-Six

She's perfect. Everything he could hope for before he went to Kate, finished her, then moved on to what he really wanted. He couldn't wait to expand his horizons. Sweet Anne had given him a glimpse of what was to come. He'd tried to hold back, but once he had her and knew there was only one more before he got to Kate . . . his restraint had slipped.

This time, he'd stick to the plan. It was working so well.

They didn't have anything substantial to tie him to the women.

He was free to continue, to indulge, to surpass his predecessor.

They still hadn't given him a moniker yet.

He wanted one.

He didn't want to end up the bad sequel to the Rose Reaper.

Once he had the freedom to explore all those lovely scenarios playing in his head, he'd show them he wasn't just some follower, a copycat.

He'd leave his own mark. He'd show them he deserved to be lauded as so much more than those who came before him.

Now that he knew who and what he was, nothing could hold him back. No one could stop him.

Not even Kate.

Because while she was the ultimate goal right now, and she'd be harder to get to because she knew he was coming for her, that just made it all the more fun.

Tonight would be a challenge. But he was up for the task.

Not here, though. The restaurant was too obvious. Too public.

He needed to be patient, pick the perfect time and place. But it had to be tonight. He couldn't wait. At any moment the FBI could move Kate. He had a plan if they did, but still, he couldn't take the chance they relocated her and switched cars and places where they hid her before he could get to her. Technology would only get him so far before he lost her.

No. It had to be tonight. Even if he risked getting caught because he hadn't planned out exactly how this would go. He needed to be on his game, look for every possible obstacle and work around them.

Once this was done, Kate was his.

But first, he'd enjoy the hunt for number six. He followed his prey's car out of the restaurant parking lot and down the street. He didn't bother to hide the fact that he was following her. Why would she think that on a relatively busy road? He did allow some distance when they entered the subdivision. He even drove right past her as she stopped outside a home and dropped off her passenger. She didn't linger and quickly drove past him. He started his car again and slowly pulled out onto the street and kept on following her.

Now that she was alone, he could grab her anywhere. Well, he'd have to watch for those pesky surveillance cameras, but he'd gotten good at noticing them without making it too obvious he was checking for them everywhere he went.

His sweet rose didn't go straight home. She stopped off at one of those all-night drugstores that sold everything from makeup to books to medicine and went inside. The parking lot was lit up like it was daytime. Too obvious and dangerous to take her here. He waited, tapping his finger against the steering wheel. She appeared a few minutes later carrying a bottle of wine. Maybe he'd drink it after he had her tied up and at his mercy.

He waited for her to back out of her spot and drive toward the road before he pulled out and fell in behind her and another car. She turned left, then made another right. They drove for a couple of minutes until she pulled into a swanky-looking apartment complex. No gate. So he pulled in right after her, slowing down, allowing her time to park in a covered and numbered spot.

He didn't see any obvious cameras. No one was in the lot, so he stopped right behind her vehicle and caught her closing the driver's-side door.

Just as she turned to him, he had the needle out, ready to slip it into her neck and take her down, but she came up swinging. He had just enough time to catch the bottle of wine on his forearm and block her from hitting him in the face.

Her eyes went wide. "It's you."

He simply grinned at her.

He went for her again, but this time she pulled a knife from her coat pocket. The blade flipped out and she swiped at him, catching his side.

"Bitch." He grabbed her by the hair, stabbed her with the syringe in the neck, and pushed the plunger.

She tried to stab him with the knife again but missed.

This rose had thorns.

He took her wrist and pulled the knife free. She was kicking at him and yelling, though he muffled that with his hand over her mouth.

The drugs were taking effect and he followed her as she dropped to her knees and fell back. He was enraged she'd slit his side. The stinging pain wouldn't cease as blood ran down to his hip, and he jabbed her knife into her chest.

He wanted to finish the job but she had her fucking keys to her mouth and blew a damn whistle over and over again before he back-handed it right out of her mouth.

He couldn't stay here.

He'd fucked this up royally.

But judging by the blood pooling and spreading over her chest, she wouldn't last much longer.

"Fucking die, bitch."

He left her bleeding out, jumped in his truck, and sped away, slamming his hand into the steering wheel, infuriated that she'd been expecting an attack.

And why not? She knew he'd already killed five others.

And tonight, he got number six.

The thought calmed him.

Maybe it hadn't gone as expected, but he'd still killed her.

They'd find her. They'd know it was him.

Even if they didn't, he knew.

And now he could go after Kate.

But first, he needed to deliver his final tribute to her. He'd planned for this and had the envelope all ready to slip in the florist's mail slot. A note for Kate, along with the cash and instructions for the delivery, all sealed together. No prints on the papers because he'd worn gloves. No DNA because he sealed it with water and a sponge. He drove to the shop, taking a small risk that his instructions wouldn't be carried out in time, but optimistic that kindness and a romantic heart would win the day, if not greed, because he'd left a hefty tip for the person who fulfilled his order.

Kate would get the roses, then he'd take Kate.

She would be the end of this and the rebirth of him.

Chapter Thirty-Seven

Kate arrived at her destination but hesitated to get out of the car. She stared at the house, the light on in the kitchen window, and wondered if she'd made a huge mistake. This was dangerous. She could get herself killed. She'd been impulsive and reckless.

But she had to know. And this felt like the only way.

If he was coming for her anyway, she was going to take *him* by surprise.

"Thank you for the ride." Kate slipped out of the vehicle and used her phone to complete the transaction. A few minutes after seven, she hoped Reed was home. She closed the rideshare app and kept another one open. In this case, she couldn't be too careful. She tucked the phone in her pocket and stared up at the house.

"In for a penny . . ." She liked Reed's place and wondered why they didn't spend more time at his ranch-style home with the contemporary updates. The house itself was white with black trim, gutters, and downspouts. The garden beds were filled with evergreen bushes and wood chips. The grass was thick and cut short. The two lantern-style lights on either side of the double front door invited you up to the porch.

He took care of this place. It was neat and tidy and welcoming.

All the houses on the street were well tended, but Reed's stood out because it was so effortlessly charming in its simplicity.

Did he want all the neighbors to believe he was just a normal guy? *Nothing to see or worry about here,* the place said to the world.

And one of the other properties he owned had the very cabin where six women's lives were cut short. The scene of her nightmare.

How could he not have known it was there?

Granted, there were acres and acres of trees concealing what lay in their depths.

There she went making excuses for him again.

Not anymore.

She wanted answers and he was going to give them to her this time.

She went up to the porch, put one hand in her purse, then knocked on the door and waited.

Was he stalking his next victim?

Had he already found her and taken her?

Was he hurting her right now?

Or was he simply out with that woman he was with today, talking about the police and how his girlfriend suspected him of being a serial killer?

Did he hate her for thinking that about him?

What would he say when he found her here at his house?

Would he lie?

Would he be able to convince her that he wasn't a monster?

It took her a second to realize he'd opened the door and stared in shock at her.

"What are you doing here?" He looked around, up and down the street. "Where is the agent watching over you?"

She really wanted to believe the concern was real.

But was the face of the man she loved hiding the monster within?

Fear that she didn't know truth from lies, she pulled the gun from her purse and pointed it at him. "I need to talk to you."

Reed went very still. "Okay. But, Kate, sweetheart, where is your guard?"

Did he want to know because he wanted to get rid of the agent? Or because he cared about her well-being?

She gave him the truth to see what he'd do. Come after her? Try to hurt her? Act like he wanted to make up with her, only to get her alone and . . . She stopped those wild thoughts and went with her gut. "I sneaked out to find you."

His lips pressed tight. "You came here alone." He planted his hands on his hips, swore under his breath, then pinned her in his direct gaze again. "You can't do that. What if he's watching the house and spotted you leaving? What if he'd taken you?" The worry in his voice matched the concern in his eyes.

"I need to talk to you," she snapped, not trusting herself to believe his upset or what she saw and heard.

Reed held up both hands. "Okay, sweetheart. Let's talk. Do you want to do it right here, or do you want to come inside?"

She wasn't sure.

"If a neighbor sees you with that gun, they're going to call the cops."

She waved the gun to get him to move back so she could walk in. "If you do anything to make me think you'll hurt me or something . . ."

Reed nodded, but still didn't move. "I would never hurt you. Ever."

Tears gathered in her eyes, but she held them back. "Go," she said, but it sounded more like a plea.

Reed walked backward very slowly, giving her time to step into the house and close the door. They stood in the entry, both staring at each other in the quiet house. "Do you want me to go into the kitchen or living room?"

"The living room." It gave her more room to put between them, along with the furniture.

He turned and walked straight forward. She followed.

Reed walked all the way to the back sliders, then turned around to face her, the sofa on her right, a chair and coffee table separating them. He held his hands up so she could see them.

"What did the FBI tell you about the cabin?" Reed asked.

"Nothing. Because there was nothing to find there except the nightmare I left behind."

"And what do you believe about me?" The question held a plea for her to believe in him.

"What am I supposed to believe?" She needed him to tell the truth.

"That I love you." He infused the words with all the warmth and emotion she was used to hearing in his voice.

Reed dropped his hands, a look of defeat coming over him as he hung his head. It took him a few seconds to look at her again. "I want you to believe me. I hate being apart from you. I hated seeing you at that place. I hate it even more that I own it. I wanted to set it on fire, or tear it to the ground with my bare hands." He held her gaze, his earnest and pleading. "I want you to know with all the certainty that I feel about how much I love you that I did not do the things they're accusing me of. Because you know me, Kate. I know you want to trust in me and what we shared, but I also know that everything you've been through, everything you've endured, all that makes you who you are now, also tells you to be cautious, to never feel like a victim again. I hope that I've made you feel safe and strong and secure in how I feel about you. It pisses me off that this guy not only made you feel unsafe in your own home but he's also made you afraid of me."

"I don't want to be," she shouted at him. "I want you to be *you*, not *him*."

He held his hands out. "I don't know how to prove it to you." His hands dropped back to his sides. "I can say the words. I can make you promises. I can hold you in my arms and tell you I love you. But none of that will make you believe me."

She shook the gun at him. "You were with all the women who were abducted."

"I was in the same place as them, sometimes at the exact same time. All but the first victim. I've thought about that a lot. Why could they tie me to all of them except her? Because he didn't know about me until after he'd taken the first victim. You didn't allow me to be at your house until later. He was always watching you. And then he started watching me."

Kate had to give her mind time to backtrack to the first time she'd received the rose. She and Reed had been seeing each other outside of their working relationship for only a couple of weeks. She'd botched the first few dates and was only just getting comfortable meeting him out at restaurants for dinner.

Reed continued to try to convince her. "It was so easy for the FBI to home in on me, the guy who came into your life when all this started happening. The second they started looking into me, they found all the connections to the victims. But he found a way to use me and my relationship with you to distract law enforcement and alienate me from you. Because he thinks you're *his*. He wants you, Kate. And *I'm* in his way."

That made a hell of a lot of sense.

But still . . . "What about the cabin? It's on your property!"

"I bought the land as an investment. Emily found out that Freddy and Henry Poole inherited the property nearby from their mother's side of the family. The FBI searched it today, too. I'm guessing Freddy and Henry used to play there as kids and fished there as adults and discovered the cabin on the property no one has used in more than twenty years. Maybe Freddy built the cabin himself for all I know. What I do know is that I had no idea it was there. Even if I did, I wouldn't have known it was the cabin where he took all his victims."

Kate swiped tears away from her cheeks. "It can't be you."

"It's not me," he assured her.

She finally got to what had allowed her to hold on to hope all this time that Reed wasn't the killer. "Victim number four. Cathy Evans."

"The cops have video of me with her in the taqueria where I get lunch at least once a week."

She appreciated his honesty. She needed more of it.

"Do you remember how we found out about her abduction?" It had taken her some time to work her way through her memories of the past many months after suspicion landed on Reed for her to be clear about the events and how they unfolded.

Reed took a moment to respond, probably like her, piecing together his recollection of that time frame. "She was the first victim we knew had been abducted right after it happened. The lieutenant called to see if you'd received the roses. It was also the first time we caught the asshole on camera. The cops think I sneaked out of the house while you were sleeping and left the roses."

"But I know you didn't because that was the second day in a row you'd woken me up before dawn." She gave him a pointed look.

His gaze heated and a grin tugged at his lips. "I sometimes can't sleep for wanting you. I like making sure you start your day with a smile, warm and satisfied in my arms."

The intimacy of those memories echoed through her. "And since it was the second day in a row I woke up happy . . . ," she prompted him.

"I couldn't have taken Cathy the morning she was abducted because I was with you. You weren't asleep at the time of the abduction. You can corroborate my alibi without the shadow that you were asleep and unaware if I slipped out and back into bed without disturbing you." Reed raked his fingers through his hair. "But will the police believe it when they keep insisting I'm sneaky enough to fool you?"

Someone threw open the front door so hard it crashed into the wall, startling her.

"FBI," the first of six men coming into the living room shouted.

Kate quickly hid the gun back in her purse before the agent spotted it.

The agent yelled at Reed, "Put your hands behind your head."

He complied immediately. One of the agents grabbed her and pulled her away from him.

Reed stood with his feet apart, hands at the back of his head, his gaze steady on her. "It's okay. Just do what they say."

While four agents held their guns up and pointed at Reed, one held her at his side, and the one who did all the talking went behind Reed, cuffed one hand, pulled it behind his back, then took his other hand, pulled it behind his back, and cuffed it, too.

Her heart thundered in her chest. This couldn't be right. "He didn't do anything."

"You're under arrest for the stabbing of Emily Bell," the agent informed him.

Reed's eyes went wide. "What? That's not possible. What? What's happened to her?"

"Don't say anything until you have a lawyer," Kate warned, shocked by the accusation and wondering who Emily Bell was.

Reed stared at her. "She's my lawyer."

Kate really needed a clear head. Anxiety and trauma were making it hard for her to think clearly. "She's the woman you were with today at the cabin?"

"Yes. She was there to make sure my rights weren't trampled when they executed the search warrant."

Agent Chapman walked into the room. "And while the cabin didn't give up any clues, your truck sure did."

Reed's eyes went wide. "What?"

"You just had to get number six over and done with, didn't you? So you could get to Kate." Agent Chapman pinned her in his gaze. "What are you doing here?"

She shrank at his tone. "I needed to talk to him."

"You could have been killed."

"He didn't do this." She knew it. Something wasn't right.

"I have evidence that says he did." Agent Chapman notched his chin toward the agent holding Reed. "Put him in my car. I'll question him at the office before we book him."

"I'm going with you." Kate tried to go, but Agent Chapman got in her way.

"You're supposed to be in protective custody."

"It's not Agent Kincaid's fault. I sneaked out. And now I'm going with you, because I know for a fact he didn't do this."

Agent Chapman shook his head. "You just don't want it to be him. But it is, Kate."

"Then you'll be able to prove that beyond a shadow of a doubt, won't you?"

Agent Chapman pressed his lips tight. "Fine. Maybe when you hear what I have against him, you'll be able to accept it and help us lock him up for good."

Chapter Thirty-Eight

Ryan found Kate alone, staring through the two-way mirror at Reed sitting in the other room, his hands handcuffed to the table in front of him.

Kate saw Ryan and sighed. "Thank God you're here."

He'd spent the last couple of hours bringing his boss up to speed and checking in with his sister and best friend, Ash, about the remodel going on at his house while he was away. He was hoping to talk to Molly again, but put that on hold to haul ass down here to be with Kate.

"Did you seriously sneak out of protective custody and confront Reed?"

"Yes. She did." Agent Kincaid joined them. "By the time I called in backup because I thought that asshole might have nabbed you, Agent Chapman was calling to update me that they'd received a call from local police about a stabbing victim. At first Agent Chapman was going to ignore it because the victim wasn't found in the river, until he heard the victim's name."

"Who is it?" Ryan asked.

"Emily Bell. Reed's attorney," the agent supplied.

Kate pressed her lips tight. "He didn't do it."

Agent Kincaid held up a paper. "I thought you might say that, so I brought the police report."

"He didn't do it," Kate said again.

"No?" The agent looked skeptical of Kate's obstinacy. "Information is still coming in from the scene, but Emily was found stabbed in the chest just like all the other women Reed killed."

"Where?" Kate asked.

"At her apartment building in the parking lot."

Kate shook her head. "That makes no sense."

"Why?" Ryan asked, wanting to understand Kate's thinking. Was she simply in denial? Or did she know something they didn't?

"So you're saying he drove home with her from the cabin earlier today, stabbed her at her apartment, then went home?"

Agent Kincaid raised a brow. "No." She looked at the report. "The call to 911 came in at 7:33 p.m."

"Had she been lying there dead for a couple of hours before she was found?" Kate looked disturbed by the prospect.

Agent Kincaid glanced at the report again, then gave Kate a quizzical look. "No. Someone heard a whistle blowing and followed the sound to investigate. They found Emily stabbed and called it in right away."

"Then it wasn't Reed. I arrived at his house a few minutes before that 911 call. I can prove it." She pulled out her phone and tapped on the screen a few times, then turned the phone to Ryan and the agent. "See. I arrived at Reed's house before Emily was killed."

Agent Kincaid frowned. "This proves what time you got to the house, but did you see Reed right away?"

"Yes. He opened the door immediately. We talked for some time before the FBI arrived and arrested him."

"How long?"

Kate tapped on her phone again, then turned it to them once more. "Twenty-seven minutes."

"Wait," Agent Kincaid said, looking more closely at the phone. "You recorded your conversation."

"Yes. I confronted him because I couldn't believe he was the killer and I also didn't want to be wrong if he was. I was feeling so confused and like nothing made sense anymore."

"That's perfectly understandable." Ryan affirmed Kate's feelings.

"I wanted it on the record if he happened to admit to doing it. And I wanted it on record if he denied it and proved it to me so that others would believe it, too."

"We'll need to verify this, but you're right." Agent Kincaid shifted her perspective. "He couldn't have been in two places at once and stabbed Emily. Maybe it was just a random act, a purse-snatching or carjacking gone wrong. The knife used wasn't long and thin like the other victims' wounds. In fact, the knife was still in her chest when she was found."

"So maybe this has nothing to do with the serial killer at all," Ryan suggested.

Agent Kincaid and Kate both looked skeptical.

Kate spoke her thoughts on the subject. "It's too coincidental. Reed didn't do it. So maybe he's right about all the rest, that he's being set up. If that's true, then killing his attorney would really point the police in his direction because he had opportunity. We all saw them together today and watched her drive him home."

"We need to work on the timeline with Reed to determine exactly when they parted ways and what Emily did once she left him." Agent Kincaid turned for the door. "I need to update Agent Chapman before he interrogates Reed."

"There's no reason to interrogate him now," Kate called.

Ryan stepped in front of Kate before she followed Agent Kincaid. "Actually, there is. They have other evidence."

Kate's brow furrowed. "But it's a lie. He didn't do it."

"They need to be sure, Kate. Evidence points to him. If they drop Reed as a person of interest and release him, and he takes and kills another woman—or goes after you—then it's on them. They can't just let him go without assessing the evidence properly and corroborating his alibi."

"He couldn't have taken Cathy Evans. He was with me that morning."

Ryan wondered how that information hadn't already been checked. "You're sure?"

"We saw the news report together that she'd been kidnapped outside her home. He'd spent the night with me. He woke me up early. Before the time the police said neighbors heard her scream." She gave him a look that suggested Reed had seduced her awake.

As alibis went, that one was good. So long as Kate wasn't covering for her boyfriend.

"Kate?"

"If it was him, I'd be the first to want him stopped. My life is on the line. Why do you think I brought a gun to see him earlier tonight?" She pulled the weapon from her purse, just long enough for him to see it before she hid it again.

"Kate," he admonished. "What if he was the killer and took that from you?"

"If I thought it was him, I'd have shot him first."

Ryan believed her. She'd had enough of being terrorized, her life being turned upside down, and if it had been the man she'd fallen for, she'd want to hurt him even more for tricking and manipulating her like that.

Agents Chapman and Kincaid returned.

"Kincaid brought me up to speed on how long you were with Reed tonight." Agent Chapman looked through the glass at Reed, still stewing in the other room. "He's got an alibi for tonight."

"And one for Cathy Evans's abduction. He was with me that morning, too."

Agent Kincaid looked skeptical. "If he was with you, and someone else is pinning this on him, wouldn't they have made sure Reed was home? Alone. With no alibi."

Kate grinned. "Maybe it looked like he was home, but he was with me."

"What do you mean?" Agent Chapman asked.

"Reed and I suspected we were both being watched. So sometimes he'd leave his truck at home, go out the back of his house into the alleyway, walk a few blocks away, and take a rideshare to my place. He'd sneak in through the back so whoever was watching would think I was home alone. That way if they tried to get me, Reed would be there to protect me without the killer knowing."

Ryan remembered Kate telling him this when they spoke at her home and had to admit they'd been smart. "Okay, if Reed isn't the killer, we need to figure out who is. Serial killers want recognition. Why is this killer using the Rose Reaper to gain attention but putting the blame on someone else? The only answer that fits, as I see it, is that he's hoping to finish what the Reaper started, kill Kate, Reed goes down for it, then he gets to continue on with whatever he's got planned next."

Agent Chapman nodded. "We've seen the shift in how he hurt Anne Murphy. He's not happy being confined to how the Reaper killed. He needs more."

Kate looked to Agent Chapman. "Ryan says you have other proof connected to Reed. What is it?"

"You can listen in while I ask him about it. Right now there's a lot of circumstantial evidence that points to Reed. But there's no clear motive for him to be the one doing this. He's well liked by friends, coworkers, even his exes. He's got no criminal background. Not a single domestic disturbance call. No indication he's violent in any way."

Ryan thought about that. "It's unusual that someone just starts killing for no reason. Not like this. Especially when the Rose Reaper last killed nearly four years ago. Copycats usually pop up within a year, maybe two from the original murders. That's not to say they don't happen later, but it's rare."

"So something triggered our killer and that somehow connects to the Reaper," Agent Kincaid filled in.

"But what?" Agent Chapman asked.

Ryan had a niggling of an idea in the back of his mind but needed more information for it to seem plausible. "Get Reed talking. Go through the evidence. Let's see if we can all figure this out."

Agent Chapman nodded his agreement. "You, Kate, and Agent Kincaid watch from here. If anything strikes you, or you can add to the conversation, text it to me. I'm tired of this case pointing in one direction that doesn't make sense."

That was exactly how Ryan saw things, too.

But that's how cases went: you built it on one piece of evidence at a time until things added up to a decisive conclusion. In this case, Reed seemed like the right suspect, but nothing they had on him was irrefutable.

Ryan felt like they were on the cusp of figuring out why the circumstantial evidence pointed to Reed and how that connected back to whoever was the real killer.

Chapter Thirty-Nine

Ryan stood beside Kate as Agent Chapman walked into the other room and sat with his back to the two-way mirror, facing Reed.

"Is Kate okay?" Reed asked immediately, his gaze not on the agent but the glass.

"She's fine. But you and I need to talk. You need to be very specific and forthcoming with your answers. This is serious, Reed. I need to know if it wasn't you who stabbed Emily Bell, then who is trying so damn hard to make me believe it was you?"

Reed's gaze shifted from the glass to the agent. "So you finally believe me. I didn't do this."

"I know you didn't attack Emily tonight. The MO is different. But then I have to ask myself, was it a random attack? And if it was, why did she point the finger at you?"

"What?" Reed looked shocked and confused. "Did she say I attacked her?"

"In a way." Agent Chapman tapped the tablet screen and turned it to Reed. "She used her blood to tell us who attacked her."

Ryan wanted to see the photo but couldn't.

Kate looked at him, then back at Reed. "We need to see that picture."

Agent Chapman probably knew they were anxiously waiting to see it. "She drew an *R* on the pavement in her blood."

Reed furrowed his brow and shook his head. "That makes no sense."

Agent Chapman swiped his finger across the screen to another picture. "Tell me why we found victim number one, Denise Simmons's, cell phone in your truck with your prints on it."

Reed's eyes went wide. "What? No. That can't be. How the hell would my prints get on her phone? I've never met her. As far as I know, I was never near her like you linked me to the other victims."

Agent Chapman swiped the screen again. "And that's where this gets really interesting. One of the agents remembered that we were able to connect you to victim number two, Kelly Russell. You two were in the same coffee shop. We had video of you standing behind her. But the video showed something else. An exchange you had with a guy in a hoodie. Kelly bumped into him, because he stepped into her as she stepped back from the counter. Was it intentional? We think so, because then he drops his phone and it appears he asked you to pick it up."

Reed seemed to be watching the video. "He never looks up enough to see his face through the hoodie."

Agent Chapman notched his chin toward the tablet. "And you barely looked at him."

Reed scrunched his lips. "I just did the guy a favor. I think he said he'd hurt his back and couldn't bend over."

Agent Chapman leaned forward. "What else do you remember?"

"He was young. Early twenties, maybe. He bought my coffee to say thanks for the help." Reed looked thoughtful. "How the hell did he put the phone in my truck?"

"That's what I'd like to know. We found it under the driver's seat."

Reed sighed and tried to sit back, but with his hands chained to the table, he couldn't manage it. "I leave my truck unlocked on jobsites all the time. I lock it when I'm home. If he's the killer and he's been following me, he could have put it in there at any time between then and now. It's a work truck. I don't clean it out very often."

"We found other evidence in your house."

Reed's face paled. "What the . . . He's been in my house?"

"In the time you've been here, the forensic team has found at least one item from each victim known to have belonged to them."

"There's no way." Reed shook his head. "It can't be."

"They were all neatly tucked into a drawer in one of the tool chests in your garage. Mostly clothes. A couple of pieces of jewelry."

"His trophies." Ryan watched this all play out, thinking about how the killer had set up Reed.

"Why would he give up his trophies? I thought killers held on to them so they could relive their kills over and over again." Kate cringed.

"Some do. In this case, the things were used to implicate Reed, so we'd think they were *his* trophies. It feels like our killer is doing this as a tribute to the Rose Reaper and his real desire is whatever comes next."

Agent Chapman swiped the screen again. "This is the video you sent us of the guy outside Kate's house leaving the flowers. Do you recognize him now?"

Reed studied the screen. "It's too hard to see his face. The hoodie is cov . . . Shit. You think it's the same guy in the hoodie in the coffee shop."

Agent Chapman shrugged. "I mean. Black jeans and hoodies don't exactly identify this guy in any way. They're common clothing for so many. Men and women. But it's something that ties these two people together. Coincidence? Maybe. But it seems we've been dealing with nothing but coincidence." Agent Chapman glanced at the figure on the tablet. "Unless it's not."

"Because I've been right all along and this guy is setting me up."

"Or he just wants to distract us with you so he can get to Kate," the agent suggested.

Ryan had to wonder if this killer's endgame included killing Kate and revealing Reed wasn't the killer so he could take the credit he wanted, or if he planned to let Reed go down for the crimes.

"Is there anything about this guy you can remember? His hair color? Eyes? Did he have a beard? A tattoo? Something?" Agent Chapman prompted.

Reed shook his head. "No. It was a random encounter. It didn't mean anything to me. I just did what anyone would do and helped the guy out."

Agent Chapman pointed at the screen. "This guy is setting you up. You need to help me out here if you want to prove it. This guy is getting close to you." Agent Chapman tapped his finger on the tablet. "He was a foot away from you. You talked to him."

Reed leaned forward. "I don't remember." His eyes filled with anguish. "He's going to get away with this fucking tribute to some psycho whose own brother let him get away with killing women like he owed it to him."

Ryan's whole being lit up with an epiphany. That thing niggling at the back of his mind didn't seem so far-fetched all of a sudden. "Wait here," he said to Kate and the other agent as he ran out of the room and into the one with Reed and Agent Chapman.

The agent glanced up at him in shock that he'd burst into the room like this and interrupt an interrogation. "Ryan?"

"Show me the video of Reed and the guy at the coffee place?" The urgency in his voice made the agent sit up and quickly swipe the screen to the video.

Agent Chapman handed him the tablet. "What are you looking for?"

Ryan watched the video, rewound it to be sure he saw what he expected to see, then handed the tablet to the agent again. "Now the one from Kate's house of the killer leaving the message."

Agent Chapman pulled it up and handed the tablet back to him.

Ryan watched, rewound it twice to be sure he wasn't just seeing things he wanted to see. "It's him."

"Who?"

"He went fishing on the river as a kid. He inherited everything from his father and his uncle. He owns the property connected to where we found the cabin. Of course he'd explore it, looking for where his uncle took his victims."

Agent Chapman raised a brow. "You think it's Phillip Poole? He's just a kid."

"He's nineteen. And every time we've seen him he does the same thing. It's a repetitive gesture." Ryan demonstrated and shrugged his shoulders.

Agent Chapman's eyes went wide. "Okay. Yeah. I noticed it, too, but didn't think much of it other than he seemed to do it to punctuate everything he said. Like talking with your hands, but this guy did it with his shoulders."

"Exactly." Ryan tapped the screen and played the video of Phillip leaving roses and a note for Kate. "Watch." He turned the tablet so the agent and Reed could both see the killer step to the gate, lean over and place the roses and note, then stand tall, shrug, then point at the camera. "Did you catch it?"

"Yeah," they both said.

Reed swiped back to the coffee shop footage. "Now watch this." He played that video. The guy in the hoodie asked Reed to pick up his phone, shrugged, then took the phone from Reed, shrugged again, thanked Reed, said something else, and ended the exchange with a final shrug before talking to the barista.

"He does it three times," Reed pointed out.

"He can't help himself," Ryan said. "It's an innate gesture. He doesn't even think about it anymore." Ryan tried to think things through. "He spent time with his uncle. He knew the man and what he was like. Maybe he didn't know everything back when he was a kid, but then his father dies and he inherits everything from both of them. He had all those journals from his father. What if they said more than he shared with us?"

Ryan thought about how Henry poured out his guilt on the pages of all those journals and to his wife in drunken confessions. He couldn't contain his grief over losing his brother and complicity in making Freddy the monster he became. Freddy had shielded his brother as much as he could, and Henry blamed himself for not being strong enough to do the same for Freddy or stop him from turning into a murderer to ease his pain.

Ryan remembered the suicide note Henry left behind and how it echoed his own thoughts now. The odd wording he'd used to express his grief struck a new chord for him now. He pulled it up on his phone. "Phillip read the suicide note to us, leading us to believe that his father couldn't live with what Freddy had done. But what if his father wrote that letter about what he saw in his own son? Something he'd already lived through with Freddy."

Ryan pulled up the picture of it on his phone and read the words again. *"I can't do it anymore. I've tried so hard to forget the past but it keeps coming back. I tried to steer things in the right direction but I've found myself right back where I started and ended."* Ryan paused and gave his interpretation. "If his son's behavior reminded him of Freddy, then he would have tried to steer Phillip away from hurting others and toward being kind." Ryan read more. *"I thought it was over. But I fear it only inspired instead of deterred."* Ryan looked at both Agent Chapman and Reed, hoping they got it, too. "He thought it ended when Freddy died, but all that did was inspire Phillip. *'I can't stay and feel what's left of my heart ravished with this darkness that is a living thing I can't stop or destroy.'* He watched his brother succumb to his darkness. He can't watch the same thing happen to his son. *'I am helpless. I am complicit. I am responsible.'* He gave life to Phillip. He can't turn in his own son. *'I need it to end so I can escape the torment that is coming.'* So he took his life so he didn't have to live with what Phillip was going to do, because he knew what drove Freddy to kill was also inside Phillip. The darkness. The need they both had to fulfill."

Agent Chapman swore.

Ryan thought more about the journals. "If the social worker encouraged Henry to keep a journal to help him process his feelings, or at least get them out, then I bet she did the same with Freddy. Maybe the reason Phillip knows so much about the Rose Reaper is because Freddy left behind a record of what he'd done and Phillip used it as a playbook and an excuse. Maybe Henry was right, it inspired Phillip, so he's paying homage to his uncle for giving him permission to unleash this part of him that maybe otherwise would have remained a dark fantasy."

"This is all speculation," Agent Chapman stated, though he looked like he believed it.

Ryan held his gaze. "It is until we prove it."

"We need to do a deep dive on Phillip, the way we did on you," Agent Chapman said to Reed.

"What if that's how he got the phone in my truck?" Reed asked. "He showed up at the search of my property. Why? He shouldn't have been there, right?"

Agent Chapman nodded. "No. He said he was curious."

"I'll bet," Ryan said. "He wanted to see us find the cabin. Maybe he even hoped we'd bring Kate there."

"And you did," Kate said from the doorway a split second before she rushed to Reed, stood behind him, and put her hands on his shoulders.

Reed immediately pressed his cheek to Kate's forearm.

Agent Kincaid also joined them. "Phillip watched her the whole time she was there."

Kate brushed her fingers through Reed's hair. "He came up to me and apologized for his uncle on behalf of the family. I didn't know what to say."

Agent Kincaid went back to the evidence. "There's nothing in the cabin that says he's been there. Just a partial footprint out front."

"That matched Reed's boot perfectly," Agent Chapman blurted out.

Ryan remembered something else. "They were wearing the same exact boots."

"Are you sure?" Agent Chapman asked.

Ryan thought back to earlier in the day. "Yes. I'm sure of it. I had a random thought that I didn't get the memo to wear rugged boots to the scene and I should have because we needed them out there. My tennis shoes were wet and I slipped a lot."

Reed looked up at him. "He could have followed me and Emily back to town, waited until after she dropped me off at home, thought I was in for the night, then went after her." Tears gathered in his eyes. "I wouldn't have had an alibi."

Kate squeezed Reed's shoulders. "But then I showed up while he attacked Emily."

Reed blinked away the moisture in his eyes and sucked in a steadying breath to ease his grief, then leaned forward. "Pull up the picture of what Emily wrote in her blood."

Agent Chapman did and laid the tablet on the table so all of them could see it.

Ryan stared at it. "What if that's not an *R* for Reed, but a *P* and her finger just slipped as she lost consciousness?"

Agent Chapman turned thoughtful for a moment, then divulged his thoughts. "It doesn't make sense the way he attacked her like that, with a knife that isn't anything like the blade he uses on his other victims."

Reed's anguished frown deepened. "Emily carried a knife with her everywhere she went," he supplied. "She told me if I was being followed by the killer and the women around me were being abducted and killed, she didn't want to be an easy target."

"Did you ever see the knife?" Agent Chapman asked.

"Yes. She pulled it out of her purse with a bunch of other stuff when she was trying to find a pen. I told her if she wanted to use it as protection she should keep it on her person in a way that she could get to it easily. It's silver and black with a clip on one side. The blade flips out really easily. She started wearing it on her hip beneath her shirts."

Agent Chapman tapped the screen a few times and pulled up another photo. "Is that the knife?"

"Yes," Reed confirmed.

"There is a vague description of the guy who sped away in a truck. Guess what it was?"

"A guy in a black hoodie," Reed, Kate, and Ryan all said in unison.

"Yeah." Agent Chapman held Ryan's gaze. "And the truck description matches that of the one Freddy Poole used to drive."

"Let me guess, Phillip inherited it." Ryan couldn't believe Phillip would use it, but he guessed it made sense since he was living out his uncle's dark deeds.

"Yes," Agent Chapman confirmed. "What else do you think he's hiding in that storage place he was so ready to show us?"

"He can't know we're onto him," Kate said. "We have an opportunity to set a trap."

"They are not using you as bait," Reed immediately interjected.

Agent Chapman met Reed's direct gaze. "If he believes Emily was his sixth victim, then Kate is all he needs to finish what his uncle started."

"Do we have any actual proof it's him, besides Ryan's assumption that this guy's body language matches Phillip's?" Agent Kincaid asked.

"When Emily wakes up from surgery, she can ID him." Agent Chapman grinned when all of them gasped.

"She's alive?" Reed asked, not believing it but looking hopeful it was true.

"Yes. Though last I checked, critical. I think she fought Phillip off as best she could. When he stabbed her, he probably thought she'd bleed out. But help got to her quickly, so there's a very good chance she'll pull through."

Reed let out a huge sigh of relief and hung his head.

Kate squeezed Reed's shoulders again. "That's all the more reason why we need to make Phillip, or whoever the killer is, believe she's dead. So he can attempt the rest of his plan. I assume he'll somehow leave the roses."

"Then what?" Agent Chapman asked.

Agent Kincaid answered, "We have local police put out a fake press release that Emily is dead. Maybe we attribute it to a random carjacking gone bad."

"He'll be furious he doesn't get the credit," Reed speculated.

Ryan shook his head. "I don't think he cares at this point. It's all about Kate now. He was so close to you today. He didn't take the time to stalk Emily and find the best opportunity to grab her without being seen. He was impulsive and it cost him. He didn't get to play out the Reaper's kill. He wants the seven done so he can move on. We saw it with Anne. He lost control. It's getting harder and harder for him to hold back. Emily dead by his hand is enough to make him move on to Kate as soon as possible. But he'll need a way to get to her. He knows she's in protective custody."

Kate gasped. "That's why he went after Emily tonight. To finish the sixth victim before the FBI moved me to a secure location. He must have overheard that I made the request today. If I'm hidden, he can't get to me, which means he's going to need to get to me tonight or tomorrow morning."

Agent Kincaid nodded. "He doesn't know you're not at the house. We'll have to sneak you back in somehow."

"Agent shift change," Agent Chapman suggested. "But this time, we'll show that we're putting more agents at the house. After all, he'll expect that because Emily is supposedly dead."

Ryan liked the plan. "We'll need to be ready for anything. Most especially Phillip trying to lure Kate out to him."

Agent Chapman looked across the table at Reed. "I can't release you just yet. If he sees you go home, he'll know something is up."

Agent Kincaid offered a suggestion. "We bring Phillip in for questioning. We say that no one except Reed saw Emily after the search of the property. We want to know if he saw or heard anything today."

"It can't be tonight," Kate said. "It needs to feel like you're still one hundred percent looking at Reed. Plus, we need to see if he actually leaves me the roses and thinks of Emily as victim number six. We can't jump the gun on this and tip our hand. He thinks he's winning."

Agent Chapman nodded. "It's going to be a long night. I'm going to have the team pulling every record we can find on Phillip Poole. I want to know how this guy thinks and what in his past can help us figure out what he'll do next."

"We need to speak to his mother again." With what they suspected now, Ryan knew Ms. Poole would be invaluable and insightful when it came to her son. If they could get her to cooperate.

Agent Chapman agreed with a nod. "I'll have her picked up and brought in first thing in the morning. I'll also put a team on Phillip."

"And protection for Emily," Reed added.

Ryan wondered if Phillip would see them coming. "He'll be watching for surveillance."

Agent Chapman shrugged. "I can't take a chance that he slips away now."

"I don't think he will." Ryan doubted Phillip could deny the compulsion to finish what the Reaper started and not kill Kate. "He has a plan of some sort. Otherwise he wouldn't have openly used Kate to tell law enforcement what he was doing. It's blatant. It invites discovery. It makes it hard for him to get to Kate. So how is he going to get her?"

Agent Chapman threw up his hands. "That's the million-dollar question."

Kate didn't look frightened or deterred at all. "We know he's coming. He doesn't know we know about him. We have an advantage. We just need to figure out how to use it."

"Leave that to us." Agent Chapman leaned over and unlocked Reed's handcuffs.

Reed rubbed at his wrists as he stood, turned, and wrapped Kate in a hug. "I'm so glad this part is over and you believe I didn't do any of this."

Kate held on tight. "We're going to get him. For all of it."

Ryan breathed a huge sigh of relief for Kate and Reed, even though this wasn't over yet. They still needed to catch the killer.

Agent Chapman picked up the tablet. "I'm going to get my team working on Phillip's background." He stared at Reed. "I'll have an agent take you to a hotel tonight. Agent Kincaid and several other agents will take Kate back to her house to wait and see if Phillip makes contact." He directed his next comments to Kate. "We'll dress you like an agent and sneak you into the house. Anyone have any questions?"

Ryan shook his head. "I'll leave you to it with your team. Kate, I'll come by in the morning and stay with you. Hopefully, this ends soon."

Ryan waited for Agent Kincaid, three other agents, and Kate, wearing an FBI hat and jacket, and they all left the building. "See you in the morning," he called to Kate as she was led to one of the FBI vehicles and he walked to his rental.

Kate waved to him and gave him a smile. She had to be tired and feeling happy that she and Reed would soon be reunited. She hadn't trusted the wrong man. The dreams and plans she and Reed had made for their future were still going to happen.

Not everyone got a happy ending. Ryan hoped for Kate's sake she got hers.

He drove back to his hotel and received several texts on the way that he couldn't look at while he was driving. He assumed it was either Molly or his sister and couldn't wait to get to his room, order something hot to eat, take a shower, and maybe spend some time on the phone with Molly. After today, he could use some mundane talk about how her day went. She'd make him laugh. He'd flirt with her. Maybe even set up a date for when he returned.

The hotel parking lot was packed, but he found a spot near the back and climbed out of the car, ready for this day to be over, when someone hooked an arm around his neck and poked him with something.

"Night night."

Ryan recognized the voice right before he blacked out and thought, *Oh, shit. I'm dead.*

Chapter Forty

Sometimes, you have to improvise and strike while everyone is distracted by that other thing that happened.

He thought about using Reed to get to Kate, but that was too obvious. They'd expect that.

No one would expect him to take the other man in Kate's life, the one who came to help her yet again as a killer took her back to the past.

Well, he was so close to the future he had planned.

Now all he had to do was get Kate to come running to Ryan's rescue.

Not that she'd save him. Or herself.

No. He had plans for her.

And what comes next.

So he made the call.

"You didn't have to call to check on me again. I'm home. I'm safe. All is well." Kate sounded so at ease and sure.

"Sorry, my rose, but Ryan's unavailable at the moment."

Kate gasped.

"Before you alert your bodyguards, my rose, you need to know that if you say a word, clue them in in any way, he's dead."

"Yes, Ryan, it was a difficult day being at the cabin."

"I bet it was. So many memories."

A door closed in the background. "I'm in my room. What do you want, Phillip?"

"Who figured it out? You? I hope it was you after we spoke today. I could see why my uncle chose you, his rose among the weeds."

"Actually, it was Ryan."

Phillip stared at his guest. "I mean, it makes sense, given his job. Right?"

Kate didn't answer. She didn't want to engage.

Well, he didn't give her a choice. "Not in the mood to play?"

"This isn't a game," she snapped. "So tell me what you want and let Ryan go. He's not a part of this."

"But he is. He's the one who got inside your head and made you spill all the Reaper's secrets. My parents always thought I needed to see a shrink. Maybe I'll hold on to Ryan for a while and hear what he has to say about me now that I can be me."

"You're sick. You need help."

"I am what I am. Now . . . if you want to save Ryan, then I suggest you come."

"Why would I do that when I know you're just going to kill me?"

"Because I know your secret. The one you didn't tell any of them." She gasped.

He smiled. "You know where to find me. Come alone, or things could get very messy. See you soon. Don't keep me waiting. I get bored. And Ryan may not be . . . whole when you get here."

Chapter Forty-One

Kate turned to Agent Kincaid, who she'd waved close to listen to the call. "Did you hear all that?" Her heart pounded with urgency to get to Ryan.

She nodded. "What's the secret, Kate?"

She caught her breath, then confessed. "I've never told anyone, not even my therapist. I mentioned it to Ryan, but I didn't tell him everything. At first, I thought it was a stupid thing to do. But then . . . it helped. And now they're both gone, so . . . I let them rest in peace and tried to move on. But now this . . ." Anxiety had her holding her hands tightly together.

"What's the secret?" the agent pressed. "We don't have a lot of time. He's got Ryan. We need to move now to save him."

"That's just it. I think I'm the only one who can."

"How?"

She could do this. She could bring down another killer. "You need to let me go in alone. I can get him to confess to everything. He wants to tell me how he's better than his uncle. I can use that. I can save Ryan." She had to save him. He was in danger because of her. "I know something about the place we're going to that Phillip doesn't know."

Agent Kincaid didn't budge. "We can't put your life at risk. Not like that."

Kate appreciated the concern. "I want to do it. I need to do it. This is my fault." She wanted Phillip to pay for everything he'd done.

Agent Kincaid's head tilted, a question already in her eyes. "How are you to blame for any of this?"

"It's always been about me. He's using Ryan to get to me."

"We speculated that if it wasn't Reed, then the killer might use him to get to you."

Kate thought so, too. "Phillip was smart to take Ryan. None of us expected that."

Agent Kincaid stepped close. "The secret, Kate."

"Everyone knows about the cabin now. It's not a secret anymore. But no one knows about the place where Freddy and Henry were tortured as children. I met Henry there the week before he committed suicide. He told me about Freddy and his mother, all the terrible things she did to them. He showed me the place she'd locked them up when they were bad for days without food and water. If Phillip is doing this to somehow connect with, or pay homage to his uncle, then that's where Phillip is holding Ryan. It's the Rose Reaper's final resting place. It's on the property you searched today, though you never found it. I think in some twisted way Phillip wants his uncle to see him kill me."

"So there's another structure on Reed's property?"

"No. On Freddy's. Well, Phillip's now, I guess." She'd been so focused on the cabin, she hadn't even thought about Freddy's underground makeshift crypt.

"And you didn't say anything?"

"I didn't think my meeting with Henry had anything to do with the murders happening now."

Agent Kincaid ran her fingers through her short golden hair. "Agent Chapman is not going to like this."

"I don't care. I need to get to Ryan."

"You're not leaving without us."

She started planning in her head, feeling the clock ticking and Ryan's desperation to be saved, because that's how she'd felt when she'd been held against her will. "He needs to see me arrive alone."

Agent Kincaid shook her head. "Not happening."

"I have a plan. But I need your help." She couldn't hide the urgency from her voice. "We'll go over everything on the way." Kate thought quickly through the logistics and alternate scenarios, didn't find any huge holes, then grabbed what she needed from her room. "It's going to work. I know it will." She needed Ryan to survive. She couldn't live with herself if he got hurt or killed because of her. "You just need to trust me. And help me pull it off." This time she wouldn't be alone against a killer.

Agent Kincaid followed her out of the room. "You're being reckless, you know that. He wants to kill you."

Fear clawed at her throat, but it didn't stop her. "What happens if I send you to him and you end up in a standoff? He'll just kill Ryan and probably do exactly what his uncle did." She wouldn't let Phillip take the easy way out. "Not this time. This time, I'm going to make him take responsibility for everyone he's hurt."

Chapter Forty-Two

Ryan woke up in increments. First he heard someone humming nearby. Then he felt the dull headache behind his eyes. He sensed that he was in a large room. It smelled dank and musty, like a basement. No. A cellar.

The chill sent goose bumps rising on his skin. The presence of someone drawing closer rose the hairs on the back of his neck, but he didn't open his eyes. Not yet. Better to stay still and calm. Especially since his hands were bound behind the chairback and his ankles were tied to the legs. The ropes were already biting into his skin.

"I know you're awake. The dose I gave you should only last thirty to forty-five minutes given your weight. Though I think my estimate was fairly close. So come on, Mr. Psychologist, let's talk."

Of course the asshole knew the dose, he was studying pharmacology. No telling what kind of twisted things he had planned using drugs to subdue his victims.

Ryan opened his eyes and stared up at Phillip. "What do you want to talk about?"

"Serial killers."

"They're all the same and different." Ryan looked around the dank underground room. Dirt floor, stone walls, crumbling in places. Rough wood beams and rotting floorboards overhead. Stairs leading up to storm doors behind Phillip. Two chairs and an old table in front of him with a lantern, two urns, and a wooden box. No windows. He appreciated the shelves off to one side that held several lanterns, their soft light chasing away the deep shadows. Ryan didn't dare turn away from the predator eyeing him to look at anything else. "Where are we?"

"I guess you'd say the place that made my uncle."

"Your grandmother made Freddy." It wasn't a place, it was a person. Someone a child should be able to trust unequivocally.

"Did she? Or was he born that way and she brought it out of him? I mean, look at her and what she did."

"I'm guessing someone, probably her mother or father, someone very close to her, did the same to her."

Phillip frowned. "Hurt people, hurt people. I've heard that bullshit."

"You don't believe it."

"Do you really think all so-called bad people are made?"

"You don't think that what your grandmother and uncle did, what you're doing now, isn't bad?"

"I used to think there was something dark and deadly inside me. Now I know I'm the dark and deadly thing."

The words chilled Ryan to the bone.

Fear made a fine sheen of sweat coat his body. But Ryan tried to stay focused.

He tilted his head and studied Phillip, who looked back, avidly interested in what Ryan might say next. "You made a choice." He kept his voice calm, steady, trying not to show an ounce of the anxiety building inside him. "You're not lashing out. You're not trying to feel something other than a pain that someone put on you and you can't let it go. You idolized your uncle. You saw the recognition he received and you wanted that for yourself. Because yes, there is something inside you that you let out. You knew it was wrong and you did it anyway. And now you can't stop. It's an unfulfilled desire you'll never quench. You tried to maintain the illusion that you were doing this as some tribute to your uncle, but really, you simply wanted to do it. And now, it's not enough to follow in his footsteps. You need to cause more pain, you need the kills to be more brutal. You need to test your limits and his MO is just restraining you. Because of what happened to him, he used those women to find control. Maybe the first one or two were to feel that relief he felt when he killed his mother. But after that, I think he killed them to show them mercy after what he'd done to them. Mercy his mother never showed him."

"I have no mercy." Pride filled those words.

Ryan felt the lick of terror race up his spine that any second Phillip could lash out and kill him. Still, he tried to remain outwardly calm and reasonable. "That doesn't make you better than him. You're a killer, just like all the others. There is no game, except the one you think you're playing. This frenzy inside you, it's what's going to get you caught faster."

Ryan hoped Phillip heard the truth, that this was not going to end well for him. He wasn't going to walk away free to continue killing to slake the need inside him.

Phillip shook his head frantically. "Kate will die. More will die."

"You should have abandoned this quest for Kate already. You shouldn't have sent those roses and taunted her. You think you can get away with what your uncle couldn't. Such arrogance. It's delusional. They know who you are now. They will stop you." Ryan hoped Phillip saw the error of his ways. "Turn yourself in, before the cops come for you. You don't want to get hurt." Phillip didn't want to find himself facing a bunch of cops with guns like his uncle.

"She got him killed!"

Ryan shook his head. "No. Your uncle should have done what you didn't do either. He should have let her go and run. Instead, he went after her. He needed to finish what he started. You have that in common. And when faced with life behind bars or death by cop, he took the easy way out. He didn't take responsibility for what he'd done. Will you?"

Phillip glared.

"You want the fame, not the consequences. Those are for other people. You want what you want and you'll take it every chance you get now."

"So that's it, there's no hope for someone like me?"

"Hope is for people who want to change. You don't. You love it. You can't get enough of it. And because of that, you'll make mistakes and you'll be caught. It's already happening."

"I'm too smart for that."

Ryan rolled his eyes. "Said nearly every person ever who thought they could get away with a crime. The FBI will never stop hunting you." Ryan looked down at himself. "And you took me. What's the plan? Get Kate here, you kill her, me, then escape?"

"Yes."

Ryan shook his head. "I'm sure you think you've thought of everything, but you haven't. But let's say you do pull this off. Then what? You go on a killing spree somewhere else. You'll be a wanted man for the rest of your life. Something will trip you up. Someone will recognize you, because believe me, your face will be plastered all over the news."

Phillip grinned. "Good. Let them make me a sensation. I'll have exceeded my uncle's body count."

"Is that what this is about? Besting him?" Ryan didn't say anything about Emily still being alive.

"Or do you just want revenge against the person who escaped your uncle?" Kate stood on the cellar stairs, her gaze laser focused on Phillip.

A shock wave of surprise went through Ryan. He couldn't believe she was here. Hope bloomed in his heart that he might actually get out of this alive.

She came down the last few stairs and stepped into what was probably a root cellar back in the day, looking confident and cautious.

Phillip walked toward her and pulled a rope. A metal door slammed above the stairs Kate had descended. "Welcome to the party. It's small and intimate. And only one of us is getting out alive." Phillip glanced over to the corner behind Ryan.

He turned and stared at the hole in the ground along with a large sheet of plastic spread beside it. His heart accelerated as his breath hitched at the sight of the shallow grave.

Phillip started humming a song or something.

Ryan turned back to the looming threat.

Kate tilted her head and squinted her eyes. "I know that song. What is it?"

"I thought you'd remember. He hummed it all the time. 'Roses are red, violets are blue. If you see me . . . it's too late for you.'"

Kate shivered with the icy chill that evoked in both of them.

Phillip grinned. "It was the song stuck in his head, the calling he had to answer. And now it's in me. And once this is done, I can continue to answer that call. Over and over and over again, racking up the body count."

Ryan thought he sounded like a gamer, playing one of those games where killing scored you points and desensitized you to violence. It was just another scene, another point to win.

Kate backed away a few steps and stood between Ryan and Phillip off to the side, her hands at her thighs, her gaze fixed on Phillip.

"You sound so sure of yourself," Kate said, looking confident.

Ryan hoped that was because she hadn't come alone. A bead of sweat trickled down from his hairline to his jaw.

"Did you leave your escort up top?" Phillip didn't seem fazed by the possibility the FBI was right outside the cellar door.

"I came alone as you requested."

Phillip tsked. "You're not a very good liar. But no matter. They won't be able to get through the locking mechanism I installed anytime soon."

If Phillip intended to keep on killing, yet they were locked in this room with the FBI waiting outside to take him down, then how did

Phillip expect to get out of here alive? Phillip had nothing to lose, but he also wanted to continue his killing spree, so he obviously didn't think he was going to die down here.

Kate seemed as much at ease as one could be locked in a room with a killer, which meant the FBI had to be here, too, and she expected them to get them out safely.

He had to be missing something.

Phillip looked Kate over. "Remove your coat and toss it to me. Slowly."

Kate complied, the shaking of her hand the only show of fear.

Phillip ran his hand over the coat, looking to see if Kate had a weapon. All he found was her phone. He shut it off. "Do a nice, slow turn for me."

Kate complied again, though she turned her head, keeping Phillip in sight the whole time.

"Now, raise your shirt and do it again so I can see you're not wearing a wire."

"Does it matter if I am? You already suspect the FBI is outside."

"Still. I don't need to make their job easy."

Kate pulled up her shirt and did the spin thing again. "But you already have by locking us down here." Kate kept her back to the wall of rickety wood shelves behind her. The rest of the room spread out in front of her.

Ryan worried the shelves with the lanterns would break, the lanterns would fall, and they'd all go up in flames.

Ryan felt a draft behind him, sneaked a peek, but couldn't see anything but a wood pallet leaning against the wall.

"Do you know where I'm standing?" Phillip asked Kate. "He told you, right?"

Chapter Forty-Three

A chill ran up Kate's spine. She needed to keep him talking so he'd confess everything he so obviously wanted to brag about with the pride she saw in his eyes. But being in this confined space with a cold-blooded killer scared her out of her mind. Still, she held it together, remembered the plan, and answered Phillip's question, even as her heart clenched at his callous action.

"You're standing on your grandmother's grave. Your father and uncle buried her here, where she used to lock them in the dark. She liked to hear them scream for her to let them out. She'd taunt them, making them believe she'd open the door after they begged. And then she'd leave them in silence for days. Hungry, desperate, they'd eat the rats that found their way down here."

Kate felt the echo of that terror, claustrophobia, and desperation locked in these crumbling walls and resonating in the earthy air around them.

"Why did he share that with you?" Phillip's eyes filled with anger.

"Your father wanted me to understand Freddy, the brother he loved, not the monster I knew."

"He wasn't a monster," Phillip snapped. "He was a predator." Such pride in those words. "You were just prey."

Kate felt the menace in his voice. "I was more than that. It's taken me a long time to find my way out of the choking nightmare to remember the details. I remember trying to find the person behind the monster." She pressed a hand to her sour stomach. "I felt his wrath in his deafening silence. And while I never deluded myself into thinking he wasn't going to kill me, I thought I saw glimpses of sympathy in him. I didn't know what that would mean for me, or for him. But it felt like a victory on my part. It felt like I'd won something after he'd taken so much from me." She sucked in a ragged breath, then went on. "I held on to my humanity even as I lost myself, because I was able to still feel sorry for him, even while I hated him for what he did to me." Tears streamed down her face as she pressed a hand to her heavy heart.

"Kate." The sympathy Ryan packed into just her name hit Kate hard.

She'd been holding that in for such a long time.

Phillip's gaze narrowed and filled with rage. "My father told you everything, didn't he?"

The resentment coming off him hit her like a brutal wave.

"Right here, you two sat and talked and he spilled all the family secrets he never shared with me. I had to find this place and everything out after he was gone." Anger and disdain filled Phillip's voice. "He shared all the secrets with you and left me with his contempt, his dis-appointment that I was like my uncle and not the good boy he wanted me to be."

Kate shook her head, sorry for the boy who wanted his father's approval, but not for the man who'd taken this deadly path. "He never said anything about you. He asked me to come here to help try to make amends for what I'd been through, to help me understand what happened to me and why."

"Because you were necessary!" Phillip breathed hard, his emotions winding up. "Isn't that what you learned?"

Kate's chest went tight with that simple truth. But there was so much more to Freddy's story. And Phillip didn't want to accept that Freddy wasn't just a cruel killer. "If that is what you think, then you are far worse than your uncle. He was possessed by your grandmother's ghost. Everything she said to him, everything she did to him, it lived inside him, gnawing away at him. All he wanted to do was kill her again and make it stop. It warped his mind, his reality, his soul. It's not an excuse for what he did, but an explanation. What's yours?"

"I am the dark and deadly thing because I was born this way."

"Bullshit." She didn't believe that for a second. She glared daggers at Phillip, showing him her anger over such a dramatic and false statement. "You're on a deadly ego trip." The biting words angered Phillip. She didn't give him a chance to respond. "You think you know him, but you don't know anything about what it's like to be treated like you're nothing but a means to an end. Like you don't matter. You have no voice, choice, or options because they've all been ignored or taken away from you. That was never your life. You had everything! And you threw it away to play a game you won't win."

Kate shook her head at Phillip, like she would to a naughty child. "Do you want to know what your dad wanted to tell me? I did have an impact on Freddy. He wasn't coming after me to kill me on that road. He was coming to take me home."

Ryan gasped, shaken, like she'd been when Henry said that to her, by that twist to the story he thought he knew about Kate and the Rose Reaper.

"You ruined him!" Phillip paced a few steps, then turned on Kate. "If you'd just been like all the rest, he'd still be here. We could have shared this. He would have understood me."

Kate shook her head slowly, disappointed that someone so smart and with so much potential wasted it. "You just don't get it. You think he liked killing."

Arms stiff at his sides, he seethed. "He did. I read it in his journal."

"Maybe you heard what you wanted to hear. Because there is a difference between a need and a want. You are all about what *you* want. He had a need that had to be fed, one that ate at him unrelentingly even as he grew to despise it and question it and wanted it to end. I originally dismissed Henry's assertion that Freddy only came after me because he wanted to do the right thing and take me home. But then in talking to Ryan, I remembered that I'd heard someone at the cabin that night. Now I know it was your father. He must have gotten through to Freddy after I escaped. But then the cops showed up and Freddy finally did end it."

Phillip's whole body went rigid, his lips pressed in a thin line. "No. You're lying."

"Your dad loved Freddy. He wanted the pain and suffering your uncle endured to stop. He confessed that he'd even thought about killing Freddy out of mercy. He said if your uncle hadn't died that night, and he went back to killing women, he'd have put a bullet in his head, then his own."

Kate glanced at Ryan. "After we spoke at my home about the cabin, a memory came back of that night on the road. Freddy put his hand behind his back. He knew the police were going to shoot him. He wanted it. And a split second before he pulled his hand out and pushed them to do it, he looked right at me and mouthed *I'm sorry*."

"No! He didn't fucking apologize for being who he is." Phillip's eyes blazed with fury.

Kate didn't back down. "In that moment he was the boy he'd been born, not the monster he'd become. I wish I had remembered that sooner. I wish you could see that you don't have to be the monster. You can be the young man your father tried so hard to raise you to be. The one he treated well and loved like Henry hadn't been as a child. You had a good life. One a lot of people would wish for, but you threw it all away on some fantasy that being a serial killer, besting your uncle, would make you . . . what? Popular? Immortal?" It disgusted her.

"No one cares about the serial killer. You're a fascination. A side-show thrill. A cautionary tale. A documentary that makes watchers feel the fear as their heart beats faster at the idea that a sadistic killer will strike without warning. And they feel better that at least their lives aren't that bad. They move on and forget the victims' names and why they ever wanted to get into the mind of someone with no redeeming qualities, the worst humanity has to offer."

Phillip's arms went rigid at his sides. "You don't know anything about me."

Kate laughed under her breath without any humor. "I know you too well. I saw the version you're just trying to copy. I'll give it to you. You're worse than him. You're merciless. You don't feel anything. And you're chasing something you'll never get again."

Phillip went still. "What's that?"

"The thrill of that first kill," Ryan supplied. "Freddy must have felt such relief and excitement and joy at killing his mother. He was finally free. He wanted to feel that over and over again. But like Kate said, he lost that thrill. You lost it before Anne Murphy. That's why you had to try something new. Anything to find that euphoria you had at the beginning."

Phillip pulled the dagger from behind his back.

The sight of it twisted her gut and made her heart pound.

Phillip pointed it at her. "I'll be all too happy to show you how much I like it when I kill you."

Kate swallowed back her fear and tried to distract Phillip as planned. "But I'm supposed to be number seven."

"You are. You will be. I guess you didn't hear. I got my number six tonight."

"No. You didn't," Kate taunted, feeling a little smug and happy Phillip had failed. "Emily is still alive. And she pointed the finger at you. Literally. She tried to write your name in her own blood."

Phillip's distress was written on his face. "You're lying."

"Not even a little bit." Kate felt the end coming and couldn't wait for Phillip to get what he deserved. "You thought you got away with it. You thought you'd set up Reed so perfectly, but you made mistakes.

Like taking Cathy Evans from her home early in the morning when Reed was unequivocally with me."

Phillip white-knuckled the knife. "Fuck."

"And now the FBI is digging all through your background, everything you own, every nook and cranny of your life. You'll get exactly what you want. Everyone will know you killed five women. They'll know you copied the Rose Reaper, hoping to make a name for yourself. I bet you have one picked out already. But none of that matters because you'll be behind bars."

Phillip's gaze narrowed. "You think you've won."

Kate took a step back toward Ryan. She needed to keep him out of harm's way. "This isn't a game. No one wins. But I'm here to make damn sure you don't kill anyone else. You will spend the rest of your life in jail."

"They'll never catch me." Such confidence.

She'd divest him of that shortly.

Kate stepped back again, this time coming up beside Ryan and putting her hand on the back of the chair.

Phillip probably thought she was trying to hide behind Ryan.

She had other plans. "You know I didn't come alone." A cold draft coming from behind her whispered across her hair and cheek.

A slight hesitation came over Phillip. "They can't get in. The door is bolted from the inside."

Kate shrugged like Phillip did so often. "And yet, they're already here."

Phillip's eyes went wide with surprise. "No! He fucking told you!"

"He did."

Phillip lunged for Kate with the knife out.

Ryan struggled to get free and somehow block Phillip from reaching her.

Kate tipped his chair to get him out of the line of fire. She fell beside him, looking up at Phillip.

Behind her, the wood pallet fell to the dirt as agents scuffled out of the hidden tunnel two industrious boys had dug in the back wall to escape the prison their mother liked to put them in.

Phillip loomed over Ryan and her, the knife raised as he brought it down to strike. Kate winced, expecting the bite of the knife, but Ryan wrenched his body sideways, putting as much of himself between her and the knife as he could. And then . . .

A loud cracking pop echoed in the dank room. A single gunshot.

Phillip collapsed and hit the ground on his stomach, then curled up and grabbed his thigh, blood oozing through his fingers.

Kate scrambled up, grabbed the knife away from Phillip, and stood over him as he wailed and swore, blood seeping out of the wound. She had zero sympathy. Pure relief overwhelmed her. "You had every opportunity to live a good life and you threw it away to follow in the footsteps of a tormented man who never got the help he needed before it was too late and the monster his mother made him took control. You tried to ruin a good and decent man's reputation. You tormented a survivor. You thought you could take me, too. I am not a victim anymore! Not his. Not yours."

Her fury spent, adrenaline waning, Kate turned her back on Phillip to help Ryan. She didn't have to imagine the terror he felt after being kidnapped, tied up, and held hostage by a killer.

Agent Chapman, Kincaid, and several others in black tactical gear poured into the room until they were standing shoulder to shoulder over Phillip. Agent Chapman rolled Phillip to his stomach with no mercy, pulled his hands behind his back, and cuffed him. Two tactical agents hauled him up to his feet by his arms. Phillip cussed and screamed because no one cared about his gunshot wound at the moment, though the FBI had an ambulance standing by outside.

Kate untied Ryan and helped him up.

He held his raw wrists and sucked in a ragged breath, probably the first real one since he woke up in this hellhole. He turned to Kate. "You knew about the tunnel?"

Kate nodded. "When Henry asked me to meet him at this property, I didn't know what to expect." She raked her trembling fingers through her hair. "In fact, I was terrified. But I also heard the plea in his voice and he promised me he could answer my questions about Freddy and why he hurt me."

"I imagine that was hard to pass up when you were processing and trying to make sense of it all. But when you told me about meeting Henry, why didn't you tell me about all of this?"

"We were focused on where the Rose Reaper had taken me, not why. I thought to tell you about all of this once the new killer had been caught. I never thought I'd be here again." Kate crossed her arms and rubbed her hands up and down her biceps to erase the shiver that ran through her.

Understanding filled Ryan's gaze. "Finding the killer was more important than why Freddy hurt you."

Kate held herself, feeling very vulnerable and unsteady now that the danger had passed. "When Henry showed me the hidden cellar doors and opened them, inviting me to come down here, I have to say, I almost bolted. He went down first. The room was lit with even more lanterns than are here now."

Phillip swore and bellowed out threats as he was hauled up and out of the cellar.

Kate didn't pay him any attention and continued. "We sat at the table. Me. Henry. And Freddy." She waved to the urns. "Henry started at the beginning. He spoke without stopping, telling me about their childhood, what Freddy did for him, what he'd endured at their mother's hands. He told me about this place. She'd bring them here and leave them for days. They could scream and yell and no one would hear them." Tears gathered in her eyes. Even now, Kate sympathized for those abused kids. "But they were smart boys. They knew they'd starve down here if she decided to just leave them, so they dug a tunnel out and hid it so that their mother wouldn't know. They'd search the forest for food and go to the river for water." She tore her gaze from the urns on the table to look at him. "Their neighbor was a fisherman. He helped the boys, no questions asked."

"He must be the one who owned the cabin Freddy used."

"Probably. Henry didn't tell me anything about the cabin on the neighbor's property. I just knew that this place wasn't where the Reaper had taken me. So I didn't think it relevant to the killer now."

Ryan's lips quirked into a partial frown. "You see Freddy as two different people. The boy who turned into the man, who became the Rose Reaper."

Kate nodded, but clarified, "He's still my nightmare." She took a second, still trying to understand everything. "After all he confessed, why didn't Henry tell me what he feared about his son?"

"Because he didn't want it to be true. He couldn't face that his son idolized a killer instead of feeling lucky for having a father who loved him. You were right. Henry gave him the best life he could and Phillip only wanted his uncle's notoriety to be his. When it all came out about his uncle, Phillip got a lot of attention. He loved it. He wanted more of it."

Kate shook her head. "That's a disturbing way to get it."

"Not enough for him to claim diminished capacity." Ryan grinned. "You got him, Kate."

"The feds got him. I just figured out how to do it." She gave him a sheepish look. "This all could have gone wrong if he knew I knew about the tunnel."

"Why would he ask you to come down here if he thought you knew about it?"

"I mean, it would have been completely stupid of me to do so. I guess his arrogance that he could get away with all this got the better of him." Kate's gaze went to the plastic sheeting lying in the corner beside the empty, narrow, shallow grave. "You got the grave. I got the river."

Ryan squeezed her hand. "Not this time. Never again. He's done."

"Five lives lost was too many to lose for his ego."

"Absolutely true. Their families will be relieved he's in custody. They'll be grateful to you for getting them justice." Ryan held out his arm, offering her comfort.

She pressed into his side as his arm settled over her shoulders and she wrapped her arms around his middle. She hugged him, grateful for his help and support.

"I take it Agent Kincaid refused you a weapon."

"I did," the agent said, coming down the stairs. "Kate didn't need any more horrors in her life. Just a victory worth celebrating."

Kate took a small step away from Ryan to address Agent Kincaid. "I was surprised you guys waited that long to take him down."

The agent shrugged. "I promised you your reckoning. And that we wouldn't shoot to kill. No sense giving him an easy out." Agent Kincaid glanced back up the stairs, then looked at them again. "Agent Chapman would like a word, if you're ready to surrender the scene to us."

Ryan stepped toward the table, curiosity lighting his gaze. "I just want to see something." He used his fingernail to flip the lid open on the wooden box on the table. It had a place of prominence between the two urns.

He stared at the thick book, roses drawn all over the cover in different sizes, but all the same image drawn again and again and again. The Rose Reaper's journal.

"Don't touch it. It's evidence," Agent Kincaid warned.

Ryan raised a brow. "You're seriously not going to let me take one peek at it?"

"I'm sure Agent Chapman will let you look at it once it's booked into evidence."

Ryan left the journal where it was and sighed. "Fine."

Kate came up behind him, snatched the book out of the box, and opened it.

"Kate," Agent Kincaid admonished.

She raised a haughty brow. "What are you going to do? Arrest me? Go ahead." Kate flipped open the book and looked at the first page. "It's covered in more roses. He couldn't help drawing them over and over and over again." Kate turned the book toward them.

Ryan stared at the page. "I wonder what else is inside, what else we'll learn about Freddy Poole and the Rose Reaper."

Kate handed the book to him. "I know all I need to know about them. I don't want him in my head anymore. Everything I need is waiting for me outside." Kate left them and this place behind.

She'd come a long way. The trauma hadn't overwhelmed her this time—it had made her strong enough to stand up to a killer and take him down.

Phillip would rot in a cell, never having reached his goal of outkilling his uncle and making Kate pay for besting the Reaper.

Kate wouldn't let them best her.

Because even in her pain and trauma, she was stronger than both of them.

Chapter Forty-Four

Ryan didn't worry about Kate falling apart. Oh, sure, she'd have her moments as she processed yet another close encounter with a killer and how he'd tried to take everything from her once again. But she knew what happened in the past and what happened now were two separate things. And this time, she'd outsmarted and put another monster in his place.

And she'd been so damn brave, coming here to save him from certain death. The whole thing felt unreal, except for the echo of fear inside him, making him amped and ready to flee. But it was over for him, too.

That single thought allowed him to breathe easier. Though he'd be dealing with the emotional fallout later. Right now, it helped to focus on the fact that he was safe, alive, and walking out of here mostly unscathed.

The nightmare of this place, that shallow grave, and Phillip's deadly intentions would haunt him for a while.

Ryan focused on the journal again. For some reason, he turned to the back pages and Freddy's last entry. He read it quickly, then sprinted up the stairs, the book still in his hand, out into the darkness and the field that separated him from the ruins of the old house that used to stand here.

He saw Kate in Reed's arms and went to her. "Kate. I think you need to see this."

He handed her the book and let her read Freddy's almost last words.

She looks at me like she's trying to find something inside me that I can no longer feel. The longer I keep her, the more I feel whatever it is poking at the blackness inside me, waking up and stretching to be free of all the filth eating at me. If her stare held defiance and rage and all the other things the others glared at me, I wouldn't care. I'd know it's my due.

But in her eyes there is something I can't ignore.

She looks into me like no one ever has, except maybe the one who was always by my side even as I protected him.

I want her to see what is buried so deep even I can't claim it anymore. I want her to see what I could have been. What was taken from me.

I want the tears she sheds to be because she mourns that which is lost in me. The what was and will never be again.

I want her to see the apology I can't speak. Because it will never be enough, even though I mean it. And I do. I'm sorry.

Tears cascaded down Kate's cheeks as she stared at Ryan. "In the end, he said the words, and I weep for what he was and could never be."

"Maybe in the end, on that road, facing you and death, he was what you allowed him to be. No one is all bad or all good. You experienced the worst of him, but he showed you a glimpse of the good that was left inside him. I don't know what you do with that, Kate, except to maybe remember that when things happen between you and other people in your life. People will disappoint you sometimes. But they'll also surprise you."

"After all this, I think I can trust the way I feel about someone when they show me who they are." She looked up at Reed, then laid her head on his shoulder, her trust and love so clear to see.

Agent Chapman joined their small group and held out Ryan's phone. "I believe this is yours."

"Thank you." Ryan tapped the screen and smiled at the text notification from Molly. He couldn't wait to speak to her.

Agent Chapman cleared his throat. "You okay?"

Ryan met the agent's earnest gaze. "Yeah. I'm good. Whatever he injected me with has worn off." Ryan didn't want to think about what he'd been through. Not right now. It was too fresh and overwhelming.

"We found the syringe and a sedative in the glove box of his truck."

Ryan turned and looked at the Rose Reaper's truck. "He wanted to be like him. He thought he and his uncle were the same."

"Weren't they?" the agent asked.

"No," Kate answered for him. "One was a lost and broken man. The other, a cold-blooded killer with no remorse. They were both guilty of the brutality they inflicted. There's no excuse for what they did. But Phillip is a different kind of beast. One who deserves a cell and to be locked away from others. He doesn't see the pain he caused. He only sees the game he doesn't want to end. He is the dark and deadly thing he unleashed and he likes it."

Agent Chapman's shoulders shook. "That's . . . dark."

Kate frowned. "He showed us who he is. And now he'll pay for what he's done. That's all I ever wanted. The families deserve that peace of mind that he will never hurt anyone ever again."

"He will never hurt you again," Agent Chapman assured her before turning to Ryan. "I've got an ambulance here. Let the paramedics check you out just in case."

"I'm fine, but okay." The relief of being rescued hadn't quite eliminated all the fear he'd felt thinking he'd meet his end down in that cellar. He still felt the chill of death every time he pictured the grave that had been waiting for him.

Kate separated from Reed and came to him. "Thank you for everything. I'm sorry he used you to get to me."

"Not your fault. And anytime. I mean that, Kate. If you need me, I'm just a phone call away."

"I may take you up on that. My therapist is good. You're better, because you were here with me. You see them. You made me see them both for what and who they are and it helps to be clear about it."

"I'm glad. Now, go home. Focus on being happy."

"And free." Kate sighed, her relief evident if not hesitant like his. In time, they'd both let the fear they felt in that cellar go. "It's finally over."

"You can truly move on," Ryan assured her.

Agent Kincaid came forward. "I'll stay with you while the paramedics check you out, then I'll drive you back to your hotel."

Agent Chapman nodded his agreement to that plan. "Come by the office in the morning before you head home. I'll need your statement about what happened tonight."

Ryan answered a call from his boss as he walked over to the ambulance. "Hello, Agent Booker."

"Ryan. Are you okay? They told me you were drugged, but not hurt."

"I'm fine. Getting checked out now." He sat on the back of the ambulance and let the paramedic check his vitals. "We got the guy. That's all that matters."

"No. It's not. My people matter. Now tell me what happened."

Ryan told her the whole story. "So, you see, it was Agent Kincaid who took down the suspect and saved me and Kate."

"She has my gratitude and I'll be sure she knows it. And how is Kate?"

"She's holding up, considering all she's been through. It was a relief to know that Reed hadn't deceived her and she can trust her instincts. She's got work to do to put this behind her, but she will. And Reed will be by her side for all of it."

"And who will be with you while you cope with this after the losses you suffered on the last case?" True concern filled that question.

"I have my family." *And Molly,* he silently acknowledged, though his boss didn't need to know about his burgeoning relationship with her.

"When will you be back?"

Ryan held up his free hand while the paramedic wrapped his wrist in gauze to protect the abrasions. "Tomorrow night. I need to tie up things here tomorrow morning. I want to check in with Kate, too, before I leave. Why? Do you have a case for me?"

"I think you've earned a couple of days off after being drugged and kidnapped."

He wanted to say he was fine, but of course he knew these kinds of things could sneak up on you once the initial trauma was over. And he had to admit, waking up tied to a chair with a serial killer standing over him . . . not a great day. At all. He could still feel the adrenaline and fear in his system.

"I'll take those couple of days." He'd spend time with his family. An in-person date with Molly would do him a world of good. She'd distract him. She'd make him laugh. And for a little while, he could just be himself and not think about the job and what was coming next. Because there would be another case. Soon.

But first, he needed to finish this one.

Chapter Forty-Five

Ryan got the all clear from the paramedics and arrived back at his hotel around eleven with a promise from Agent Chapman that he'd get to read through the Rose Reaper's journal in the morning and possibly be in the interview with Phillip Poole once the doctors were finished patching up his gunshot wound.

Amped up after everything that happened, he ordered food, then took a quick shower. The hot water eased his tense muscles. By the time he toweled off, put on a pair of sweatpants and a T-shirt, rewrapped his sore wrists, and took delivery of his soup, salad, and rolls, he was feeling drained.

He didn't want to think about what happened anymore, but he did want to talk to someone. He tapped her number and waited, hoping she picked up.

Molly's sweet voice eased him. "Hey, stranger. It's late. Long day?"

He settled on the sofa. "Actually, yeah." It was quiet in the background, so he guessed she wasn't at the bar. "Sorry to call so late."

"I'm glad you did. I was hoping you would. How was your day?"

"Nearly fatal. How was yours?"

Dead silence filled the line.

He shouldn't have said it that way. "Molly, sweetheart, I'm sorry. That was—"

"Are you all right?" she cut in. "What happened? Are you hurt? In the hospital? Where are you? I can be there if you want me to—"

"Hey. Stop. I'm fine. Really. I'm okay." He felt like a dick for doing that to her, but the reality had hit him and he'd blurted out the blunt truth.

She breathed out a huge sigh of relief.

He had to admit, it felt good to know she cared that much.

"Let's start again." She paused. "Tell me everything you can share about what happened today."

It was that kind of understanding that loosened the knot in his gut and softened his heart. "I don't even know where to begin."

"You talk, and I'll listen."

He sighed and picked up his spoon, his gut not really feeling the whole food thing at the moment, but he took a bite anyway. The hot loaded-potato soup and cheesy flavor hit his tongue and he changed his mind. Soup was always comfort food for him and he'd been glad to hear it was the special on the menu tonight. Feeling incrementally better because of the sustenance, but most especially having Molly's ear, he let the words fall from his lips like a confession. "We found the cabin we'd been looking for this afternoon." It felt like days ago, not just hours. "All the evidence pointed to our suspect, but it didn't feel right. And Kate, the woman I came here to help, she was so strong and courageous to go there and see the place where her nightmare took place."

"She had you there to help her."

He'd helped her see that it was only a place.

And then tonight in the dank cellar, she'd seen two very different killers, monsters, but two different kinds of beasts.

He didn't know how long he spoke. Molly his captive audience. Quiet, yet intent, he sensed, as the story flowed out of him.

"Do you feel any lingering effects from the drug he gave you?"

"None. The sedative wore off a couple hours ago."

"You sound tired, though. You've had a long day. And Kate . . . I can't imagine how she's feeling right now."

"I know she's home with Reed. She's where she needs to be. With him. Now that they've shared this experience together, I think it will make their relationship even stronger."

"I mean, taking down a serial killer like that . . . She should feel like everything else in life is easy."

Ryan raked a hand over his head. "She saved my life."

"I think she'd say the same thing about you. You helped her when she needed someone most. You made the unimaginable understandable. Sometimes all a person needs is to quiet the lingering questions. Sometimes all you need is the answer to why."

"In this case, why was different for each of the killers."

"The answer doesn't always have to make sense. It won't make sense to the families. They lost someone they loved. That's not easy. And in this case, it's tragic."

They'd talked a little about loss when he was working his sister's case and they met. But Molly hadn't been forthcoming with any specifics. "Who did you lose, Molly?"

It took her a second to answer. "My brother."

He'd lost his sister and knew just how that tore a piece of your heart to shreds. "I'm sorry for your loss."

"It's been years. But time doesn't make us forget or feel the absence any less, does it?"

"No. I miss my sister."

"I miss my brother. His birthday is coming up," she said sadly. "It's always a tough day for me, thinking about what was and what might have been for him if he was still here."

"I know exactly what you mean."

"I know you do." She sighed. "Did you finish your dinner?"

He took the last sip of his beer. "Yeah."

"Feel better?"

"The food was good. The company outstanding."

"I wish you were here." The sentiment came through loud and clear.

"I wish I was there. I'll be home tomorrow evening."

"I work the early shift, so I'll be off at nine. You could come by my place. If you want to."

He did. More than anything. "I'll be there."

"You should get some sleep."

"I'll try."

"Want me to stay on the phone?"

He appreciated the offer and almost took her up on it. "I'd love that, but I think we both need to call it a day. If I know you're still with me, I'll just want to talk to you more."

"Sweet dreams, Ryan."

"You too, sweetheart." He'd take her with him into sleep. Her sweetness, his need for her, would black out all the bad.

Tomorrow he'd focus on the case. Tonight, he imagined the woman he desperately wanted was in his bed.

Chapter Forty-Six

"Authorities have captured the man responsible for the kidnapping, rape, and murder of five women over the last ten months.

"All the women's bodies were found in the river and have been identified as Denise Simmons, Kelly Russell, Tina Parker, Cathy Evans, and most recently, Anne Murphy.

"We reported last night that Emily Bell was stabbed outside her apartment. Initial reports stated that Emily had died at the scene, but the FBI has confirmed those reports were false.

"Emily underwent emergency surgery last night and is reported to be in stable condition this morning and expected to make a full recovery."

"Fucking NO!" Phillip raged from his hospital bed. He went to reach for the water pitcher on the table, but the handcuffs prevented him from grabbing it, making him even more frustrated. He pulled at the restraints, only making them clink louder and bite into his wrists.

He'd asked the nurse to turn the TV to a movie or something, but she'd put on the news and left without speaking to him.

The two guards outside his door kept everyone else away. They barely glanced at him as he thrashed in the bed. They didn't care.

"The suspect was taken into custody last night after he kidnapped a psychologist consulting with the FBI and tied to Kate Doyle, the seventh and sole surviving victim of the Rose Reaper, who the suspect, Phillip Poole,

has been taunting and terrorizing by leaving her roses after he kidnapped each woman, counting down to when he would come for her to finish what his uncle started years ago. But Phillip Poole"—they kept using his name. No moniker. He'd earned it, damnit—*"won't get the chance to complete his deadly game, as he'll be released from the hospital today after he was shot in the leg by a federal agent during his apprehension and booked and charged for all his crimes. The families of his victims can rest easy that this killer will remain behind bars for the rest of his life."*

The other anchor at the news desk gave a sympathetic look right into the camera. *"A chilling story, Susan. We'll be back with weather and traffic after a quick break."*

That's it? He'd killed five women and that's all they had to say about him? What about giving him his own fucking name? What about dedicating a whole fucking show to how he did it?

No, it's just *He's off to jail and we'll let you know if it's going to be fucking cold or hot today.* Motherfucker!

He tried to slam his fists down on the bed, but the shackles kept him from doing anything but hurt himself more.

A knock on the interior window facing the hallway had him spinning his head in that direction.

He spotted Kate and her boyfriend standing together and glared her down.

Kate slapped the note he'd forgotten he'd sent her with the flower delivery this morning on the glass and smiled at him.

They'll never catch me.

Kate pointed to herself, then at him, and mouthed, *I got you.* She crumpled the note in her hand and walked away.

"Come back here, you bitch! I'll fucking kill you!"

She didn't turn around or even acknowledge him.

He thrashed in the bed, making his thigh hurt like hell from the bullet wound the surgeon had cleaned and stitched closed last night before they cuffed him to this damn bed.

One of the agents guarding him popped his head into the room. "Calm down and shut up."

"I need more meds. My leg is killing me."

"Then I suggest you be still. You've still got ninety minutes before your next dose."

"When is my mother supposed to get here? I want to see her now."

"You'll see her when we say you can see her." With that, the agent closed the door, though not all the way, so they could hear everything he did.

It was going to be like this for the rest of his life now. He'd be in someone else's control. They'd get to decide everything about his life. What he ate, when he slept, what he wore, who he got to see and when. Everything.

The control he'd wielded was gone.

He was the one at others' mercy now.

The agonizing pain in his leg was nothing compared to that appalling reality.

Chapter Forty-Seven

Ryan met Kate and Reed in Emily's hospital room and found them and Emily all smiles and laughing. "Please, clue me in because I could use a good laugh."

Kate turned to him, looking vibrant and happy. "P.P.—that's how I'm referring to him now, even if it's childish and makes me want to giggle a little bit—sent me flowers this morning. Six of them."

Ryan raised a brow. "He must have set that up before or right after he stabbed Emily." He turned to her. "How are you?"

Emily looked tired but alert. "Sore. Dazed because of the good drugs, but I'm going to be fine and that asshole is going to prison."

"We're all happy about that," Ryan agreed, then focused on Kate again.

"The roses came with a note. *They'll never catch me.*"

"Arrogant," Ryan supplied.

"So I asked the nurse to turn on the news in his room at the top of the hour, when I knew P.P. would be the lead story. And guess what he learned."

"Everyone knows he got caught and didn't kill you."

"And P.P. never got the moniker he wanted." Kate nodded her appreciation of that.

Agent Chapman joined them. "I made sure the FBI press liaison expressed how sensationalizing a killer, making him some kind of celebrity by giving him a name, only diminished the victims and made them less important than the killer."

Kate snickered. "I held up the note he sent to me to his window and told him I got him."

Ryan wanted to congratulate her, but erred on the side of caution. "Kate, you don't want to taunt someone who's fixated on you."

"I just needed to get my shot in. I'm done. With him. With all of this. Reed and I talked last night. I'm going to sell my house. He's going to sell his. And we're going to buy a place together."

"Right after I have that cabin torn down to the ground," Reed added. "I'll be speaking to a Realtor I know this afternoon to handle the sale of the house, plus that land."

Kate leaned into Reed and stared up at him. "We're going house hunting. Then we're getting married."

Reed's eyes went wide for a second, but the smile came just as quickly. "I'll get right on that, sweetheart."

"You better. Because I want it all. The house. The ring. The happy life I know we'll have together." Kate's smile, her joy, infected them all.

"Congratulations," Ryan said, Agent Chapman and Emily adding theirs to his.

Kate released Reed and walked toward Ryan until she was close enough to wrap him in her arms. He held her loosely and tipped his head so she could whisper in his ear. "Thank you for coming. I don't know what I would have done without you."

He stared down at her. "Exactly what you did do, Kate. Survived."

Kate hugged him again.

He let her loose and added, "Don't forget to send me pictures of the wedding."

Reed pulled Kate back to his side. "When do you leave?"

"In a few hours. Agent Chapman and I have a few things to tie up." Ryan glanced at Emily. "Kate has a great therapist who specializes in trauma and PTSD. While you're healing in the hospital and at home, remember that your mind needs a chance to process everything that happened, too."

Emily nodded, though it appeared she was losing energy quickly and fading on them. "I will. I've never been through anything like this. I'm still trying to believe it's real."

"The hospital bill will remind you of that," Agent Chapman quipped. "If you'll excuse Ryan and me, we have some things to discuss."

They said their goodbyes and left Kate, Reed, and Emily, and walked down the hallway toward the unit where Phillip was being guarded.

As they walked, Ryan took out the journal they'd found last night in the cellar. "I looked through it this morning. It's chilling. The Rose Reaper . . . Freddy . . . his thoughts are candid and uncensored. He's drawn that rose in there so many times it's almost impossible to keep count. But what he writes . . . it's the thoughts of a tormented mind. He has bouts of remorse, then writes about the need he has to find another rose among the weeds and make her his so that he can find some peace."

Ryan opened the book and flipped through a couple of pages as they walked and ended up outside Phillip's door. Ryan heard the humming through the crack and stepped into the room and read the Reaper's poem. "Roses are red, violets are blue. If you see me . . . it's too late for you."

Phillip grinned. "It's stuck in my head now."

Ryan studied Phillip. "You're not him. I hope one day you realize that. Maybe then you can begin to see what you did to all those innocent women was nothing more than you making a conscious decision to hurt and kill them."

"I was born this way."

"You made yourself into this," Ryan corrected.

"My father saw it in me."

"He saw a troubled teen who fixated on a man who didn't deserve your adoration. All those video games you play, all the violence you see on the TV news and in shows and movies, numbed you to the fact that real people get hurt. They feel. The people in their lives feel. But you stayed focused on one thing. The need to win."

"You don't know anything." Phillip sounded like a petulant child.

"It was all about the number. You wanted to beat your uncle. You thought if you could get that seven, kill Kate, you'd somehow win. But there's no prize for this. There's no top score that gets you anything."

"Immortality. My name, known by all."

"Except you didn't get that either." Agent Chapman pressed his lips tight. "We made sure of that because we've learned that violence glorified only begets more violence. You're the perfect example of that. So you will be transferred to prison and incarcerated for the rest of your life, surrounded by like-minded individuals who will have as little remorse or empathy for you as you showed your victims." Agent Chapman turned for the door.

Ryan followed.

"Wait. That's my book."

Ryan held it up. "It's evidence in a federal case." He walked out on Phillip's threats and cursing and stood with Agent Chapman in the hallway and waited for Ms. Poole to reach them.

"Oh, good, you're here," she said to Ryan.

"I'm sorry, why?"

"You're here to help my son, right?" She looked so hopeful.

"I'm sorry, Ms. Poole, but I specialize in helping victims and witnesses, not serial killers."

"But . . ." Confusion filled her eyes. "Then why are you here?"

"I was checking in on Emily Bell, the woman your son stabbed last night, and Kate and Reed to be sure they were okay this morning after the ordeal we all suffered last night."

"He's not in his right mind. It's the Poole family curse. They're all nuts," Ms. Poole rationalized.

Ryan shook his head. "Your son is very much in his right mind. He knew what he was doing was wrong and did it anyway. He's smart and conniving. He planned and executed his crimes multiple times. While I certainly believe he needs mental health help and that therapy could help him see the error of his ways and possibly feel remorse for what he's done, it won't change the fact that he will spend the rest of his life in prison for the choices he made." Ryan didn't have a lot of patience for Ms. Poole this morning. She wanted to help her son. But her son had drugged and kidnapped him last night, so he wasn't feeling very charitable.

"I don't know what to do. They're going to take him away from me." Her distress softened Ryan, because she'd been through a lot. The life-changing and shattering realization that her brother-in-law was a serial killer that had disrupted her whole world almost four years ago, the divorce and subsequent suicide of her husband, and now the surreal reality that her son had followed in his uncle's footsteps, and she was alone.

"Ms. Poole, I understand that everything feels out of control and upside down right now. My best advice for you is that you let Phillip take responsibility for his actions by letting him work his way through this on his own. Don't let him drag you into the mess he made. He can get an attorney and face the charges like the adult he is. I'm not saying you don't offer him moral support if that's what you want to do, but don't make this next part of his life your job. You need to live your life, because from now on, he won't be a part of it the way he would have been if he'd stayed in college, found a job, and made a life for himself in society."

"I can't just turn my back on him."

"He turned his back on you," Agent Chapman pointed out. "You taught him right from wrong. You gave him a good life. He threw it all away. There's nothing more you can really do for him, except love him the way you always have because he's your boy. He's just not the one you hoped he'd be."

Ms. Poole fidgeted with her hands clasped in front of her. "The last few times we've spoken, he's been mean and demanding and not anything like the boy I knew. I just can't take it anymore. I don't want to go in there."

"No one expects you to. No one says you have to." Agent Chapman lightly touched her shoulder. "Maybe now isn't the time to see him. Maybe you need time to decide what kind of relationship you want with him going forward. Maybe you wait until he reaches out to you in a respectful way that feels like you two can have a real and honest conversation."

Ms. Poole gave a firm nod. "I think you're right. That's probably best." She hurriedly walked away, like if she didn't get out now, she'd be locked in that room with Phillip, too.

Ryan bumped his fist to Agent Chapman's arm. "Really good advice you offered there."

"I have a teenager with attitude. My wife and I have used a lot of de-escalation tactics to stop the yelling and get to why we suck." Agent Chapman grinned. "And also why our teen feels like the world is ending over stupid shit, which isn't stupid to him at all."

"I feel like I rubbed off on you the last time we worked together."

"Why do you think I welcomed you back so quickly? Watching you listen and talk to people, it's not an easy thing. I know you wanted to tell Phillip to fuck off after what he did to you, but instead you told him exactly what he needed to hear, even if he didn't want to listen to it."

"Most people just want to be right."

"Or they care about what people will think," the agent said. "Ms. Poole doesn't want to be seen as a bad mother. But she needs to get away from all this. I know it's family and it sucks, but sometimes you have to walk away from a situation. Like you should do now, too."

"This hasn't been like one of my usual cases."

"I imagine you spend most of your time in an interview or hospital room talking to people, not getting drugged and tied to chairs."

"It could have been worse." Ryan fought the instinctive chill up his spine. He didn't want to think about what happened right now.

Agent Chapman notched his chin toward the journal in Ryan's hand. "Do you want to take some time to read that?"

Ryan held it out. "I don't need the Reaper's dark thoughts in my head. It's enough to know that this is how Phillip copied him so well. I'll leave it to the psychiatrists who study serial killers to make what they will of Freddy and Phillip Poole."

"I think you nailed them both perfectly. One was made a monster, the other chose to be one." Agent Chapman turned for the elevator with Ryan following. "We found the boots Phillip wore to the cabin when he took the victims there and the rose brand in the truck. We also matched the knife he had at the cellar to the victims. It's the same width and length the coroners had suspected it would be. Phillip must have found the journal and knife in the box in the cellar or with his father's things. It's kind of creepy that he kept both his father's and uncle's urns in the cellar."

They entered the elevator and Ryan punched the lobby button. "Henry told Kate their mother used to hide them down there when they were bad and she wanted them out of the way. Maybe Henry realized his son wasn't the only one who idolized the Rose Reaper and didn't want a marked grave where someone could visit him, so he hid Freddy away where he could finally rest in peace."

"I still can't believe the nephew just decided one day he'd start killing."

"It wasn't just one day. He had three years to think about it, plan, and fixate until just thinking about it wasn't enough anymore. I'm sure during that time he tried to assuage his urges in other ways. The video games he played. Maybe some rough sex with willing partners. Maybe he even practiced killing on small animals. His father and uncle used to take him fishing. Maybe he took up hunting. This is Maine. Lots of places to do that here and for a wide variety of birds and game."

"I bet we'll learn a lot more about Phillip Poole as we finish the investigation and throughout the trial."

They stepped out of the elevator and walked toward the lobby exit.

"Good luck with all that."

"You have a new case yet?"

Ryan shook his head. "No. But I'm sure there will be one soon."

"Mind if I call on you again in the future if I need you?"

Ryan held his hand out. "Not at all." He shook the agent's hand. "Take it easy."

"Thanks for coming."

"Not a problem." Ryan split off from the agent in the parking lot and climbed behind the wheel of his rental, drove out of the hospital, and headed toward the airport.

He couldn't wait to get home and see his family and Molly. He didn't want to tell his parents and sister about his experience here. They worried about him enough. But he couldn't keep it to himself. If they ever found out, they'd be angry he didn't share it with them.

Normally, his job wasn't so in the thick of it, but this one and the last one had put him right in it. He hoped the next case was something easy, less traumatic.

And maybe he should be careful what he wished for, because in his experience nothing in this job was ever easy and trauma came with the nature of the cases he was called in to help with.

Still, maybe next time he could stay at the police or FBI building and leave the fieldwork to law enforcement.

Yeah, right.

Chapter Forty-Eight

Ryan knocked on Molly's door just after 9:00 p.m. holding a bottle of wine and anxious to see the blue-haired beauty. He'd been home long enough to drop his bag at his place, send the report he'd typed up on the plane about the case to his boss, and update his mom and dad that he was home and couldn't wait to see them and Thea for brunch on Sunday. He'd showered and changed, grabbed the bottle of wine from his fridge, and assuaged the driving need inside him to see the woman who'd made this case and being away from home a little easier to bear.

Molly opened the door wearing a black tank top, a tight black skirt that hit her midthigh, and black boots, her hair vibrant with soft waves and her easy smile. "Hi. You're here." The excitement in her eyes made him grin and amped his ego.

He was happy to see her, too, and held up the bottle of wine. "I come bearing gifts."

She grinned at the wine and waved her hand out. "Come in."

He desperately wanted to get his hands on her, but settled for leaning in and kissing her on the cheek.

She gave him a shy smile.

He stepped into the combo living and dining room area and turned to her. "Thank you."

She closed the door and raised a brow. "For what?"

"Being the perfect long-distance date. I've never had that good a time without being in the same room as the person I'm with."

"Are you with me?" she asked.

He answered honestly, so there were no misunderstandings. "Yeah. If you want me."

She closed the gap and stood an inch away from him, her face upturned and her soft gaze meeting his. "This is how much I want you." She wrapped her arms around his neck, pressed her body against his, and kissed him.

He felt everything she poured into it. *I want you. I need you. I missed you.*

He lost himself in her arms, in her bed, and in the amazing moment they shared and forgot about everything else but her.

It was nice to just feel safe and wanted and unencumbered and alive.

He needed this. Her. Because he'd have another case soon. Another victim or witness to help.

He just hoped the next case didn't put him directly in harm's way again.

ABOUT THE AUTHOR

Photo © Steven Hopkins

Jennifer Hunter explores the darker side of life with her Ryan Strickland thriller series, which includes *The Lost Victim*. She also writes suspenseful contemporary romance and women's fiction as *New York Times* bestselling author Jennifer Ryan. Her deeply emotional stories are filled with unforgettable characters, secrets, betrayals, and page-turning suspense. For more information, visit www.jennifer-ryan.com.